GHOST DANCE

When the mirror swung open there was darkness beyond. He thought that if he tried hard enough his eyes could pierce it, but he didn't want to know what he'd see. In that moment of fear his mind released the image and the door swung shut, closing with a soft *click*.

The glass was a mirror again and Morgan could see the reflection of a woman – but it wasn't Kate. This woman's cheeks were rounder, her eyes a paler, washed-out blue. Her gaze passed over Morgan without seeing him. She was studying herself, mouth squeezed shut as she applied her lipstick.

Morgan noticed the man behind her at the same time she did. He was watching her in the glass. His hair and eyes were the same dark brown that was almost black and though he was dressed in jeans and a T-shirt, Morgan thought he belonged in uniform. He recognised a soldier when he saw one, the tense shoulders and loose arms, aggression held on only a light leash.

The woman gasped, then turned and smiled. Morgan fought the futile urge to shout a warning. This was her killer and she didn't know it and wouldn't realise until it was too late.

An Abaddon Books™ Publication
www.abaddonbooks.com
abaddon@rebellion.co.uk

First published in 2010 by Abaddon Books™, Rebellion Intellectual
Property Limited, Riverside House, Osney Mead, Oxford, OX2 0ES, UK.

10 9 8 7 6 5 4 3 2 1

Editor: Jonathan Oliver
Cover: Pye Parr
Design: Simon Parr & Luke Preece
Marketing and PR: Keith Richardson
Creative Director and CEO: Jason Kingsley
Chief Technical Officer: Chris Kingsley
The Infernal Game™ created by Rebecca Levene

ISBN: 978-1-907519-03-1

Printed in the US

THE INFERNAL GAME

GHOST DANCE

Rebecca Levene

Abaddon
Books

WWW.ABADDONBOOKS.COM

Dedicated to David Bailey, Jon Pollard and Gramsci, who are brilliant friends and – not entirely coincidentally – great cooks. They also had a lovely apartment in San Francisco and were foolish enough to let me stay in it.

PROLOGUE

When he looked in the mirror, George W. Bush looked back. The mask was expressionless, blank – the way he felt inside.

He'd laid the guns out on his bed after his mom left for work. There was the Beretta 391 semi-automatic shotgun which he'd stolen from Joshua Heligman's house, from the gun drawer his dad was supposed to keep locked but never did. Joshua had told him about that in Home Room, his pimply face flushed with excitement. Joshua claimed he used to take the gun into the woods and use the rabbits for target practice.

The holster for the Beretta fit on his hip. He slung the Browning A-bolt across his back, where it bulged out the leather of his duster. The material creaked in protest as he moved and released its distinctive smell. Musty – as if the curing hadn't quite halted its decay. He'd stolen the rifle from a freshman whose name he couldn't remember. His parents had given it him for his fifteenth birthday, a present no one would forget.

The two little pea-shooters in his pockets had come from Christine Dunn's house. They didn't have much stopping power, but he was saving them for her. He wanted to imagine her parents' faces when the cops told them their stuck-up little bitch of a daughter had been shot with their own guns. He enjoyed picturing everyone's faces.

The phone rang, but he ignored it. That would be the school secretary wanting to find out where he was. She'd know the answer soon enough.

The sun was bright, the sky flat and the air dead as he walked the half mile to school. Old Mrs Corry stared as he passed, probably trying to guess the face behind the mask. She hadn't spoken to him anyway since the day she found her little kitten's guts smeared all over her microwave door. She'd known it was him, but not been able to prove it. That made him laugh as he passed her and he heard the clacking of her pumps speed to a half jog as she hurried away.

There was no one at the school gates. He'd waited long enough to ensure Mr Atkinson was back inside, no longer lurking to pounce on tardy students. No one would stop him. This was really going to happen.

He'd thought he might experience things differently today of all days, but he couldn't see this place through fresh eyes. He felt the same dull ache of hatred as the doors swung open onto the gloom inside. He squinted, momentarily blind. The squeak of rubber soles on linoleum told him he wasn't alone, and when his eyes cleared he saw Mrs O'Grady striding towards him, red ringlets swaying.

He let her get very close before he drew the Beretta and he waited to see the fear in her eyes before he put a bullet between them. The silencer muffled the retort to a dull *thump*, but he still froze, momentarily stunned by what he'd done. The bullet hole in her forehead was surprisingly small. It looked like that mark – he couldn't remember the name – the red dot that some of the Indian students wore.

When she fell to the floor it was with a thud that startled him out of his paralysis. And there was the blood he'd anticipated, spreading in a scarlet halo around her head. The exit wound would be far larger than the entry and suddenly he wanted to see it. He used his foot to flip her head to the side and the blood leaked on to his shoe, alongside skull fragments and fatty brain matter. There was nothing left of the back of her head.

He expected to feel something. He'd been sure that this, at least, would penetrate the dense fog that softened everything he saw to the same white nothing. But it was... disappointing. Maybe he'd rehearsed it so many times in his mind, he'd already sucked all the marrow from the bones of the experience. Or perhaps he hadn't hated Mrs O'Grady enough.

He flipped her over and saw her face, slack in death. Back again, and there was the mess and the gore. He could smell it too, along with the shit and piss that stained her dress. He left her like that, exit wound exposed, the truth that was the dead meat, not the lie that had been her face.

He moved deeper inside the building, drawing the rifle from his back to join the Beretta in his hand. Now he'd notched up his first kill he didn't have much time left and he had to make it count. He removed the silencer from the Beretta's barrel, wanting to make a noise – to be heard.

Classroom 4B was on the second floor. As he took the stairs two at a time he realised he felt weightless. Was this the elation he'd been waiting for? It hadn't occurred to him that happiness was something so foreign he might not recognise it if he felt it. A kid scampered towards him as he rounded the second curve of the stairs. It was no one he recognised, just some jock senior with a thick neck and dumb eyes. They widened when the boy caught sight of the semi-automatic in his hand.

He took a moment to savour the raw terror in the jock's face and then fired. The trigger was lighter than he'd realised and a hail of bullets shattered the silence before he released the pressure. The senior's body danced and jerked, just like in the movies.

When the bullets stopped the screams started. A door to his left opened then quickly slammed and he knew that the cops would be called very soon – but not soon enough. There was the wooden door to 4B, pitted at the bottom where generations of feet had kicked it open. He added his own toe print, a little memento of his existence that would be lost amidst the bigger legacy he was leaving.

It was Mr Skeet's class. He'd planned it that way. Skeet had once taken him aside and told him that he had a real talent for physics. He'd asked if there were problems at home, if there was anything he wanted to talk about.

There were no problems at home, that *was* the problem. There was only the destructive blandness of it all.

Mr Skeet was the first to die. Then ten more in the first wild volley of bullets. He'd read about other school shootings, and the thing that had shocked him was the survival rate. It seemed to him those other guys hadn't done their research. But he'd read an airport thriller about Navy SEALs once and he knew they never took a kill for granted.

He didn't either. Brittany was bleeding from a wound in her shoulder. It seeped a rich dark blood through the fingers she'd curled protectively against it. When he took a step towards her she said his name and he wondered how she recognised him behind the mask. But he found it gratifying that she did. He *was* memorable – hell, he was unforgettable. He winked at her through the mask as he rested the barrel of the gun against her ear and pulled the trigger.

It became almost mechanical after that, each kill a little less of a high and more of a chore, like the fourth hit of Ecstasy when the pleasure was gone and you were just looking for the energy to go on. When he'd finished there was blood *everywhere*. He placed himself in the middle of it, feet planted in the deepest pool. He lifted a hand to his mask and considered lifting it. But no, the crime-scene photos would be so much more memorable if he was still wearing it. The media would love it. They'd fucking eat it up.

The barrel of the gun scalded him even through the mask as he rested it against his temple. All that heat from the bullets, the transformed kinetic energy. That was something he'd learned in Mr Skeet's class. He took a deep, final breath as his eyes slid shut.

They snapped open again when he heard the footstep behind him. His finger tightened on the trigger of his second weapon as he spun, but the chamber clicked empty and the man just smiled. For a moment he thought this must be his father. The shape of the face was the same, and the wide hazel eyes. But this man was younger, and his father had never worn quite that knowing, cynically amused expression.

The man nodded at the gun in his other hand, the one still pointed at his own temple.

"If you knew where you were going," he said, "you wouldn't be in such a hurry to get there."

The man was waiting for Alex outside the front door of the school. She walked right past him into the bitterly cold Manhattan morning, cellphone pressed to her ear as she made an appointment with her manicurist, only for him to grab her wrist and swing her round to face him.

"What the hell do you think you're doing?" she said, jerking her arm futilely in his grasp. "And while we're on the subject, who the hell do you think you are?"

He was a tall, dark-haired Native American, with a quality of stillness about him so intense that it was hard to tell if he was even breathing. "I'm an agent of the federal government, Miss Keve," he said. "And I'm arresting you. I can put on more of a show if you like. Mirandize you, handcuffs, the works. Or you could just come quietly."

She was so shocked that she let him pull her unresisting down the steps and past the stunted, winter-bald oak trees to the car park out front. It was only when she saw Jenna leaning against her Porsche, eyes unreadable behind dark glasses as she waited for her ride home, that Alex returned to her senses. She dug in her heels, skidding a few inches against the sidewalk before pulling him to a halt.

"Not so fast, Agent Orange," she said. "How about you show me some ID? And how about I get my constitutionally mandated phone call and use to it call my dad? Who, by the way, is a senior 9th circuit judge, in case no one mentioned that to you."

He raised an eyebrow, unperturbed. "Have it your way, kid. You have the right to remain silent. Anything you say can and will be used against you in a court of law–" He pitched his voice loud enough to carry across the entire car park. Jenna's head jerked up at the sound, looking shocked when she caught sight of Alex.

"Shut up!" Alex hissed. "I'm coming, OK – just shut the hell up."

The rest of the walk passed in silence, but he didn't release her wrist and she felt eyes on her, boring into the back of her head. Kids at West Village High didn't get arrested. It just wasn't that sort of school.

Alex waited until she was inside his black Ford before she turned to him again. She'd decided on a new tactic, and it required her to look friendly. Her smile was so stiff it made her jaw ache.

"Look, this has to be some mistake," she said. "Why don't you drive me home, have a word with my dad – I'm sure we can clear this all up." She was sure her father would be furious, but dealing with his anger seemed like the least bad option right now.

"Here's the thing," he said. "Most people, when they're told they're under arrest, ask what the hell for."

"I..." she trailed into silence.

"You need to work on your poker face, kid. Too many tells."

He was right and he knew it and there was nothing she could do about it. After a second he clicked on the radio to some college station, tapping his finger against the wheel just out of time with the music. She looked at her reflection in the car's tinted window, long blonde hair bleached to ash and pale skin, ghost-like. She didn't look like an innocent person taken against her will. She looked like a guilty person who'd been caught.

"I have a problem," she said eventually. "I'll get help. I'll go into rehab. I'm not hurting anybody except myself."

He nodded almost imperceptibly, eyes fixed on the road and finger still tapping.

"What do the FBI care about a little recreational drug use, anyway?"

"They don't," he said. "But thanks for the heads-up. I'll make sure to have local law enforcement search your home and locker."

After that she sat in silence, fists clenched and jaw working soundlessly. She'd walked right into it and she only had herself to blame, but that didn't stop her fury. And beneath that, quivering in her belly, her fear. Because she really hadn't done anything other than attend a few pharma parties and maybe score X a few times when they hit the East Village clubs. There was no reason why a federal agent should have dragged her out of school and into his unmarked car. And though she'd asked for ID, he'd never shown it.

He was bigger and stronger than her – if she reached for her cellphone, he might hurt her. She thought about screaming, but there was no one to hear except him. She had the horrible feeling it would just make him laugh.

She stared out of the window instead, trying to memorise their route, imagining repeating it to a cop, a real one, when she made her escape. The West Village passed by, leafy and quiet, dull Chelsea, the sprawling campus of Colombia and then the shabby-hipness of Harlem. They were on 130th, somewhere between Lennox and 5th, when the car finally slowed.

Alex hoped they'd stop on the street where she'd have a chance to call for help, but her captor pressed a button on the dash and the doorway to an underground garage opened onto darkness. She banged against the glass of the window as the car slid down, but all it did was bruise her palm and no one looked round.

"I'm not going to hurt you," the man said mildly as he reversed the car between two identical black Impalas.

"You haven't even told me your name."

"You can call me PD if you want."

The underground garage was empty, dank and dripping. Her heels caught in the cracked concrete as she walked beside him, but he didn't take her wrist again and she let herself believe that was a good sign.

"PD," she said, "are you really with the FBI?"

"I never said that I was." He turned to stare at her, head cocked to one side, considering. "Listen, kid – you're in trouble, but not the kind you think. You'll be walking out of here alive.

Whether you're walking out a free woman or in cuffs is up to you."

He led her to a rusted metal door and punched a number into a keypad lock before swinging it open. The corridor beyond was white-painted and strip-lit, clinical and unwelcoming. Her footsteps echoed on the tiled floor but there was no one around to hear them.

The room he brought her to contained nothing but a table and three chairs. PD gestured at one of them and settled himself beside her so that she had to twist her head to see him. She was sure it was deliberate, an interrogation technique. But what the hell did he want to interrogate her about?

She tried to keep calm and not let the waiting get to her the way it was clearly intended to. She tried to convince herself this was all a trick of her father's, something he'd cooked up with his contacts in the NYPD in an attempt to scare her straight. It was almost plausible enough that she could buy it.

When the door opened behind her with a whoosh of air she couldn't suppress her start of surprise. She forced herself not to look around as the newcomer paused behind her. PD's head lifted and she knew the two were exchanging glances.

A few seconds passed before she heard a soft sound which could have been a laugh or maybe just a sigh, and the newcomer moved to sit opposite her. He was thin, old and white with a friendly, almost avuncular face and eyes such an odd, pale blue they appeared blind. But the most striking things about him were his hands. He held them steepled in front of him, slender, desiccated fingers tapering into hooked nails. They were a skeleton's hands covered in only the thinnest parchment layer of skin.

"Miss Keve," he said, "My name is Hammond. You must be wondering why you're here."

She nodded, not trusting her voice.

"The Patriot Act's a marvellous thing, Alexandra. It gives us a freedom we never had before. It allows us to listen in on a populace that once valued its privacy above its safety. And, as the conspiracy theorists have correctly surmised, Al Qaeda operatives aren't the only people we're searching for."

Alex's heart raced as she tried to recall the hundreds of phone conversations she'd held in the last few weeks. Had she said anything incriminating? But they already knew about the drugs and didn't seem to care.

Hammond read her expression and smiled. "No need to rack your brain, young lady. I can tell you exactly what you said that interested us."

He nodded to PD, and a moment later the sound her of own voice filled the room. It was a little slurred in places, over-enunciated in others. It was clear she'd been wasted.

"Hey," her voice said. "Is that the – what's the word? Is that the NBC *complaints division*?" There was a brief pause, but no reply came. She'd probably reached an answering machine and failed to realise it.

"Well, anyway," her voice continued, "I've got a complaint to make. I'm – it's late, I'm a little – I'm watching the news right now, and it's some piece about a high-school football team raising money for some 9/11 charity, and that's supposed to be uplifting, right? I mean boring, but uplifting. But there's *blood everywhere*."

There was another pause, and in this one you could hear her sob. "He killed them all – he shot the whole fucking lot of them. Jesus, I don't know, maybe that's news or whatever, but did you have to show the bodies? That... that girl with her head blown off, and the guy in the George Bush mask, that's just sick." A shuddering breath, and then her voice was a little steadier. "So yeah, that's what I wanted to say. Just stop showing it, all right. Please stop showing it."

There was the hiss of static, and then a long stretch of silence. Alex had no memory at all of making that call, but she knew when it must have been: 10 days ago exactly after that night at Jenna's where they'd all tried ketamine and god knows what else and none of them had had a very good time on it, but she'd had the worst. "Down the K-hole," Jenna had said, and after that it was all blank until Alex woke the next morning with a pounding head and a feeling of sick, unfocused dread.

Alex didn't generally follow the news – she didn't give a shit – but she'd seen the piece about the school shooting in Iowa, where an unknown boy in a George Bush mask had murdered 27 of his classmates. The police still hadn't confirmed the identity of the killer, but then it was only *three days* since the shooting.

"I didn't know it was going to happen!" she said. "It was – I don't know, a crazy coincidence or something. You can't possibly think I was involved. I've never even been to Iowa!"

"It was no coincidence," Hammond said.

PD's chair squeaked against the floor as he shifted. He was watching her through narrowed eyes.

"You weren't bullshitting me," she said. "You really work for the government."

Hammond shrugged. "For the... let's say for the CIA."

She'd moved beyond fear into a kind of frozen calm so brittle it could shatter at the slightest pressure. "Look," she said. "I was high. I'd taken... all kinds of stuff and I had no idea what I was saying. I don't even remember saying it."

Hammond's thin lips pressed together. "But you did. You did, Alexandra, and I find that very interesting indeed."

She wondered what they would do with her. Were they going to ask her to identify her accomplice, the boy in the George Bush mask? Would they offer her a deal if she did? She could lie, just make up a name. If it was common enough there'd probably be a boy at the school in Iowa who had it. But that would be an admission of guilt and she wasn't ready for that. She was innocent, and some part of her that still believed in the pledge of allegiance and America the Brave and all that shit, thought that ought to count for something.

"You want to know what I think happened?" Hammond said. "Those drugs – whatever it was you took – opened a doorway in your mind, and for a brief moment you were in the spirit world, where time has no meaning."

Alex stared at him. "You think *what*?"

"There really was a broadcast about that school on NBC the night you called. And when you saw it in that state, you saw... well, to say the future would oversimplify things. Time in the spirit world isn't unidirectional. But you saw the psychic scar that the events to come would leave."

There was no hint of madness in his pale eyes and when she looked at PD he nodded encouragement and agreement.

"OK," she said. "Right. So you're saying I *didn't* have anything to do with that shooting. So why the hell have you brought me here?"

Hammond reached across the table to rest his dry, skeletal hand against hers. "You're a spirit traveller, Alexandra, the first of your generation. That makes you very rare and very valuable indeed. In the right hands and with the right training you could be an enormous asset."

PD shifted in his seat, and for the first time Alex noticed the bulge of the jacket at his hip, the tell-tale shape of a handgun beneath it.

He followed the direction of her gaze. "I told you I won't hurt you, kid."

"That's the last thing we want," Hammond said. "Our aim is to recruit you."

She jerked back, pulling her hand from beneath Hammond's. "*Recruit* me? I'm sixteen!"

"Oh, we'd want you to finish school, of course," Hammond said. "You wouldn't enter active service for a few years – though we'd train you in the interim, and perhaps make occasional use of your unusual abilities. What do you say, Miss Keve?"

Her chair scraped shrilly against the tiles as she stood. "No! More no than you can possibly imagine! You're crazy, this is crazy and even if it wasn't there's no way I'm working for the federal fucking government. I've got thirty million dollars in trust – I'm not going to work at all!"

Hammond suddenly didn't look friendly or avuncular. "I'm not sure you fully understand the situation here. We have evidence – quite solid evidence, I imagine, since the search warrant on your house was executed a few minutes ago – that you've been engaging in illegal activities. We also have testimony from several of your friends that you have, on more than one occasion, supplied them with controlled substances. I don't have to tell you that's a felony. How do you think you'd enjoy prison, Alexandra – with or without your thirty million dollar trust fund?"

Alex took in a shuddering breath. "My dad–"

"Hasn't always been a model of integrity. We have files that could end his political career for ever. Don't think he wouldn't sacrifice you to keep them buried."

"You bastard!" she said. But she knew he was right. Her father wouldn't pull strings to save her if it cost him his job.

She pictured prison, the shame and the boredom and the fear – every woman in there knowing her father was a judge. Her life would be over, maybe literally, definitely metaphorically. She tried to imagine Jenna standing by her, or Ryan or any of her friends, and knew they wouldn't. Their complicity in her crime would drive them away from her. And her dad would be so stern and cold and disapproving, and her mom would say all the right things to the press and nothing at all to her.

She let herself sink back into her chair. "You win. But I guess you knew that."

Hammond smiled wide. "I'm pleased to hear it. Welcome to the Bureau of Counter-Rational Warfare, Alexandra."

CHAPTER ONE

Morgan missed the smoke. The last time he'd been out drinking in London was before the ban and he still associated the taste of beer with the chemical fog of other people's cigarettes. He ran his palm across his cornrows and wished he was somewhere else.

"Get that down you, for god's sake," Ian said, slapping a pint on the table. "You've got a face like a pit bull licking piss off a nettle." His own face was open and smiling, darkened to the colour of teak by a summer tan.

"Must be the company that's making me miserable." Morgan managed a smile but it wasn't really a joke. He'd forgotten how to *be* with people, even now he finally could.

"You called me, man," Ian said. It was true. Morgan *had* got in touch with him, an old almost-friend from the care home on Coldharbour Lane, one of the few who'd done all right for himself with a job at John Lewis and a council flat he was close to buying.

Kate had assured Morgan it was OK to have friends now he was no longer a mortal danger to those around him. And maybe she hadn't meant it that way, but he'd taken it as an order to *get* some friends. He didn't think he was proving very good at it.

"So..." Ian said a few moments into the awkward silence. "The army, right?"

Morgan nodded. "Yeah, well, kind of. Got out a few months ago."

"Oh." Ian's face fell. "Look, man, I don't think there's any openings on the Oxford Street branch."

It took Morgan a moment to realise what Ian had assumed. "Oh shit – no, that's not... I don't need a job. I've been gone a while, I just thought it'd be good to get back in touch. Remind everyone I'm still alive. You know."

Ian laughed, relieved. "That's cool. Middle of some desert for five years, then you're back here – that's gotta be strange."

"You've got no fucking idea."

Ian studied Morgan with unsettling thoroughness. "Did you kill anyone?"

Morgan wondered how to respond, but Ian spoke before he could. "Sorry – don't answer that, it's a stupid question."

"It's not. I was a soldier. That's what we're for, isn't it?"

"That's not what I meant."

"But it's true. I killed a lot of people, Ian. A lot. And now I'm back here, and I look around, and all I can think is how nobody understands a fucking thing. If they knew what I knew, if they'd seen what I've seen..."

"You've gotta give it time, man," Ian said. It was probably a phrase he'd heard on *Jeremy Kyle*, Morgan thought. But knowledge wasn't like grief; it didn't fade with the weeks and months. Some things couldn't be unlearnt – hadn't Tomas told him that?

The memory of his dead friend cut like a knife, and for a moment Morgan wanted to tell Ian everything. He wanted to describe the year when he really had been just another squaddie in Afghanistan and the incident which had ended all that, when a round he'd meant for an insurgent had found one of his own lads instead.

He wanted to talk about being recruited by the SIS, training as a sniper, the missions they'd sent him on which they'd been careful never to call assassinations. He wanted to describe what it felt like to see someone's face in the sights of your rifle and know that a second later you were going to put a bullet through it.

Most of all, he wanted to tell Ian about the Hermetic Division. The trip across Europe with Tomas and Anya when all his certainties had been ripped away. He needed to talk about Tomas, who'd died twenty years before and come back for one final mission. And he desperately needed to talk about his father, Nicholson, who told Morgan he'd been born out of death and carried it with him. Nicholson had *created* Morgan to be an agent of evil. And Morgan thought he'd rejected that destiny, but every day since he wondered if he really could.

Morgan wanted to tell Ian all of it. He might not believe, but he'd listen and even saying the words would be a relief. Morgan watched the bubbles rising to the surface of his pint, paler than the gold lager, and knew he never would.

There was a man reflected in the glass. The image was blurry and distorted, but there was no mistaking the ragged cut in his neck. It had probably been made by a broken bottle. Morgan had to suppress the urge to look behind him. He knew the man wasn't really there. But he had been. Once, Morgan was a danger to everyone around him. Someone told him he emitted mortality. That had gone along with his birthright, but it hadn't left him normal. Now he *saw* death.

If Morgan told Ian he might believe, but he'd never understand, not really. And he'd be safer and happier not knowing.

The ringing of his mobile cut through his thoughts. The caller ID told him it was Kate. "Sorry," he told Ian, "I've gotta get that."

Ian shrugged and Morgan thought he was probably relieved at the interruption.

"What?" Morgan snapped into the phone.

"And a very good evening to you too," Kate said.

Morgan moved away from the table, feet sticking slightly to the beer-clogged carpet. "Tell me this isn't you telling me I've got to go to work, and I'll tell you good evening."

He could hear the smile in Kate's voice as she said, "You know me too well. I need you to get yourself over to University College London – that's on Gower Street in the centre of town. Just go to main reception and I'll meet you inside."

"What's the emergency?"

"Why spoil the surprise? I'll see you there, Morgan."

The call cut off before he could ask anything further. He shook his head, sure she was paying him back for his earlier cheek. And it occurred to him that he'd known Kate only two months and Ian more than a decade, but he felt closer to his boss than he ever did to his childhood friend.

Ian looked up from his pint as Morgan approached. "Something happened?"

"Work called. Sorry, man, I've gotta go."

He was halfway to the door when Ian called out, "What you doing now, anyway? You never said."

Morgan hesitated a moment, studying the other man, the smile lines starting to form around his mouth and the wide innocence of his eyes. "No, I didn't," he said finally. "You have a nice life, Ian."

He could feel Ian watching him as he weaved between the tables to reach the door, but he didn't look back.

Night had fallen when an hour and two buses later Morgan reached Gower Street and strode through the front gates with a confidence he didn't feel. The moon was full above the white buildings and the grand central dome of the university, but its light was drowned out by the glare of London.

He didn't spot the cops until he was nearly on top of them, a cluster of uniforms at the foot of the staircase leading inside. "It's closed, mate," one of them said. "Crime scene."

"That's what I'm here about," Morgan guessed.

"Yeah, and who are you?" The policeman scowled beneath his blond crew cut. Morgan saw that he had a Celtic knot tattoo circling his arm to disappear beneath the short sleeve of his shirt.

"He's with me," Kate said, striding down the stairs towards them. "This way, Morgan." Night time erased the wrinkles around her eyes and blurred the silver in her hair so that he could see her as the striking young girl Tomas had fallen in love with, not the weary, middle-aged woman she'd become.

"Crime scene?" he said as they ducked into the foyer. "What crime?"

"Murder."

When they turned left, he saw the body perched upright in a wooden case against one of the walls. It was dressed in an old-fashioned frock coat.

Kate raised an eyebrow as he turned towards it, then smiled. "No, that's not it."

Closer to, Morgan could see she was right. The face was wax, not flesh, the rosy glow of the cheeks painted on. "What is this?" he said. "Fucking Madam Tussauds?"

"Actually, the skeleton *is* real. That's Jeremy Bentham – he was a philosopher. When he died in 1832 he left his body to the University, but his will stipulated that the corpse had to be preserved and displayed. It's supposed to attend annual board meetings, too. Bentham called it his Auto Icon."

She shivered, and Morgan knew she was thinking about Tomas. They turned their backs on the body and walked deeper inside the building, past the public spaces and into a dingy corridor with blue-and-white police tape stretched across one end. Morgan followed Kate as she ducked underneath.

The room beyond was larger than he'd expected, a lecture theatre with a semi-circle of raked seating facing a lectern and a screen. The screen was lit-up, the headline 'Heteronormative Influences in Elizabethan Alchemy' followed by a block of writing which made even less sense. The police appeared to have been and gone, a latex glove and a dusting of fingerprint powder on one of the wooden benches the sole relics of their presence. The insect-whine of a computer fan was the only sound in the room.

The woman's body was sprawled beside the lectern, eyes open but unseeing. She looked almost the same age as Kate, but less pretty. She had the sort of face that inspired affection rather than desire; round-cheeked and friendly.

"Doctor Jane Granger. Cambridge academic due to give a guest lecture at UCL tomorrow," Kate said. "Apparently she was nervous, so she decided to rehearse it. The killer must have known where to find her."

Cause of death wasn't hard to guess. There was a slash across Granger's throat so deep it had cut through her windpipe and into the bones of her spine. They shone white against the red flesh and Morgan had seen enough death to know that was odd. Blood should have masked the wound, but there was none either in the cut or pooling on the floor around her head.

"Can I?" he said, leaning closer.

When Kate nodded he reached out a hand to tip the woman's head. That was when the smell hit him, the stink of scorched flesh. Close to, he could see the burn marks around the cut and the bubbling blisters on the skin of her neck. The tissue around the wound was blackened and smooth – cauterised.

He rocked back on his heels. "What the hell happened?"

"We were hoping you could tell us." She nodded at the back wall of the lecture theatre, where a mirror hung in a chipped frame.

Morgan knew what she was asking and hesitated. There was a part of him that still wanted to deny the hidden world and accept the comforting illusion of normality. "I can't guarantee I'll see something," he said.

She smiled at him. "Just try, Morgan. Granger died violently here – there's a good chance her spirit's hanging around, reliving the moment. Isn't that how it works?"

He shrugged. "Maybe. I still haven't figured it all out."

His knees cracked as he rose. The mirror was thick with dust, reflecting the room through a haze and bleaching the brown of his skin to a faded sepia. He wiped the glass with his sleeve and the picture sprang into sharper focus: his own face framed by geometric circles of seating.

For a long moment that was all he saw. He'd tried forcing it before, clenching his muscles because he didn't know how to tense whatever part of his mind allowed him to do this. It was always useless and he didn't bother this time, relaxing instead and letting his thoughts drift.

As they had before, they drifted to Richard, the man who'd first shown Morgan this could be done – and summoned his long-dead sister on a night train to Berlin. "I only open the door," he'd said. Morgan didn't think Richard had meant it literally, but he'd learnt that in the other world metaphor could be as powerful as truth. He let his eyes lose focus until the glass of the mirror was just a grey blank – then imagined pushing it. He thought how cold the glass would feel under his palm, and he pictured it moving, the creak of hinges.

When the mirror swung open there was darkness beyond. He thought that if he tried hard enough his eyes could pierce it, but he didn't want to know what he'd see. In that moment of fear his mind released the image and the door swung shut, closing with a soft *click*.

The glass was a mirror again and Morgan could see the reflection of a woman – but it wasn't Kate. This woman's cheeks were rounder, her eyes a paler, washed-out blue. Her gaze passed over Morgan without seeing him. She was studying herself, mouth squeezed shut as she applied her lipstick.

Morgan noticed the man behind her at the same time she did. He was watching her in the glass. His hair and eyes were the same dark brown that was almost black and though he was dressed in jeans and a T-shirt, Morgan thought he belonged in uniform. He recognised a soldier when he saw one, the tense shoulders and loose arms, aggression held on only a light leash.

The woman gasped, then turned and smiled. Morgan fought the futile urge to shout a warning. This was her killer and she didn't know it and wouldn't realise until it was too late.

The man took a step towards her. His mouth was moving, but the glass didn't transmit sound and the woman's back was to the mirror now, her expression hidden. Morgan could read the sudden stiffening of her spine, though, and knew that whatever the man had said alarmed her.

But not enough. The man took another step closer and she stood her ground. It was only when he drew his knife that she tried to make a run for it and by then it was too late. The man grabbed a fistful of her hair, bending her head back and resting his blade against the vulnerable skin of her throat. The knife looked like ordinary steel and leather, but where it touched her skin Morgan saw a wisp of smoke curl into the air. He imaged he could hear the sizzle of burning flesh.

Her mouth moved, still soundless, but Morgan knew she was begging the man to let her go. Morgan's jaw clenched as he forced himself not to move.

The man pressed the knife harder against the woman's throat, using the flat of the blade to cause maximum pain with minimal risk of accidental death. His face remained dispassionate. There was no hint that he enjoyed hurting the woman. There was no pleasure in it for him, it was purely about getting results.

White blisters bloomed on her neck, ichor leaking into the hollow of her clavicle. Her lips moved again and Morgan could read them now, "Oh god, oh god, oh god," over and over again. Saliva sprayed from her mouth, droplets speckling and blurring the mirror's surface.

There were flecks of her spittle in the man's eyelashes until he blinked them away. The movements of his mouth were smaller and more controlled, but Morgan could read them too. "Where is it?" he said. "Have you found it?"

She spoke for longer this time, gabbling so Morgan couldn't follow what she was saying. The man cocked his head as he listened, probably assessing her honesty. But the woman was too terrified to lie and her attacker seemed to realise that. He smiled a little. Then he looked back at the woman and the smile died. Morgan closed his eyes as the knife slashed and the woman's mouth stretched wide in its final, silent scream.

When he opened them again the woman's body had slumped out of sight and only the man remained. He was frowning, one deep upright groove in the centre of his forehead as he stared at the mirror. And Morgan knew it could only be a trick of perspective, but in the instant before his image disappeared from the glass, the man seemed to be staring right at him.

CHAPTER TWO

PD was waiting for Alex outside the School of Native American Studies, and for a second she flashed back to their very first meeting. In the seven years since he'd changed very little, only the first hint of crow's feet seaming the skin around his eyes. He must have been a young man new to the Agency when she'd first seen him, but to her 16-year-old eyes he'd seemed ancient.

He nodded a greeting and she raised a lazy hand in response. The classmate walking beside her shot her a questioning look. "Old family friend," she told him, her stock answer. "He and I are going away for a few days – road trip. I'll catch you when I get back."

"Hey, kid," PD said. "Looking for some action?"

She suppressed a smile. "Kid? Really?"

His gaze raked her quickly up and down, frankly appreciative. But when he met her eyes again there was something odd in his. "No, I guess not."

PD didn't speak again till they were in the car together, the latest in a long string of black Impalas. "I hear you got the lowest score ever recorded on the shooting range last month."

She shrugged, hiding her half smile behind her long blonde hair. "I guess I'm just not cut out for life in the CIA. Must be why I keep failing my finals. Shame you don't want me to start work for you till I graduate."

"Isn't it," he said. She'd grown accustomed to him in all the years he'd been dropping in and out of her life, but she still hadn't learnt to read him. She thought he seemed tense, though, and his tension gradually transmitted itself to her until she realised her hands were balled into tight fists.

"So what's the plan for this little outing?" she asked. "LSD? Prescription pain-killers? Crystal meth? It's kind of ironic, if you think about it. I've taken more drugs since I've been working for the government than I ever consumed as a private citizen. "

"And yet you've never seen anything worth telling us." He kept his eyes on the road as he took a right towards the Manhattan Bridge exit.

"Well, I did see an amazing light show when you made me take five hits of X in a night."

"But no visions, no insights into the spirit world."

She let him see her smile this time as she shook her head. They'd been playing this game for a long time. The fury she'd felt when they first recruited her had faded with familiarity and PD had become something like a friend. But she was ready for the game to be over. The Agency had to tire of wasting its money on her soon, didn't it?

It better, said a voice inside her head that wasn't quite her own, and she felt her smile dropping. The visions had been getting stronger with every drug she took and it was growing harder and harder to deny them. She hadn't quite come to believe in this spirit world Hammond was so desperate for her to access, but she saw *something*.

She was staring out of the window, mind drifting, when she finally registered the route they were taking. This wasn't the way to the isolated cottage in the Catskills where they usually performed their tests.

"We're taking a flight," PD said. She realised his attention had been on her the whole time.

"A field trip," she said. "Are we going somewhere exciting?"

He didn't smile and she noticed for the first time how stiff his face looked. They'd reached the messy sprawl of JFK and PD swerved the car into the nearest space and pulled on the handbrake. His seatbelt undid with a snap as he turned to look at her.

She took a breath, bracing herself, but he just smiled and said, "Happy birthday."

"Oh," she said. "I didn't think you knew. But then I guess you've got access to my personnel files, right? And the rest. You probably know what my favourite colour is."

"Blue. So, any nice gifts? Another Porsche? Your own tropical island?"

Alex shrugged, suddenly awkward. "My trust fund matured two years ago. After that, mom and dad said I could buy whatever I wanted for myself."

"Yeah, that's what I thought. What do you get for the girl who has everything? Something cheap."

He reached across to flick open the compartment on her side of the dash, his palm grazing her thigh as he dropped a paper-wrapped package in her lap.

She stared at it for several seconds. "You bought me a birthday present," she said.

He nodded, no longer looking at her.

She hesitated a moment, then tore it open. "A French phrase-book. You shouldn't have." She tried to sound dry but wasn't sure she succeeded. She couldn't quite believe he'd remembered.

"I know you wanted to study it, before we... sidetracked you," he said. He was looking at her again and his expression froze her. "I've done what I can, Alex. They wanted you to get in the game the second you turned 21. I told them to let you finish your degree, and when you made it clear that was never gonna happen, I told them to wait till you were willing – that we'd get the best out of you that way. But they've run out of patience and you've run out of time."

She dropped the phrase book to the carpeted floor of the car with a muffled thump. "I can't work for you if I can't do the job, can I?"

He sighed. "Hammond's not a fool. He's gone all in on you and there's no chance he's going to fold now. Alex, how could you think he'd just take your word for it? Your food at night was laced with sodium pentothal. Our best interrogators sat you down with our best hypnotists and they found out everything."

She had to swallow twice before she could speak. "I don't know what you're talking about."

"We know about the second selves you see, a black bear for Hammond and the coyote for me. We know about the fire in the house two blocks away, the one you saw burning three weeks before it happened. We know about the raven who speaks to you. He wants to be your spirit guide, only you won't let him."

"You know everything," she said.

He opened the door, warm air wafting in to replace the air-conditioned chill. "You can fail all the shooting tests you like, and you can fail out of college as well if you want, but this is happening. So you might wanna learn how to fire a gun straight, because from now on it's real, and you're part of it."

The airfield was a strip of pitted tarmac in the middle of a forest, a grey streak in the endless green. Alex felt her ears pop as the plane landed and the sound of the engine changed from a muted rumble to a fierce roar before spluttering into silence as they taxied to a halt.

Her legs were cramped from the long journey and they ached dully as she descended the stairs to the airstrip. The drooping trees looked as weary as she felt but she forced her back to straighten as the car drew to a halt beside them.

PD sat beside her as they were driven away, staring out of the window. She didn't know what time of day it was or in which country they'd finally ended their flight, and she refused to ask. They were in Eastern Europe, she knew that much, and the tired quality of the sunlight suggested the day might be drawing to a close. The journey took less than an hour as dusty woodland scrolled by outside. Alex's stomach felt uneasy and her mind hazy with a combination of sleep deprivation and fear.

When the car finally braked PD grasped her arm, his fingers transmitting the anxiety he kept from his face. "Listen to me, kid.

Hammond didn't get where he is by being a nice guy. If he can't have you, he won't let anyone else. And officially, this place doesn't even exist."

The warning hung unanswered in the air as they drew to a halt outside their destination. It was hidden in the heart of the forest, an old Soviet prison repurposed for the War on Terror. Decaying walls were topped with new razor wire but the aura of despair felt like it had hung over the place for centuries. Despite the stifling heat, Alex shivered as she and PD exited the car.

A sentry with sunburn and a Kalashnikov slung across his hip waved them to a stop outside the gate. The planes of his face shifted seismically as he frowned down at their IDs, and he looked twice between their photos and them before standing aside.

Another soldier led them to the officers' mess, deserted at this time of day. He gestured at a small plate on which Alex could see a pile of the dried brown flakes she'd learnt to recognise as peyote. His expression was openly curiously but PD just smiled and thanked him and waited for him to leave the room before looking at Alex.

"OK," he said, "You know what you have to do."

She picked up a fragment of the dried cactus and turned it in her fingers but didn't put it in her mouth. "This is a bad place," she said. "If I take a trip here, I won't see anything good. I'm not bullshitting you, PD, I'll do what Hammond wants – just please, not here."

He studied her. She knew from the small mirror in the plane's restroom that her hair hung lank and greasy and the foundation she'd applied did little to disguise her pallor. She looked sick, at the end of her endurance.

PD's expression softened. "It has to be here, they want you to look at some of the prisoners, tell them what you sense. It won't be so bad, kid. It's just a vision – nothing you see is really real."

She couldn't articulate why that was wrong, why reality wasn't the right metric by which the world of her visions should be measured. So she just nodded, then put the drug in her mouth and swallowed, scrunching her face at the bitter taste. PD's eyes didn't lower and she ate another piece and then another, until the plate was empty – a far greater dose than she'd ever taken before.

"Sit down," he said. "Relax. It'll be a while before they're ready to see us or you're ready to see what they want."

She couldn't cope with his kindness. She wanted to hate him for his part in this, and he kept making that impossible. She opened her mouth to tell him that, then closed it again when she realised the drug was already taking effect, faster and more powerfully than anything she'd previously experienced. Colours writhed at the edge of her vision, struggling to free themselves from the shapes which confined them.

She could sense the peyote inside her, a living presence that wasn't quite a possession. She imagined it as warm water, flowing through every part of her. And every part of her it touched, it changed. Her hands felt looser and lighter. They throbbed in a pulse that was like a heartbeat, but not hers. She could see the bones shining white beneath her skin. She shifted her gaze and there was PD's skull, grinning at her as all skulls did.

A blink of her eyes and his face was back, worried and unsmiling beneath short black hair. Another blink and she saw his other face with its long muzzle and lolling tongue. The creature was his companion and also a part of him, the contradiction of being both self and other somehow perfectly reconcilable in this parallel world.

The coyote looked a little sad, its yellow eyes downcast. Alex thought it was because PD couldn't see it and wouldn't acknowledge it. "Look at yourself," she told him, but he just frowned and she knew he didn't understand.

"Are you ready?" he asked her.

She didn't reply, her eyes straining for what she knew would come next. She heard its cry before she saw it, a dry *caw-caw* that was halfway between a cough and a laugh. She didn't know its true name, but it always came, the guide she didn't want to a world she'd prefer not to enter. Recently she'd begun to sense it flying in her shadow in the real world.

"Raven," she said and realised this was the first time she'd ever openly acknowledged it.

The bird lifted its head from where it had been picking at its glossy black feathers. Its face was incapable of human expression but she read a smile in its bright, knowing eyes.

"Are you ready at last?" Raven asked, and this time she said, "Yes".

The bird flew down a long corridor that was also a path through the woods. Tangled briers caught at her heels as she followed. PD held her arm to guide her but Raven knew the way. Ahead of her she could see another figure – a man, she thought – hurrying away from her. She found her steps dragging, sure for some reason that she didn't want to catch this other traveller in the spirit world. But when they reached the cells, the figure was gone.

The soldiers who were waiting for them had wolf spirits. Their teeth glittered white as they smiled and Raven laughed, unafraid of these earthbound things. Alex dismissed them too, beta males who only knew how to follow.

The bars of the cage were cold iron, a brand on the world. Alex flinched away from them as she slid through the door of the cell, but she felt their chill. Inside it was worse. Terrible things had been done here, and the spirit realm never forgot. Alex felt Raven's weight settle on her shoulder and its beak brushed her ear as it ducked its head towards her. Its claws dug into her as she studied the three men in the cell. Their dark hair dripped with water and a sheen of it glittered across their faces. They had been drowned once, or more than once, and in their minds they were still drowning.

"What the hell have you done to them?" Alex whispered.

"You know, you know, you know," Raven cawed in her ear.

"They've been questioned," PD said. Though his human face was expressionless, she read a flicker of shame in the coyote's eyes. "We need to know if we can believe what they've told us. Tell us what you see."

"I don't see any–" She broke off, spitting blood, as if the words had sharp edges which had cut at her throat as they came out.

"Fool, fool, fool," Raven croaked in her ear. "Lies hurt the liar here."

"I see them drowning," Alex said.

"And before that?" one of the soldiers asked. He was different from the others, a silver-haired human whose wolf shadow was broad and powerful, the alpha-male of the pack.

She looked at the prisoners again. Their eyes were haunted and hollow behind the glitter of water, and for a second she saw their spirit selves, the part of them that torture had almost obliterated. They were mountain goats, tough and agile – prey, not predators.

But the soldiers didn't want to hear they'd been torturing innocent men. They wouldn't believe her and she might end up taking the prisoners' place – she understood that this was Hammond's unspoken threat if she didn't do as he asked. She realised suddenly that she didn't care. She was damned if she was going to let them feel good about the unforgivable things they'd done to these people.

"They're innocent," she said. "They're not Al Qaeda. You've hurt them for nothing."

The commander glared at her and PD frowned. "Don't play games, Alex," he said.

"I'm not. You wanted me to show you the truth, you forced me to. Don't blame me if you don't like it."

"No more truth," Raven said. "No more, no more. " It leapt from her shoulder and through the canopy of trees in the forest that was now all she could see. Its small body faded into the black of the sky and her consciousness faded with it.

* * *

She woke in a hospital bed looking down at the white sheets folded beneath her armpits. PD was asleep in a chair beside her, slumped inelegantly with one arm hanging at his side, knuckles grazing the floor. She took a moment to study his face and was reassured to see that it was fully human. The last of the drug must have washed out of her system and the spirit world along with it. Her throat was still sore, though, and she shivered as she realised Raven had been right. The lie she'd told had physically hurt her.

PD grunted as he shifted in the chair and his eyes blinked open to stare straight into hers. His face was still relaxed from sleep and it looked momentarily younger. For the first time, she noticed something wounded in his dark eyes. He opened his mouth to say something, but before he could speak Hammond pushed through the door behind him. PD kept his eyes on her, only tearing them away when the older man shuffled impatiently, holding the door open for PD to leave.

"Feeling better, Alexandra?" Hammond asked once they were alone. His thin face twisted into an expression that was probably meant to be caring. PD's had been more convincing.

Alex shrugged. "The visions have gone. I don't know if that counts as better in your book."

"Right now it does. I have another job for you and I need you compos mentis for the briefing."

"I've just *done* a job for you – what more do you want?"

Hammond tossed something on the bed beside her: a thick leather wallet. "That's your badge. I would give you a gun but I suspect you'd shoot yourself in the foot and I need you on active duty. Welcome to full-time service, Agent Keve."

She opened her mouth, ready to protest that she had classes tomorrow and drinks with a friend arranged that evening. "I don't think I'm ready for another day like today," she said instead.

"We don't intend to burn you out, Alexandra. I've told you before, you're too valuable for that. And we will permit you return to your studies if you prove you can apply yourself."

"Yeah, why wouldn't you?" she said. "You were the one who forced me to major in Native American History in the first place."

Hammond rubbed his fingers against his temples as if she was giving him a headache. "We believed the subject would prove useful to you – the way being able to fire a gun would prove useful. We have your interests at heart."

"Where they coincide with yours."

"Of course. We're the government, not a charity – what did you expect?"

She sighed. "Exactly that. So what the hell is it you want me to do?"

"Have your heard of the Croatoans?"

Alex nodded. "Some bat-shit crazy Californian cult."

"But do you know anything about them?"

She shook her head.

"They possess the archetypal quality of being easy to join and very hard to leave. Their leader – who calls himself Laughing Wolf – claims he can teach his followers to transport their souls into the bodies of animals."

"And can he?" She'd meant the question to be sarcastic but Hammond took her seriously.

"We must hope not," he said.

Alex steepled her fingers in an unconscious imitation of Hammond's own habitual gesture. "So what if some loser gets to wander around as a racoon for a while? What do you care?"

The old man smiled. "We care because you're one of a kind, Alexandra – and you work for us. We're keen for things stay that way and we'll do whatever it takes to ensure they do. You might do well to bear that in mind."

CHAPTER THREE

Morgan spent two days expecting to be contacted by Kate and hearing from no one except telemarketers. When he'd been recruited to the Division he'd found himself a new flat, nearer to Borough and with furniture that came from Ikea rather than Argos. It was light and – unlike his old place – it was clean, but he was sick of the sight of it by the time the call came.

"About bloody time," he said when he answered the phone.

Kate chuckled. "Sorry. Took us a while to identify the killer."

"You know who he is?"

"Come into the office and I'll fill you in." As usual, she ended the call without saying good-bye.

The office meant a run-down Edwardian terrace house near the Oval. Morgan got there in a near jog, dodging pedestrians and the occasional surly cyclist. September was drawing to a close but the air was hot and humid as if summer wasn't quite ready to let go. By the time he arrived, his sweaty T-shirt was plastered to his back and his hair felt stiff with salt.

Kate answered the door herself. In all the weeks he'd been coming here, Morgan had only met one other member of the Hermetic Division and he'd clearly been a low-grade clerical worker. When he asked Kate she'd laughed and said, "This isn't the kind of organisation that has office parties. The less our agents know about each other, the safer everyone is."

As usual, the house was deserted. Kate led him through to the living room, a gloomy space with a carpet which might once have been blue. The sofa had been replaced with office chairs, the TV with a computer. Kate pulled one of the chairs close to it and gestured Morgan to do the same.

"Cup of tea would go down really well," he said as he slid into place.

She rolled her eyes, but disappeared into the kitchen to make one.

"You're such a pushover," he said when she returned.

She cradled her own cup in her hand as she booted up the computer. "Maybe it's just that you're so charming."

"Nah," he said. "You're a soft touch."

She smiled at him affectionately, but he knew it was second-hand. She cared about him because Tomas had and she seemed to feel that looking after Morgan was a way of paying back her lover for his sacrifice.

When the computer finished loading, the screen showed the sketch an artist had drawn from Morgan's description of the murderer. It was a good likeness, capturing the hard line of the man's mouth and his hawkish nose.

"Have you found him?" he asked.

"Found no, but we have identified him." She clicked the mouse and another image opened on screen. This one was a photo, but it was recognisably the same man. "Meir Porat, known as 'Lahav'. That's Hebrew for both flame and sword – it's not hard to guess why he got the name, is it? He's an agent of the Mossad, the Israeli secret service. They call his cell the Shomer Hamikdash, the Temple Guard."

"Like their version of the Hermetic Division?" Morgan said, and when Kate nodded, "But what are they doing killing some university professor over here?"

"That's the question."

"And that knife of his – what the fuck is it?"

"I don't know. If our intel's right, the Shomer have put a lot of resources into tracking down the lost treasure from the Temple in Jerusalem. The Romans sacked the place in 70AD and a group of very powerful artefacts were lost to history. We don't have concrete evidence, but rumours suggest the Israelis have already found one, a prayer shawl that protects the wearer from occult harm. It's possible the knife is another."

Morgan digested that. "And do you think that's why he's here? He's looking for more of these artefacts?"

"Maybe. Some of the treasure could have made its way over the Channel in the chaos following the fall of the Roman Empire. That could be where our murder victim fits in." She tapped the mouse again, and the woman's photo appeared on screen, a page from the University of Cambridge website. "Dr Granger's a fellow of Trinity College, a member of the history department and a specialist in Tudor England. She's never been arrested, never mixed with any unsavoury types and never previously come to the attention of the Hermetic Division. But if the Shomer Hamikdash are interested in her, then so are we."

"He wanted something she had – or he thought she had," Morgan remembered. "He asked her if she'd found it."

Kate nodded. "So his next stop's likely to be Cambridge."

"You want me to go there, see if I can track him down?"

"And find out what you can about Dr Granger while you're at it."

Morgan skimmed the rest of the webpage but it was written in impenetrable academic language and seemed mainly to consist of a list of publications. He shrugged and pushed his chair back, the wheels catching in the grubby carpet as they rolled. "OK, but how do I get access? Some posh Cambridge college isn't gonna let me just wander around."

Kate flipped him a leather wallet. When he opened it he saw that it held a police badge in his name. "You work for the government. We know how to make things happen."

She was gazing at him fondly, a half-smile on her lips.

"Listen," he blurted, speaking before he'd realised he intended to. "I wanted to ask you about – about me. About the things Nicholson told me." *That I was born without a soul*, he thought, but he didn't say it. It was too painful to articulate.

Kate curled her hands together in her lap, looking suddenly serious – or maybe uncomfortable. "Nicholson was... He wasn't a good man, Morgan. And he was trying to convince you to do what he wanted. I don't think you should pay much attention to what he said."

"I get that, but it doesn't mean it wasn't true. I'm not normal, am I? I reckon we can agree on that."

"Normal's overrated."

He shrugged and thought it was easy for her to say, who'd never had to spend a day worrying about who or what she was.

"But you're the government," he said. "You can get things done – and you can find things out. Can't you find out more about me?"

Her eyes shifted away from his and it occurred to him that they were already trying to find out about him. Of course they were. But if they didn't like what they found, would they ever tell him? If he was what his father had said he was, would they even risk letting him live, however useful he might be?

"Forget it," he said, rising. "It was a stupid idea. The trains to Cambridge go from King's Cross, right?"

Kate's hand on his arm stopped him as he made to leave the room, her palm warm against his skin. He hesitated a moment, then turned to look at her.

"Morgan," she said. "You're a good person. It doesn't matter how you were born, it's the choices you make that define you."

"I used to think that," he said. "All that stuff about good and evil and souls and hell, I thought it was so much shit, but we both know it isn't. And if it's true, maybe I can do as much good as I want, and it won't help me. Maybe I'm already damned."

Kate held his eyes this time. "I refuse to think the world works like that. I won't believe life is so unfair."

Morgan used his other hand to gently prise her fingers from his arm. "But if the world was fair, Tomas would still be alive, wouldn't he?"

He turned away from the sudden tears in her eyes and left before she could answer.

*   *   *

The journey to Cambridge was far quicker than he'd expected. In his mind, the university was at some opposite pole of existence from London and his rough, grey childhood in Lambeth. But forty-five minutes after setting out, the train pulled into the station.

It was a disappointingly characterless building, modern but slightly rundown and utterly charmless. It would have looked at home in any number of drab English towns. A taxi rank waited outside but Morgan chose to walk, though the earlier sunlight had given way to drizzle.

The first college he saw was a substantial golden building with a clocktower over its gatehouse. Morgan knew he looked like a tourist as he stopped and gawped but he didn't really care. It was such a peaceful place, despite the shoppers squeezing past on the main road and the gaggle of Americans being lectured by a woman holding a red umbrella. He tried to picture what it would have been like to spend the last few years here, instead of where he had, but his imagination failed him.

Kate seemed to think he could turn himself into someone else if he chose. How could he, though, when he couldn't even picture who that other person might be?

He hurried the rest of the way to Trinity College, through the centre of town and past a collection of equally picturesque colleges that he barely spared a glance. Trinity turned out to be one of the larger buildings, more imposing than welcoming ,though it was built from the same warm stone.

A tall man, dressed absurdly in a black jacket and bowler hat, stopped him at the gate. "Sorry, sir – only organised tours at the moment, I'm afraid."

"I'm here on business." Morgan pulled out the fake police ID. "Can you show me the way to Dr Granger's room?"

The man frowned. "Dr Granger lived outside college, near Chesterton. I believe officers have already been to her house."

"She's got a place here too, right?" Morgan guessed. "Somewhere she meets her students?"

"You think her murder might have something to do with the college?"

Morgan shrugged. "Just exploring possibilities."

"Of course. I'll take you up there now, sir."

He led Morgan through the front gate and into a courtyard that seemed to stretch for a mile in either direction. The central lawn was manicured as neatly as a golfing green and Morgan was led on two sides of a square to reach their destination, rather than cutting across the grass.

The room was on the second floor, at the top of a rickety wooden staircase. His guide turned an old-fashioned mortis key in the lock and Morgan smiled his thanks, then stood in the doorway until the other man huffed and left him alone.

Inside, it was smaller and shabbier than he'd expected. The furniture was old but not antique, the kind of stuff you could pick up at a second-hand shop down Walworth Road. The computer was modern, though, and he saw that it was still on. When he jogged the mouse, the screen lit. It took him a moment to see that Dr Granger had been in the middle of composing a letter, something dull to the Department of History. There was a half-eaten apple beside the keyboard, slowly shrivelling. She must have left for London in a rush.

Morgan was struck by the sudden sense of a life unfinished. Granger had expected to return, write the end of her letter, throw away her apple. He shivered and turned to scan the bookshelves. They were packed, books ranked in a double layer and others sitting on top. Some of the volumes had Dr Granger's name on them. He pulled one out – *Alchemical Transformations* – and read the blurb on the back, but it seemed to have been written for someone who already knew what the book was about.

A lower shelf proved more interesting, a whole stack of books with the words 'magic' or 'occult' in the title. *Did* the professor involve herself in the supernatural? But then how had she managed to stay off the Hermetic Division's radar – and at the same time attract the fatal attention of the Israelis?

Morgan's head jerked round at the sound of the door opening and he felt a moment of panicked guilt before he remembered he had every right to be there.

The young man paused in the doorway, blinking at Morgan.

"Oh," he said, "I thought I had my supervision now. Is Dr Granger not around?" He had curly brown hair cut short in a vain attempt to tame it, and wide hazel eyes that made him look permanently startled.

"I'm sorry," Morgan said, "Dr Granger's dead."

The young man's eyes widened even further. "What the hell happened?" he asked. Morgan realised he had an American accent, one of those flat, bland ones which were hard to place.

"She was murdered." Morgan took a step closer, studying the young man's reaction. "If she's your teacher, how come you haven't heard?"

"I'm her PhD student – I don't see her all that often and I live out of college. Jesus Christ! Murdered? Who'd want to do that?"

Morgan showed him the police ID. "That's what I'm here to find out. And you are..?"

"Coby, Coby Bryson. Like I said, I'm studying for my doctorate with Dr Granger. I mean, I *was*. Jesus – sorry, it's just a lot to take in."

Her PhD student, Morgan realised, probably knew more about Granger's field of study than anyone else. He pulled out the office chair for Coby, then perched on the prickly, over-stuffed sofa opposite him.

"What can you tell me about Dr Granger?" Morgan asked. "She was an expert in–" he flashed back to the powerpoint display she'd been preparing before her death "–Elizabethan alchemy, right?"

Coby swallowed, then nodded. "Yeah, but she was particularly interested in Dr John Dee. Have you heard of him?"

Morgan shook his head.

Coby leaned forward, hands on knees. He looked suddenly confident and enthusiastic – a man in his element. "John Dee was probably the most famous alchemist of his age. He was a scientist too, but people today aren't so interested in his conventional experiments. They tend to focus on his more esoteric fields of research. Not that I'm sneering, that's what my PhD is about too; his search for the philosopher's stone."

Morgan vaguely remembered that had something to do with *Harry Potter.*

Coby read his expression. "It's the search for eternal life," he said. "Dr Dee believed he was close to uncovering the secret of immortality."

CHAPTER FOUR

The flight back from Europe took even longer than the journey out, crossing a continent this time as well as an ocean. By the time they landed in San Francisco, Alex felt like she hadn't slept in a week. Her hair was greasy, her skin too, and she concentrated very hard on these minor discomforts to avoid thinking about any of her real problems.

"You need rest," PD told her when he'd reclaimed his luggage.

"I need some clothes, too," she said, watching him sling his black bag over his shoulder. "And a toothbrush. I have nothing with me except my purse."

"Then I guess you'd better put some of that thirty million dollar trust fund to work. I'll fix us a room and you can pay a visit to the Croatoans in the morning."

"*Two* rooms," she said. "You can snatch me away from home and conscript me into an army I never wanted to join, but there is no way you can make me double up with you. You slept on the plane and you snore like a landslide. Call me when you've booked us in."

She walked out of the arrivals hall without giving him a chance to respond and slid into a cab before he could catch up with her. "Downtown," she told the driver.

She'd been to San Francisco on a school trip back in junior high. She remembered its quaint gingerbread houses and tree-lined streets descending to the water which surrounded it on three sides. But now the leaves looked limp on the branches and the shadows of the Market Street high-rises seemed too sharp, as if they could cut the city to pieces. It felt like enemy territory, as if she'd never left the prison in Eastern Europe, or had brought something of it back with her. She hunched her shoulders and headed towards Union Square.

She was signing a credit-card receipt in Saks when PD finally called. "I'm claiming all this back on expenses," she said before he could speak.

He laughed and she realised it was the first time she'd heard him do so in a long time. "Two rooms at the Hilltop Express," he said. "The federal government doesn't stretch to boutique hotels – and it doesn't stretch to a clothes allowance at Saks Fifth Avenue, either."

"How did you–?" she said, but he just laughed again and ended the call.

She hated the fact that the contact with him had warmed her. She debated staying out till midnight then retiring to her room without having to spend any time around him. But she was in a town full of strangers. She didn't want to be alone and there was no one she could talk to – no one who'd understand. She'd already called her mom to let her know she'd been sent away on an unexpected field trip for an American history class. Her mother was in Europe, where she spent most of the summer these days, and she hadn't seemed terribly interested. Even if she was, Alex couldn't tell her the truth. It was too implausible and – worse – too dangerous. Hammond had made it clear she was *his*, his asset. She didn't like to think what he'd do to anyone who threatened his possession of her.

That ruled out her friends too. Only PD was left, the one person in the world who knew exactly what she was going through. The fact that he was partly the cause of it seemed almost an irrelevance in the face of her sudden, hollow loneliness.

The hotel looked better than its price tag, keeping up with the high-class Joneses of its Nob Hill location. PD was waiting for her in the lobby and he took her shopping bags without a word, only quirking an eyebrow at the number of them.

Alex lay on the queen-sized bed in her room and watched as PD unpacked her shopping for her and carefully hung each item in the wardrobe.

"Is this your way of saying sorry for ratting me out to Hammond?" she said. "Because as apologies go, it sucks."

"I didn't have a choice, kid."

It was the answer she'd expected. "So, PD – I guess we're partners, huh? Is that how this works? You've got my back, I've got yours, you'll break all the rules if I'm in trouble, hand over your gun and badge when the boss tells you to back off?"

His face was bland as he turned back to her. "You've been watching too much TV."

"*Are* you my partner?"

"Yes."

She rolled over, crooking an elbow to support her head as she looked at him. "So, partner, tell me about yourself. What does PD stand for anyway? Peter David? Prancing Dog? Perennial Dick?"

He looked at her through narrowed eyes and she thought she'd angered him. Then he smiled. "It stands for Positive Discrimination."

"What – seriously?"

"It was John's joke, my first partner. He said the CIA got to tick all their minority recruitment boxes in one candidate with me."

Alex frowned. "You mean because you're Native American?"

"Don't try that politically correct bullshit, kid – it doesn't suit you. Just Indian will do. And Jewish."

She gawped at him. "You're *Jewish?* But..."

"You know the stories – how one of the lost tribes of Israel came to America."

"I thought it was only the Mormons who thought that."

"Nope. My mother's tribe believe it. Claim they've got some of the lost Temple treasure, too. There's a box in the chief's hut where they keep it. Of course, no one except the chief gets to look inside – you know the drill."

"And do you believe it?"

He perched on the bed, close enough for her to touch. "When I was a kid I thought it was so much bullshit. It used to embarrass me – my primitive people and their dumb fairytales. But since I joined the Agency... It's like you go through life thinking you're playing five-card stud. It's a tight game, only one hole card per player and you can guess what it is. There aren't many secrets or surprises. But instead you find out you've been playing Omaha all along and deuces are wild. There are too many combinations to figure and you think you know the odds, then fifth street shows a possibility you hadn't even considered. Everything that matters is hidden. Do you understand what I'm saying?"

"Not a word." She sat up, hands around her knees. "I don't get any of this. I don't get what we're supposed to be doing. Even if the stuff I see when I take the drugs actually is the spirit world, so what? The real threats are out there in the real one. Christ, I'm a New Yorker. I know that."

"No. They're not. Did you hear what went down in St Petersburg a couple of months back?"

She frowned. "There was some kind of terrorist attack, wasn't there? And an international incident when the Russians refused foreign aid for the victims."

"It was no terrorist attack. From what I heard, it was almost the end of the world. One of our agents was involved – a girl called Belle. The Brits blamed her for what happened, almost refused to give her back to us. Hammond put pressure on to get her released, but now he keeps her on a tight rein. She's... there's something dark inside her. If you took the peyote and looked at her, you'd see it. That's why you're so valuable." He rested a hand on her knee, his palm warm and a little rough. "This isn't a bad job, kid. It might not beat hanging around the lower East Side living off your trust fund, but it's important. You get to make a difference. And you get to see something no one else can, the true world behind the illusions."

She looked down at his hand, the flecks of dirt caught in the corners of his fingernails. "The place I see when I take the drugs isn't some fairy-tale land, PD. It's not somewhere anyone sane would want to spend any time. And what would you know about it, anyway? You've never been there."

His expression shifted, a closing off of something she hadn't even realised was open. He lifted his hand from her knee. "No. I'm just your caretaker. I guess it's dinner time – I'll see you in the lobby in ten."

He exited before she could ask what the hell she'd said that pissed him off. She gnawed her lip for a moment, then shook her head. What the hell did she care, anyway?

Haight-Ashbury looked like it belonged in a different city, somewhere shabbier and meaner. Tourists sweated in the Fall sunshine as they peered at the tat filling every store as if they couldn't wait to be fleeced. Fake Goths coveting knock-off T-shirts of bands they were too young to remember, Alex thought. Or buying bongs to smoke some Bay Area bud and see a pale imitation of the terrifying world the drugs opened to her.

She shook her head, trying to shake away her mood and concentrate on the job. PD had told her that the Croatoan recruitment centre was near the junction with Delmar and she knew it was approaching, but she tried not to seem as if she was looking for it. She'd wanted PD to come with her – almost begged him to. He'd told her a pretty white girl and an older Indian guy would attract the wrong kind of attention. "Don't worry," he'd said, "I've got your back."

That was what partners did, she supposed, however much he might have scoffed at the idea when she'd suggested it. They looked out for each other. The thought was odd, a shape she couldn't quite slot into a convenient category in her mind. Her parents had looked after her, of course, but they hadn't looked *out* for her. And her friends... She'd never forgotten that her old school friends had given her up to the police to save their own skins.

As she crossed Delmar she made herself glance at her watch rather than the recruiters waiting to pounce on passers-by from beneath the awnings. For a moment, she thought they were going to ignore her. Then a hand on her elbow startled her and she looked up to see an attractive blond man with surfer hair and a beach-bum tan. The other recruiter idling by the curb was a pretty young woman. No doubt she'd pounce on any likely-looking straight men who passed.

In the time Alex took to assess him, the recruiter drew her to the side, beside the door to an anonymous blue-painted building.

"Hi," he said, "how are you enjoying your visit?"

Alex frowned. "How do you know I don't live here?"

He laughed. "No one who lives here comes to Haight-Ashbury. It would be like a New Yorker spending her Saturday up the Empire State Building.

His pinpointing of her origin unsettled her, but she managed a smile in return.

"Listen, do you have a spare minute?" he asked.

"I'm on vacation," she told him, "I've got a spare day."

"Awesome." He squeezed her elbow. "I've got something really incredible I'd like to tell you about, but it would be easier if we moved this inside. Is that OK?"

She frowned suspiciously, which she imagined was the normal reaction at this point. "I don't know..."

"Don't worry – it's just through here, and there'll be plenty of other people about. I can get you some ice tea, too. You look hot."

She shrugged. "Sure, why the hell not."

"Hey – I never asked your name."

She held out her hand. "Alexandra – but Alex will do."

His hand held on to hers just a little too long. "And I'm Phil. It's really good to meet you."

When she followed him through the small lobby, she saw that the building was lit by hundreds of candles. The effect was pleasing but a little disorienting and she thought maybe that was the point. Her companion led her to one of several tables, seating himself opposite her.

"That ice tea would taste good right about now," she said and he smiled and stood again, giving her time to study the room in his absence.

It looked like it had been decorated by someone who'd read dozens of half-assed New Age books about Native American culture and believed every single word of them. The ceiling was painted in a pattern that mirrored Indian designs with stripes of orange and ochre and brown, but the tones were just a bit off, the pattern a little too geometrically precise. The walls were strung with dream catchers, as if they expected to mop up industrial quantities of nightmares. Alex saw that some of the other people in the room – all of them white – were wearing feather headdresses and wondered what the hell PD would have thought if he'd joined her.

"What do you make of it?" Phil said as he returned, following the sweep of her eyes around the room.

"I don't know *what* to make of it. What exactly is going on here?"

He rested his hands on the table between them and she saw that it too was covered in fake Native American artefacts: beads, obsidian arrow heads and what might have been intended as a peace pipe.

"Have you heard of the Croatoans?" he asked.

She widened her eyes in mock surprise. "So you're *those* guys."

"I guess you've heard some pretty disparaging things about us, huh?"

"Oh well... I've kind of heard you called a cult."

"A cult's just what people call a religion they don't understand. The Romans said Christianity was a cult when it first started."

"Well, I guess that's true," she said, smiling coyly at him. She was surprised how easy she found it pretending to be something she wasn't. She'd never considered herself much of an actress, but maybe she'd been playing a part for longer than she realised.

Phil leaned back, his expression and tone softening. "Don't worry, we're not here to convert you. In fact, we don't want anything from you at all – unlike some other groups that get called cults, we just want to help you."

"Help me do what? I have to tell you, my life's pretty good right now."

"I'm glad to hear that, Alex. But don't you sometimes feel – I don't know, like there might be more to life, if only you could figure out what it was."

"Sure. But doesn't everyone feel that way?" *Make them work for it*, PD had told her. *Just enough so they don't get suspicious.*

Phil didn't seem put off. "You know what, Alex – everyone does feel that way. And that's because there *is* something missing from pretty much everyone's lives."

"And you think you know what that something is."

"I know I do. Because I've seen it and I'm here to tell you, Alex, it's the most incredible thing there is."

She leaned forward, as if he'd hooked her and was just beginning to draw her in. "Seen what?"

He lifted the elegant black and white curve of an eagle feather from the table. "The flesh is earthbound, Alex, but the spirit flies – or it can if we let it. There's a whole world out there, behind the world we see with our eyes, and I can tell you how to explore it."

For the first time, she felt a genuine flash of interest, and a beat of apprehension. There *was* a world behind the world, and she understood why Hammond thought people like this shouldn't have access to it.

"Do you want to see that world?" Phil asked. "We can show it to you, if you want."

"I do. But is it dangerous?"

"It doesn't need to be, if you find the right guide. Would you like to find yours?"

She heard the flap of raven wings and swallowed before she answered. "I'd like that very much."

He led her deeper inside the building, down a corridor lined with doors until they reached the furthest. The room inside was small and dark. There were no candles here, only an oil lamp flickering on the table.

He gestured her to a seat, but this time drew out the one beside her. She could smell the faint odour of his sweat and the masking scent of his cologne. It was expensive, she could tell, subtle and complex. Before he sat, he put his hands together and bowed towards the opposite wall. She realised that a painting hung there, veiled in shadow. It showed the back of a man dressed in a white robe, his curly brown hair falling over its collar. Two coyotes threaded themselves between his legs.

"Our leader," Phil said. "Laughing Wolf."

"Is he here? Can I meet him?"

Phil shook his head. "The Grand Shaman is only an occasional visitor to this plane of existence."

It was absurd and yet she couldn't find it funny. Her eyes returned to the painting and she knew she didn't like it. There was something about that hidden face which troubled her. She remembered the figure she'd seen in the spirit world in the Eastern European prison and, though she didn't know why, she was suddenly certain it was the same man.

Phil seemed to sense her unease. Maybe it was a common reaction in people coming here. But Alex wasn't afraid of the unknown. It was what she knew that terrified her.

"Don't worry, this is painless," he said. "It's not a full spirit journey – you'll have to study with us for a while before you're ready for that. This is more like looking at a map to plan your route than going on the actual journey."

"What map?" she said, looking again at the painting. She knew she didn't want to follow where that figure led.

Phil laughed. "I guess that was kind of a metaphor. I'm going to help you get to the edge of the spirit world, but we'll stop there, and then we'll wait for your spirit guide to find you."

"Oh." There was no sign of any peyote, not even any weed to help her get in the right state of mind. Maybe they weren't needed. Maybe they were like training wheels, something you could manage without once you knew what you were doing.

Phil put a finger under her chin, the touch curiously asexual, and turned her head until she was looking at the oil lamp. "Just gaze into the flame," he said. "Don't look at it – look through it, into the world beyond."

She tried. The flame danced, a tantalizing randomness that felt as if it might reveal itself as patterned if she only looked long enough. Her eyes began to water and when she blinked them the tears blurred the flame to a soft glow. She let herself sink into it, no longer straining for meaning but letting it come.

There were shapes in there, she could see them if she didn't look for them: a curve that might have been a petal and an oval that could have been an eye. Was this really a way into the spirit realm? It was gentler than the path she'd used but who said the journey had to be a painful one?

"Tell me what you see," Phil said.

"I can see... it's not clear, but I think there's an eye, a flower..."

"That's good, Alex, that's very good. And what else?"

She had to fight to keep her eyes unfocused, to let the flame dictate what it wanted to be. "There's an apple," she said. "And something that looks kinda like a map of Manhattan."

"OK then." There was a slight catch in his voice, a note of what might have been impatience. "And how about any animals? Can you see any of those?"

She squinted her eyes until the lines of her lashes strobed across the yellow flames. "There might be, I don't know, maybe a cat's face."

"Awesome!" Phil said. "The lynx. There's your spirit guide."

"And if you believe that," a voice croaked in her ear, "you'll believe anything."

Her head spun so quickly she felt her neck click, but she saw only the shadow of black wings fading into the distance. Then there was just Phil, staring at her with an expression of alarm which he quickly schooled into concern.

He put a hand on her arm, meant to comfort and also, she thought, to restrain. "It's OK, Alex. He's your guide, he isn't going to hurt you – he's on your side."

"My guide?" she said. "A lynx?"

Phil's grip on her arm loosened a little and she pulled it free with a jerk.

"That's what you saw," he said. "The flame doesn't lie."

Lies hurt the liar here, Raven had said.

"No," Alex said, "but you obviously do. Thanks for your time, Phil. I've seen enough."

He didn't try to stop her as she slammed the door and hurried from the recruitment centre.

CHAPTER FIVE

Morgan woke with the idea of using the university's resources to find out a little more about Dr John Dee before returning to Kate in London. He wanted to prove his worth, he supposed, prove that he could do more than just use this unwanted gift his father had bequeathed him.

The university library was easy to find. It loomed over the nearby college quad, its centre topped by a tower that looked more industrial than academic. Morgan wasn't sure what he'd imagined the place might look like, but it definitely wasn't this. The building reminded him of Battersea Power Station, and it was dauntingly huge.

The elderly man guarding the entrance waved Morgan through when he showed his police ID, not offering to help him find his way. Even at this time of year, with the students absent, the place was packed. There were a dozen people Morgan could have asked for directions, but he took one look at their smooth, confident faces and walked on. He stumbled on the catalogue room by pure chance and sat at an unoccupied computer, glad he'd found something he knew how to handle.

A search for John Dee yielded hundreds of results, but when he paired it with other search terms – alchemy, philosopher's stone, eternal life – he narrowed down the list. He scribbled the titles on a scrap of paper, his handwriting cramped and awkward, an atrophied skill. Beside each title he wrote the library code, a collection of numbers and letters.

Then he sat and stared at them.

"Took me weeks to figure out the system here," a quiet voice said behind him.

He snapped his head round. The young woman standing by his shoulder pulled back and smiled, her sunny expression framed by spiky blonde hair.

"I'm getting the hang of it," he told her.

She nodded, but he could see she didn't believe him. "You're that policeman, aren't you? The one who's looking into Dr Granger's murder?"

"How the hell did you know that?"

She rested a hand against the back of his chair. Her fingers were delicate, but he saw that the nails were bitten to the quick. "Don't worry, I haven't been stalking you. Coby told me about you. His description was spot on."

Morgan leaned back, elbows against the desk. "Oh yeah?"

She nodded but didn't elaborate and he wondered just what Coby had said. Nothing flattering, he was sure.

She squinted at the list of books he'd noted. "You're researching John Dee? Coby said you were asking about Dr Granger's research."

"Just getting some background detail."

"Want some help? It's just I'm going up there myself, so we could find the books together. Though I've got to warn you, most of them are as dull as dried dog shit. Actually, I could just précis them for you. No reason both of us should suffer through it, is there?"

Her eyes sparkled into his and he found himself nodding.

"I'm Julie, by the way. I'm Dr Granger's other PhD student. God, sorry, I should have said that straight off." She scratched her short nails against the back of her neck, frowning.

"OK Julie," he said, "show me the way."

She led him up a long flight of stairs. Her gait was fast and relaxed, the material of her jeans pulling tight across her arse with each stride. He alternated between enjoying that and studying the view from the windows. As they climbed he saw aerial snapshots of the town, odd, mismatched angles on trees and buildings which made it seem as if the library was moving location as he climbed.

She finally left the stairwell at what must have been the sixth or seventh floor, plunging into a maze of rooms. The bookshelves were packed so tightly they were concertinaed together. Morgan couldn't figure out how anyone reached them, until he saw a gangly young man push two shelves aside to create a space between them and he realised they must be fixed on rollers.

He'd been told this was a copyright library and that it received one of every single book published in the world, but he hadn't really thought what that meant. He was used to the internet, data without form or location. It was odd to think of all this knowledge having a physical presence, solid and destructible.

The room they ended in was unoccupied. Julie perched on the end of a wooden table, her legs crossed at the ankle.

"Welcome to my home from home," she said. "It's OK for the psychologists and the chemists, all the stuff they need is in journals, they can do their research online. Us historians still need to look at primary sources and out-of-print editions of books no one's ever heard of. I've spent more time in this place than in my own room."

Morgan perched on the other side of the table, the shape of his body a mirror of hers. "I can think of worse places to be."

She looked uncomfortable, scratching at her neck again in what he realised must be a habitual gesture. "Yeah, sorry. I know I'm lucky to be here."

"Bet you worked your arse off for it, though."

She grinned and he felt himself flush. He realised he'd started running his own hand across his cornrows and he brought it to his side. "So tell me about your research. That guy – Coby – he said Dr Dee's big thing was immortality."

She laughed and he watched her T-shirt ride up her abdomen to reveal an inch of thin, pale stomach. "Yeah, he would say that, it's what his PhD's all about. But Dr Dee had his finger in a lot more pies than that. Back then it wasn't like it is now. These days I start out in humanities and then I specialise in history, I narrow that down to the Tudors and now I'm just researching one man's life. Not even all of it, just a tiny corner. There's so much knowledge in the world, no one can know very much of it.

"But back then, humanity knew less and individuals knew more. A man – and it was always a man – could be an expert in *everything*. People who called themselves natural historians saw the whole of existence as their field of study. And they didn't see the world the way we do now. They made no distinction between the natural and supernatural. Astronomy and astrology were viewed as part of the same discipline, the position of the stars being related to their predictive powers. The same methods could be applied to discover the distance of the earth from the moon, the secret of immorality, or the exact date of Noah's flood."

"And is that what your PhD's about?" Morgan said. "Noah's flood?"

"No, that wasn't actually Dr Dee's thing. His central obsession – even beyond the search for immortality, or maybe as a route to it – was figuring out a way to make contact with the spirit world. He had a... well, not really a friend. These days we'd probably call Edward Kelly a con man. Even back then, he'd had his ears cropped for forgery. But Kelly convinced Dee he was a medium and that he could train Dee to be one too. They used crystal balls and later scrying mirrors – there's one in the British Museum made from obsidian. It's kind of beautiful."

"And did it work?" Morgan asked. "Did they really contact spirits?"

She looked at him oddly and he smiled to make it seem a joke.

"Well," she said. "Dee believed he did. He wrote extensively about his conversations with discarnate entities. Angels. *That's* what my dissertation's about. The angel Uriel in particular had a long-term link with Dee and it caused him no end of trouble. People thought having dealings with spirits was ungodly. A religious mob sacked his house in 1583 and a lot of his most prized possessions were stolen or destroyed."

It was funny, Morgan thought. She was the expert in Dee, she'd read every book about him, knew when he was born, where he lived, who he married and when he died – but she didn't know the single most important thing there was to know on the subject. She didn't know that a person really *could* contact the spirit world and that mirrors really were the way to do it.

"Sorry," she said, studying his expression. "Was I..." He knew she was trying to find a way not to say 'going too fast for you'.

"That was really helpful," he told her.

Her fingers crept up to her neck again as she blushed. "I just – I have to teach part time, you know, to make ends meet. Sorry if that was a bit of a lecture."

"It was great, really."

"I don't see what it's got to do with Dr Granger getting killed, though. I mean, it's not likely to be a rival don jealous that she got an article accepted in *History Today*." She frowned. "Is it?"

"I can't discuss the details of the case, I'm afraid." It sounded stiff but she seemed to buy it. She'd probably watched the same cop shows he had.

"You wanted some books, didn't you?" she said, glancing at his list then pulling volumes from the shelves. "You can't take them out, but if you've got time you can sit and read them here. Or–" her blush deepened "–I could go through them with you. Point out the important bits. You know."

Morgan could hear his old squadmates – *you're in there, mate.* He was, he could tell. It had been a while, but not that long. So what if she didn't know the real him? Everyone had secrets and some of them had to be worse than his.

"That would be great," he said. "When I start going cross-eyed from all the reading I can take you out for lunch to say thanks."

"Yeah, I think that's the least you can do." She grinned and he smiled back. She was pretty and she was flirting with him and later tonight, she might be fucking him. The day was going a lot better than he'd expected.

She seemed to read at least some of that in his expression because he saw her pupils swell as she cleared her throat then said, "There's one book on your list that's on a different floor. Give me a few minutes and I'll fetch it."

He nodded and watched her arse as she walked out. A second later he blinked and looked down at the pile of books. They smelled faintly musty and there was a green tint on the edge of the pages. He wondered how often they were actually read.

The first contained extracts from Dee's own writings and some reproductions of the original manuscripts. Morgan was still trying to read the crabbed, old-fashioned handwriting when he heard the scream. It was piercing and terrified and he was sure it was Julie.

He was out of his seat and out of the door before the sound died, hand reaching to his hip for a gun that wasn't there. He cursed and kept running, elbowing a student out of his way. He saw a snapshot of the boy's startled face, but the kid didn't complain. He'd heard the scream too.

Morgan felt like the endless shelves of books were pressing in on him as he raced back to the staircase, shoes slapping heavily on the marble as he climbed. There was a babble of voices ahead, but no more screams. Morgan knew that wasn't good. Fuck, it was very, very bad.

He'd lost some of his physical condition since he'd left the army, or maybe he was just running faster than he'd ever run before. The air rasped against his lungs with each breath and he could feel sweat sluicing off his body.

There were more people on the next floor, milling and confused. He wanted to know what they'd seen, but he couldn't waste time asking. He pushed them aside, sending one girl tumbling against a bookcase and the books themselves falling to the floor. Another boy flung himself out of Morgan's path and then he was through that room and into the next – and suddenly there were only two more people, and one of them was already dead.

The Mossad assassin was kneeling beside Julie, head turned towards Morgan as if he'd been expecting him. His face smooth and olive-brown. Only a frown of irritation crinkled his brow. Beneath it, a droplet of blood hung suspended from one eyelash. Julie lay on the floor beside him, her face turned away from Morgan. He was glad he couldn't see it. He had a good view of the slash in her throat, the one that should have been bleeding and was smoking instead. The room was full of the smell of scorched flesh.

Morgan only froze for a moment. The instant he flung himself towards the killer the man moved, lithe and confident as a cat. Morgan felt something crunch beneath his foot as he hurled himself in pursuit and he realised, with a nauseous lurch, that it was Julie's hand.

The assassin fled deeper inside the library, away from the crowd of students and their frightened eyes. Even in the dim lighting his white T-shirt shone bright against his dark skin. Morgan followed it through room after room, always only a few paces behind, but never quite close enough.

The Israeli still held the knife in his hand. It looked like an ordinary army-issue weapon, but Morgan could see its edges glowing yellow. Their outline led him through a long, stone-floored corridor, down one flight of stairs and then another as the glow slowly faded through orange to a sullen red.

He was faster on the stairs than the assassin, vaulting them recklessly until his ankle buckled on the second flight. He felt the creak of cartilage pushed to the breaking point and gritted his teeth as he leapt again, his leg burning but still working. And now he was only two paces behind his quarry.

Morgan could hear the man's laboured breathing. He smelt his sour sweat and beneath it the copper hint of blood. His belly clenched with fury and though they were still ten feet above the next landing he bellowed and flung himself from the stairs, diving through air to catch the killer round his waist.

The man let out his own roar of rage, bucking in Morgan's grip. There was a sickening moment of free-fall, then the jarring impact of landing. Morgan tasted blood as his teeth snapped shut on his own tongue. His knee slammed agonisingly into the wooden floor and he couldn't suppress a gasp of pain. But the killer's body took the brunt of the fall and Morgan heard the whoosh of air as it was all forced from the man's lungs.

The assassin was silent, sprawled like a ragdoll. Morgan pried the knife from his limp fingers. As he lifted it free, the last heat seemed to dissipate from the metal, leaving it lethal but mundane. He tightened his hand on the pommel and used his other to flip the killer over, tearing the white T-shirt he used for leverage.

As he rolled, the man's eyes flicked open and for a second Morgan thought he saw a red fire burning in their depths, the same sullen glow which had earlier lit his knife. Was this another demon, one of Belle's kind? Morgan shuddered as he remembered the little girl who'd housed something monstrous inside her. His hand tightened on the knife and he pressed the flat of the blade to the killer's throat. The thick tube of the man's windpipe compressed and Morgan knew that the slightest tip of the knife, the first pressure of its razor-sharp edge, and the Israeli's life would end as he had ended Julie's. Morgan's hand shook with the effort of not doing it.

The killer's eyes were locked on his. He didn't look frightened. "Morgan Hewitt," he said, his accent strong and slightly harsh. "I tried to keep you out of this. I tried to act polite, to conduct my business out of your sight, but you had to interfere. And all because you were thinking with your penis and not your head. Are you really the best of the Hermetic Division?"

Morgan's fingers clawed around the handle of the knife and in the moment when rage broke his concentration, the killer moved. His legs jack-knifed beneath him, knees thumping into Morgan's stomach.

Morgan fell back, gasping for breath. His legs were useless, his body too weak to move, but his arms still worked just fine. He slashed out with the knife, aiming for the killer's throat and catching his chest instead as the man rolled and rose. A bloom of blood flowered beneath the man's T-shirt and he let out a grunt of pain. But he kept moving and when Morgan slashed again the blade caught nothing but cotton, a neat white strip of it floating to the floor like a feather as the assassin disappeared round the curve of the stairs.

Morgan had to get up. He *had* to get moving. He groaned as he rolled to his knees, head hanging between them for a moment while he gathered his breath, a tight pain in his chest telling him that ribs were bruised, maybe broken.

It didn't matter. He staggered to his feet and ran. Pain jabbed his side and the leather hilt of the knife was slick with sweat but he held it tight. The stairs flew by beneath him and he could hear the killer's footsteps echoing up the stairwell. They were drawing away – Morgan was losing him.

And then he heard the clatter of scores of shoes on the stairs, heading up. They were two floors, one floor beneath him, and then they were right there and there was nothing he could do to stop himself barrelling into them. He only had time to turn the blade of the knife away before he knocked two of the men to the ground, his fall once again cushioned by someone else's body.

His ribs screamed their agony and he probably did too. His consciousness blurred for a moment and when it came back he felt arms lifting him up, a hand easing open his own and prying the knife out of it. He didn't resist. He was massively outnumbered and even in his haste he'd seen the uniforms.

The officer facing him was plain-clothes, with the silver-yellow hair and wrinkles of a lifelong smoker.

"Listen," Morgan gasped. "That bastard's getting away. Let me get after him. Fuck – *you* get after him."

The policeman's eyebrow arched in question, and Morgan's stomach clenched because he knew that look. He'd received it often enough when he was a teenager in Brixton. He could see the knife he'd held being dropped into a plastic evidence bag – the knife which now had his fingerprints all over it. Another hand dug through his pockets and pulled out the fake police ID Kate had given him. That was bagged and labelled too.

The hands on his arms lifted them up and forward and he saw the glint of metal before he felt the cold snap of cuffs around his wrists. For a moment his muscles tensed and the hands on him tightened. Then he sighed and slumped, knowing it was useless.

He looked the lead cop in the eye and the man flinched a little from his expression. "You," Morgan said, "are going to be really, really fucking pissed off with yourselves in about two hours. But not as pissed off with you as I am, because you morons are letting a murderer escape."

The hands holding him jerked him roughly as they led him downstairs, but he barely registered it. In his mind's eye he could only see Julie's body, her face turned away from him, no blood dripping from the fatal wound in her throat.

CHAPTER SIX

When Alex left the Croatoan building the weather had switched in that odd San Franciscan way; fog rolling in from the hills to smother the streets in a grey blanket. No one tried to stop her as she shut the door behind her, and she guessed they were used to people walking out on them.

PD was waiting for her on the opposite side of the street. He leaned against the wooden slats behind him, arms folded and face impassive. He looked just like one of those old, un-PC Red Indian statues people used to put in front of their houses, and she smiled as she moved to the crosswalk, intending to tell him so.

The man and woman stepped in front of her as PD caught her eye. She saw him frown, suddenly tense, but the pair didn't look threatening. They didn't look much of anything, just an ordinary, middle-aged Hispanic couple, both shorter than her and a little stocky.

"Can we talk to you?" the man asked. His threadbare T-shirt was too loose round the arms and too tight over his paunch. She realised that he was holding a hand-written placard reading: 'Don't Let Them Suck YOU In!'

She flicked a reassuring smile at PD as he hurried across the road towards her, then said, "I'm sorry, I'm in kind of a hurry."

The woman put a hand on her arm, restraining her with surprising strength. Her face was harder than her husband's and there was a desperate light in her eyes. "You had time to go and talk to those bastards, you've got time to talk to us."

Alex raised her eyebrow haughtily and the woman dropped her arm but didn't get out of her way, even when PD brought his muscled bulk to stand beside her. "Everything OK?" he asked.

Alex nodded as the woman said, "Sir, are you with this young lady?"

"He's my friend," Alex said, then grimaced, not sure she really wanted to call PD that.

PD grimaced too as the woman gripped his arm. Her fingers clawed into his skin. "If you're her friend, you'll stop her going back in that place," she said. "You make sure she never goes near them again."

"Oh," Alex said, suddenly understanding the placard listing to the side in the man's slack hand. "No, you don't need to worry about that. They're a joke."

"A joke? Is that what you think? Is it a joke that our Maria joined them three months ago and she hasn't spoken to us since? Is it funny when she acts like she doesn't even know us?'

Alex shook her head, embarrassed by the tears gathering in the woman's eyes. "I'm sorry. But I promise you, I have absolutely no intention of joining."

"Your daughter?" PD said, his words overlapping hers. "What exactly happened to her?"

"The Croatoans happened," she said. "They changed her so she isn't our Maria any more."

PD locked eyes with Alex and she sighed at the spark of interest she saw in them.

Caesar and Sofia had the basement of a narrow house in the Mission. Alex could see the yard through the kitchen window, sunless and damp. The couple had filled the space with pots, but the plants within were wilting.

PD shook his head when Caesar offered him a beer and Sofia poured them coffee instead, the smell chasing away the lingering scent of tomatoes from the room. This was the couple's home but they didn't look at home here. Something more essential than the plants had died in the spirit of the place.

Alex leaned her chin on her hand and watched PD as he stretched his long legs beneath the table. "Tell me about Maria," he said. He nodded across the room at a framed photo of a dark-haired, almond-eyed teenager. "Is that her? She's very beautiful."

Sofia's face softened for the first time. "She is. So beautiful. She could have been a model, I always told her so, but she wanted to be a nurse. She had a heart the size of the earth, that one. She thought she could heal the world. But you don't want to hear this – what do you care about my little girl?"

PD rested his fingers against the woman's. "I have to be honest with you, we're part of an organisation that debunks cults. That's why Alex was there. Know thy enemy, you understand?"

Caesar leaned forward. "This is true? You're working against the Croatoans, trying to stop them?"

PD gave Sofia's hand a final squeeze as he let go. "Yes. So anything you can tell us about them would be great."

Caesar rubbed his back, wincing as he rose to his feet. "It's easier to show you. Here."

He returned to the table with a photo album. The cover was that bobbled fake leather which seemed designed to catch dust, but there was none on this. It was obvious the couple looked at it frequently, probably daily.

Sofia flicked it open. The first page was one big photo, a baby too young to smile held in the arms of a woman who must have been Sofia, but looked forty years younger. "She was born July 4th, 1988," Sofia said. "We thought it was lucky, a sort of blessing – we called her our little Miss America. "

Caesar gently took the book from her and flipped forward through nearly three-quarters of its width. "They don't want to see that. I'm sorry, it's just, we..." his words trailed into silence and Alex saw him swallow twice.

"I understand," PD said. "Tell me about the last few months, just before Maria joined the Croatoans – and just after."

Caesar swallowed a final time and nodded, flipping forward a couple more pages in the album. "This was her twenty-first birthday party. That was the day before she – before she walked into that place."

Maria was instantly recognisable, glowing in the centre of the photo surrounded by laughing young women. She was dressed in jeans and a blue blouse, and she had rosy cheeks and a glowing white smile. The small gap between her front teeth only made her seem more appealing, an endearingly human flaw.

"She *was* beautiful," Alex murmured.

Sofia glared at her. "She *is* beautiful. She still is."

"But she's different," Caesar said. He flipped through a few more pages and Alex saw more pictures of the party and a few other casual shots that looked like they'd been taken at a park somewhere, maybe Golden Gate.

"We went out the next day for a family picnic," Sofia said. "It was one of those spring days when the sun shines and the wind doesn't blow. It was perfect. And then..."

"She went for a walk on her own. She said she wanted to see the city before she left. She was going to go to UCLA, you see – a scholarship." Even through the pain in Caesar's voice, Alex could hear the pride. "This was her last weekend in the city. She'd gotten a job in her uncle's store in Modesto and she planned to work there a couple months, save some money."

PD leaned back, folding his arms. "But she never went." There was a tight muscle jumping in his jaw. Alex could tell he thought this was important and couldn't imagine why. It was horrible, but it was what cults did. They took people away from their families. They changed them.

It was what PD and Hammond were doing to her.

Caesar flipped to the next page in the album and suddenly she wondered. The woman staring back at them was obviously Maria – the gap between her front teeth was the same. But nothing else about her was recognisable, from the sophisticated designer clothes to the slightly stiff way she held her body.

"When was that photo taken?" she asked, her voice tight.

Sofia nodded, as if satisfied with her reaction. "That's a month after she walked into the Croatoan centre. It was the first time we saw her after she left."

"She never came back from that walk," Caesar said. "We reported her missing and the next day we got a phone call from her, telling us that she was fine, not to worry. Those bastards, they must have links to the cops. They knew we'd made the report and they didn't want any trouble. They wanted to keep us quiet."

"But we wouldn't let it go," Sofia said, a sort of bitter pride in her voice. Alex could imagine her at the precinct day after day, never making a scene but not letting them brush her off, either, driving the officers crazy.

"We thought she'd been kidnapped, you understand," Caesar said. "We thought someone had a gun to her head when she told us she was all right."

PD nodded. "But then you found out the truth..."

"The police gave us her address eventually," Sofia said. "Just to shut us up."

As she spoke, Caesar flipped over the next page to a picture of a mansion in what looked like the Hollywood Hills. There was a high fence surrounding the property and he must have used a telephoto lens to get the shot. Alex wondered how much he'd spent on the camera and whether he was still paying off the debt. At the back of the house she could see a blue smudge which might have been a swimming pool.

"That's her house," Caesar said. "Our Maria's."

"Forgive me," PD said, "but are you telling me she bought it?"

"They gave it to her," Sofia said. "The Croatoans, just two weeks after she joined them."

Alex sat up straighter. "Hang on. You're saying that the cult *gave* her money? That... that doesn't make any sense."

Caesar flicked through the remaining pages of the album, all of them containing photos clearly taken at a distance without the subject's consent. He'd been stalking his own daughter, but Alex didn't blame him. The woman in the photos bore so little resemblance to their child: eating at top-of-the-range restaurants with a mix of beautiful people her own age and moneyed men and women two generations older; at a movie premier, stepping out of a limo; attending what appeared to be a polo match.

"We don't know any of these people," Sofia said, looking at the last photo, a picture of Maria at some society function. "Maria didn't either. Three months ago, she would have been cleaning their houses to pay her way through college and they wouldn't even have noticed she was alive."

"We know what cults are," Caesar said. "They con people out of their money."

Sophia reached across the table, grasping Alex's palm in one hand and PD's wrist in the other. "So you tell us, please. What did our little girl do for those people to be given all this in return?"

Working for a covert government agency had one advantage, Alex thought sourly. If you wanted to violate someone's fourth amendment rights, they were the go-to guys. It only took two phone calls with Hammond to track Maria down to an upscale restaurant near the Bay Bridge. Apparently, Maria was stopping off in the city after a visit to her winery in Sonoma – another part of her vast and inexplicable new fortune.

"I don't see why I have to be the one to do this," Alex said as they waited to be seated. "You're a better liar than I am."

He raised an eyebrow.

"Oh come on," she said. "You've got that whole blank-faced, inscrutable Indian thing going on. I can never tell what you're thinking."

"I'm thinking you're near Maria's age. She's not going to believe she used to be at middle school with me."

"Except, you know, that I wasn't at school with her either, and she won't remember me."

"She'll be too embarrassed to admit it. Kid, take it from a good liar, the secret is confidence. It doesn't matter what you say, just say it like you believe it."

He lapsed into silence as their server approached, smiling as he led them through the restaurant. Dim lighting reflected warmly from the wood-panelled walls.

"She's there," PD said, nodding at one of the better tables near the windows overlooking the Bay. "The man next to her is Jacob Marriott. He's old New England money. I don't have any intel on the other two, but it's even odds they're Croatoans too."

The nameless couple were blonde and blandly pretty, around Maria's age but from a different social class altogether. Jacob Marriott was far older, improbably dark-haired and with the over-tight skin of a man who'd had too much plastic surgery. Alex had seen his face before beside Maria's in Caesar and Sophia's photos. She made to rise, but PD put a restraining hand on her arm.

"Food first," he said.

"I'm not hungry." She felt like she'd been living on adrenaline for several days.

"You don't need to eat much, just this."

He pushed a small packet across the table and she realised with an unpleasant lurch in her stomach that it was peyote. She darted a nervous glance around to see if they were being observed and closed her fist around the packet but didn't draw it any closer.

"Funny," she said, "you didn't mention this earlier."

His expression softened. "You'll be safe. It's public and I'm watching. There are no bad memories here to colour the spirit world."

Her fingers tightened round the drug, crushing the flakes of cactus into a fine powder. "Don't you think she might notice I'm as high as a kite?"

"Take half the packet. The lighting's dim so she won't be able to see your eyes. Just keep it short. I want to know what you see, not what you hear."

Alex nodded numbly as the waiter approached and didn't protest when PD ordered for both of them. They sat in silence until the food arrived, PD's eyes on the table and hers on Maria. The other woman seemed to be enjoying herself, chatting with her companions. She looked at ease – not like she was there under duress.

Alex jerked her eyes away when their food arrived. PD had ordered soup for her. The flakes of peyote were barely visible, brown flecks in the red, but the bitter after-taste lingered in her throat each time she swallowed.

She felt PD watching her as their main course arrived, lamb shank for him and fish for her. It was served whole and she saw its eye blinking up at her accusingly. *I've died for you*, it seemed to say, *and you aren't even enjoying me*. Its mouth gulped open, drowning in air, and when she looked up PD nodded. She didn't know what her expression was but she knew he'd understood it.

"It's started," he said.

She felt the pressure of claws against her shoulder and the warm weight of a body. She knew what she'd see if she turned her head, but she chose not to. "There are no beginnings," Raven said in her ear.

"I'm ready," she told PD.

It was the coyote's face that stared back at her as he said, "You look OK, just try to blink a bit more. Go on – she's finished her dessert. They'll be going soon."

Her chair seemed to float away from her as she pushed it back and she was vaguely aware that it had toppled over, but she didn't try to lift it. She was afraid she might fall down beside it. Her body felt both weightless and profoundly heavy. She had to stand and think carefully for a minute before she remembered which muscles she needed to tense in order to walk. She saw a figure moving away from her, hurrying to the door. His curly brown hair bounced against the collar of his shirt, and she thought about calling out to him, but realised that she didn't want him to turn around. She sighed in relief when he disappeared from sight.

Time moved in fits and starts. Her foot inched forward and when it came down she was standing beside Maria's table. She tried to look at the young woman and felt a physical ache in her face as she attempted to wrench her gaze to the side. She couldn't do it. She knew if she did she'd see Maria's true face, and that was too horrible to contemplate. She looked at Jacob Marriott instead.

"Hi," she said. Her voice sounded odd, as if it was coming from a long way away. "Sorry to interrupt your meal."

"Do I know you?" His accent was refined but the face behind his human facade was feral. *A wolf in sheep's clothing,* she thought.

"I know your friend," she said. "It's Maria Vargas, isn't it? We went to middle school together."

He frowned over at the young woman and Alex knew she should have looked at her too – that it would make more sense to say this to *her* – but she couldn't do it. Even thinking about it made a cold sweat prickle on her skin. In the corner of her eye she could see Maria's dark hair. She flinched away from it and looked at the blonde couple beside her. They reminded her of Ken and Barbie, plastic and perfect.

"Your face definitely looks familiar," Maria said.

"It's Alex," she said. She tensed her shoulders and legs and finally forced herself to turn towards her.

"Of course, I remember now. How lovely to run into you." Maria smiled and it was the most ghastly thing Alex had ever seen.

She'd only taken a small dose of the drug. The real world was still clear and in it Maria looked just as she'd been in her parents' photos, a beautiful young woman with almond eyes and a charming, gap-toothed smile.

In the spirit world, another face looked back. The skin stretched tight over the skull beneath, broken in places so the white bone shone through. Her hair was thin, grey and brittle. Patches of her scalp were bloody and bare where it had torn away.

In one socket, the bloodshot eyeball swivelled beneath a lidless brow. The other was a dark cavity. As Alex watched, a maggot crawled out of the hole, its blind white head swinging from side to side, searching for more flesh to burrow through.

"Memento mori," she said, remembering the medieval paintings she'd studied in her history of art class, the images of death hidden in scenes of decadence and luxury.

For just a second Maria's human face looked shocked. Then she hardened it into a blankness as inexpressive as the skull beneath. "Are you feeling all right?" she said. "You look a bit pale."

Alex's laugh caught in her throat. She knew she was making a mess of this but she couldn't seem to control herself. PD thought the peyote changed how she saw the world. He didn't understand that it changed her too. The world of spirit was a world of truth where lies threatened the liar.

"I'm pale because I see you," she told Maria. "You're dead inside."

The skull grinned as Maria's bow lips sneered. "Oh, you're one of those, are you?" she said. The blond man opposite her waved his arm, gesturing to someone Alex couldn't see.

A moment later hands closed around her upper arms, rough enough to bruise. The breath of the men holding her was hot against her cheeks.

"You're going to have to leave, miss," one of them said.

They had the faces of dogs, loyal and not terribly bright. She guessed they'd been sitting at a nearby table, guarding Maria from a discreet distance.

She wrenched her arm free. "You have no right to throw me out." Her voice was over-loud, echoing through the sophisticated quiet of the restaurant. Nearby diners turned to look at her and a frowning waiter hurried over.

She looked for PD and saw a group of men surround him too, trapping him at his table. A swell of panic rose in her chest.

The waiter put a soft hand against her cheek when he reached her and she expected him to ask how she was, but he said, "I'm sorry, I'm afraid you will have to go."

She looked at him in shock as his face strobed between human and animal; man and cat.

"I haven't done anything," she said.

The waiter's cat eyes were slitted and cruel. "We know who you are, Alexandra Keve. Laughing Wolf wants to meet you. He's waiting for you."

The two bodyguards led her from the restaurant. Outside, there was a car waiting. It had pulled up to the kerb only feet from the entrance, tinted windows shadowing whoever was inside. But the spirit realm offered a clearer view and Alex flinched back from the burning eyes watching her from a skeletal face. The hands on her arms tightened as the men dragged her towards the car.

She began to struggle in earnest, but the men holding her were far stronger and the drug had killed her coordination. When she briefly freed one hand, the punch she threw sailed wide of her captor's face, aimed at the muzzle of his spirit form. The dog winced in phantom pain, but the man didn't release her and now they'd opened the back door of the car.

There was a commotion behind her, raised voices and grunts of physical exertion, but she could see nothing except the car in front of her, the darkness inside and the burning eyes waiting for her. She tried to scream and a hand clamped over her mouth. She bit the fleshy palm and heard a cry of outrage but the hand didn't move, and now they'd pushed her head inside the car and other hands were levering her legs to follow. The skull-faced man in the front passenger seat turned to face her, the blunt nub of a gun pointing at her from his bone hands. Beside him, the driver turned the key and the car purred.

She kicked out desperately and felt the satisfying impact of her heel connecting with flesh. Then her ankle was grabbed and her shoe torn from her foot. She cried out as her leg bent back against the way it was meant to go, and then the door slammed shut and the engine gunned as the car gathered power with her inside it.

There was the squeal of rubber on tarmac as something heavy hit the roof above her. She hunched down into the leather seat. The car swerved, still gathering speed, and she was flung against the door. She heard a shout from the front seat and knew that her captor had been flung aside too. For a second his gun wasn't pointed at her and she scrabbled desperately at the door, searching for the lock.

Her fingers hooked into plastic and she was afraid it was stuck fast, secured from the front. But whatever had attacked them had struck too soon after they'd moved and her nail bent then held as the lock popped open.

Above, she could hear the painful screech of metal against metal and she realised what had happened. Someone had jumped onto the roof of the car and now clung on as the driver spun the wheel from side to side and the car veered like a horse trying to dislodge its rider. It was PD, she was sure of it, but he couldn't possibly hold on much longer.

She heard a noise from the front and saw that the passenger had turned back to face her, the long teeth in his skull bared in a humourless smile. He'd raised the gun again but the movement of the car jerked it from side to side and she knew she'd have to risk it. She didn't have any choice. She pressed down on the handle, then pushed.

The door swung open, dragging her arm with it. For a second she hung suspended, face-down above the tarmac. She watched it rush by with terrifying speed. Her shoulder burned with pain and her breath was coming in ragged pants. If she let go, the surface of the road would rush to meet her and the tarmac would take all the skin from her face. She couldn't do it. Captivity was better.

Then the car swerved again and she didn't have any choice. The door swung wider, her arm went with it and her legs tumbled after. They bounced once, twice against the surface of the road. Her ankle twisted as her foot snagged. And then she released the door handle and only instinct stopped her face smashing against the ground as her arms jerked to protect it, and she rolled over and over, stomach heaving with nausea and adrenaline.

When she opened her eyes the blue rectangle of sky framed by dark buildings was crazed, as if she was seeing it through cracked glass, and for a moment of confusion she thought she'd somehow shattered her eyes. But then the fragments swam and merged into a whole picture and she realised it was only her mind which was fragmented. A vicious pain burned behind her temples and she groaned as she tried to sit up. Her hands felt as weak as water and her legs were so shaky she wasn't sure she'd be able to stand.

A second later, she was jerked to her feet by her arm and her heart lurched then thundered with sudden fear until she saw that it was PD. His face was dripping blood from a scrape along his cheek. He must have flung himself from the roof of the car when she'd fallen out of the door.

The moment she thought of the car she heard it, an accelerating roar as it turned to race back towards them. The skull leered at her from the front seat and she froze on the edge of the sidewalk, waiting for it to catch her – until PD dragged her into an alley between buildings too narrow for the car to follow.

He ran and she followed, spurred by the sound of car doors opening and closing to their rear.

"Hang on," she gasped. "They can't just... kidnap someone. We... should call... the police."

PD's grip on her arm didn't loosen. She was watching him, not the road, and she didn't know where he was leading her, between wooden buildings and across deserted streets until suddenly they emerged onto a major road. The noise slammed into her with a shock that felt physical, the growl of traffic and the shouts of pedestrians. PD finally released her bicep and slung a casual arm across her shoulders as if they were just any tourist couple out for a stroll.

She studied his battered face and thought that no one was likely to believe that. But this was San Francisco. No one was likely to say anything, either.

"We can't call the police," PD said. "We can't let the Croatoans know the Agency's involved."

She nodded, though she didn't really understand. They were the government, weren't they? They could do what they damn well pleased. They had with her.

PD stumbled against her and she realised for the first time that he was limping.

"You're injured," she said.

He shrugged then winced, as if the movement pained him.

"Thanks for rescuing me," she added.

He smiled and cut his eyes at her. He was a mess: hair mussed, sharp suit torn and dirty, eyes bright with adrenaline. She liked him better this way. He didn't look like a company man now, just a man. A good-looking one. The coyote's eyes peered out behind his, whiteless and inhuman, and the brown-grey of its fur lightened his hair, but she found she didn't mind. The creature was a protector and it had protected her.

"Don't worry about it," PD said. "That's what partners are for."

She tangled her fingers in his hair and pulled his lips down towards her. He resisted for only a moment, then his mouth opened over hers. He pushed her against the nearest building and the brick hurt the bruises on her back but she didn't complain. They'd tried to take her away and do god knows what to her. But they hadn't. PD had saved her life.

He tore his mouth away from hers, panting. "Jesus," he said. "We shouldn't."

She took his hand and pulled him towards a hotel sign she could see on the next block. She knew they couldn't return to the one they'd stayed in last night. The Croatoans had known her name. They'd find them there.

"Alex," PD said, pulling back, but not hard enough to stop her.

She tightened her hand around his until she felt the bones shift beneath her fingers. "No," she said. "This is something *I* get to decide."

The hotel was much shabbier than their last but Alex hardly noticed the scabbed yellow paint or the balding carpet as PD slipped the keycard into their door then staggered back as the weight of her body pushed him inside, hands already fumbling at his jacket and shirt.

He had a good body, sculpted and strong, but it was the imperfections which intrigued her. She ran her fingers over the mole beside his left nipple and traced the ridge of an appendectomy scar across his stomach. His fingers explored her arms, pausing to circle the tattoo of a butterfly on her shoulder.

His breath hitched then speeded up as he dragged her dress over her head, tugging as it caught on her hips. He smiled when he was done and combed his fingers through her long hair to tidy it.

"Promise me this is real," she said.

"It's real," he told her, and though she saw the flash of the coyote's fangs through his smile she believed him and let him draw her down to the bed.

CHAPTER SEVEN

Morgan called Kate. It went straight to answerphone and he stammered for a moment before saying, "Yeah, hi. It's Morgan. I'm in trouble. There's been another murder – one of Dr Granger's PhD students. Same guy did it. I tried to catch him and now the cops have picked me up for it. You'd better do whatever you do and sort it out."

He let the dial tone buzz in his ear for a second after he ended the call before he put the phone back in its cradle. As soon as he did one of the uniforms approached, eyes narrowed and hostile.

The officer led him to an interrogation room, a plain white cubicle with nothing but four chairs and a desk with a tape recorder on it. The same man who'd arrested him was waiting for him, his dirty grey hair looking even yellower in the harsh lighting. He introduced himself as Detective Inspector Spalding and told Morgan – as he'd been told already – that he was entitled to legal advice.

"Just get on with it," Morgan said, dropping into the chair opposite.

The inspector nodded and switched on the tape recorder, telling it who was present in the room. Morgan had been arrested once before when he'd been caught smoking a spliff on the street as a teenager. He'd been frightened then and trying to hide it, but he was a different person now.

"To start off, how about you tell me what you were doing in that library," Spalding said. "You're not a student at the university and – whatever that badge of yours might say – you're not on the force, either."

"I was looking for some books," Morgan said.

Spalding raised an eyebrow. "Really? And what's your particular area of interest, Mr Hewitt? You don't strike me as the intellectual sort."

Morgan bit back an angry retort and shrugged instead. "Maybe I wanted to improve myself."

Spalding thumped a fist on the table, making both it and Morgan jump. "This isn't a game, son. A girl's dead."

"Yeah, and I didn't kill her. There were witnesses – they saw me running into the room after she was murdered. You've got the wrong person."

"Oh, I know that." Spalding slouched back, stiff posture relaxing.

Morgan pushed himself to his feet. "Then what the fuck am I doing here?"

The other man's lips curved in a close-mouthed smile. "Waiting for your bosses at the Hermetic Division to spring you."

"You work with us? You're with the Division?"

Spalding stood. As Morgan watched, puzzled, his fingers began twisting open the buttons of his nylon shirt. "Not exactly. But you and me, son, we're on the same side. Or we used to be."

He pulled open the unbuttoned shirt, revealing a hollow chest matted with wiry grey hair. The black tattoo stood out starkly against his pale skin, an inverted pentagram to the left of centre, covering his heart. "Belle sends her love, by the way. She told me she's been watching your career with interest."

Morgan kept his eyes fixed on the man as he sat back down. "You sure you want this recorded?"

Spalding shrugged. "I've got a funny feeling an electronic malfunction is going to erase the whole thing. Just one of those glitches."

"You can't touch me," Morgan said. "You won't get away with it."

"I don't want to hurt you. I want to talk – that's why I brought you in."

Morgan studied him, this ordinary looking middle-aged man who'd given himself to a terrible cause. "I was never on the same side as you," he said. "I was just ignorant. Once I knew the truth I made my choice."

"Maybe. But the thing is, son, the difficult decisions are the ones you don't just get to make once. You have to keep on making them, over and over, every day of your life. It's like a relationship, isn't it? The movies tell you that you meet some bird, fall in love, get married, end of story. That's how fairy tales work, not the real world. Love is about commitment. Are you *committed* to the other side, Morgan? Do you even really know what they are?"

"I work for the Hermetic Division. That's my side – and I'm committed to them."

Spalding's infuriating, smug little smile widened. "Render unto Caesar – isn't that what their book says? You've chosen your side in the mundane world, but that's not the one that matters. There's a hidden war, too, and in that battle no one gets to be Switzerland."

"I don't need a fucking philosophy lesson. What do you actually want? You're gonna have to leave the job, maybe even the country now we know who you are. So what's the point of all this? You're not gonna change my mind and I don't think Belle was *that* keen to send her good wishes."

"I want you to stop chasing the man who killed Julie Kirkpatrick and Jane Granger," Spalding said. "And I want you to know exactly who he is."

"Yeah, because I'm really inclined to believe anything you tell me. I'm guessing he's one of yours."

Spalding began to rebutton his shirt. "He works for the Mossad."

"So? My father worked for the Hermetic Division."

"You're right, son. And Lahav is a soldier in that other war – but not on our side. Your murderer works for the opposition."

"Bullshit," Morgan said. "If he works for them, why do you want me to leave him alone?"

"Because there's a few things heaven and hell agree on, and this is definitely one of them. Just let him get on with his job."

"And help you? I don't think so."

Spalding shrugged. "But you'd be helping them too – and if both sides win, neither does, right?"

"Forget it," Morgan said, "you're just trying to mess with my head."

Spalding's head was cocked, listening, and Morgan realised he could hear footsteps approaching. "He's stronger than you," Spalding said, suddenly hurried. "That knife of his can cut through anything, any flesh – even yours. He's never been defeated and you won't be the first. Go back to the Division and tell them this isn't their concern."

The door opened and Morgan knew from the faces of the men there – tense and angry – that Kate had secured his release and pissed off the cops in the process.

He rose, fixing his eyes on Spalding as he left the room. If he saw him outside the station, Spalding was dead and Morgan wanted him to know it.

The other man smiled, unperturbed. "Nice meeting you, son," he said. "Remember what I said, won't you?"

The last glimmer of twilight had faded from the sky when he left. The nearest street light was broken and the moon was below the horizon, leaving only a smattering of stars to freckle the sky. Morgan blinked, momentarily disoriented. The town looked different in the dark, the shadows obscuring the signs of modernity and making it easy to picture the long centuries of its history.

He needed to tell Kate what had happened, but he couldn't use his mobile. The police had taken it from him while he'd been in custody and he couldn't take the risk that Spalding had tampered with it. He called from a payphone instead, keeping it brief. She told him to find himself somewhere to stay and that they'd be sending someone to debrief him tomorrow. He wasn't sure if there was disappointment in her voice, but he imagined it. He'd let her down and he knew it. There was another dead body and no more leads on the killer.

He remembered Julie's flirtatious smile and the way she scratched the back of her neck when she was nervous. He'd let his guard down with her because some part of him wanted to believe what Kate had said, that he could have a normal life if he chose it. Well, so much for that.

The bed and breakfast he found was shabby and unwelcoming. The scuffed, floral-patterned carpets and peeling flock wallpaper made it feel neglected rather than lived in and his room smelt cold, as if it had stood empty for a long time. He curled up beneath the orange bedspread and closed his eyes, hoping for rest he didn't really expect. Wakeful brooding merged with uneasy dreaming and when he rose at seven the next morning he barely felt like he'd slept at all. His joints creaked as he dressed and his eyes felt dusty.

Kate hadn't said when the agent coming to debrief him would arrive. He looked around the dingy hotel and knew he couldn't bear to stay in it another minute. Kate's man could be hours yet. And there was still a murder – two murders – to investigate.

He needed to know more about John Dee, but he couldn't face returning to the library. He leafed through the information the police had reluctantly handed over before releasing him and found they knew even less than the Hermetic Division. They didn't even know the identity of the killer, though his latest murder had left enough witnesses to provide them with a description.

There was only one piece of information in the files that was new to him: Dr Granger's home address. The police had searched her house and found nothing, but they hadn't been looking for the things Morgan wanted. He pocketed the address and left the hotel.

Her house was on the outskirts of the town, a bus ride from the centre. As Morgan leant against the bus shelter, waiting, he felt a prickling between his shoulder blades, the indefinable feeling of eyes on him.

The side of the shelter was clear plastic filled with an out-of-date advert for Pepsi. The day was grey and there was only the ghost of a reflection in the surface, his own wan face but nothing beyond it. He turned around as casually as he could and raised his eyes lazily to let his gaze sweep the street.

There was no one there, just an elderly woman hurrying into a shop, wheeled trolley pushed in front of her. He lowered his head and scanned the street again from beneath his lids. Still nothing.

Was it possible the observation he felt was something else, eyes watching from the occluded world? He wished, suddenly and strongly, that Tomas were with him. Tomas would have known what to do – he'd been at this game a long time. He'd pretty much started it.

Morgan sighed, closing his eyes completely and leaning his head against the wall of the shelter until the bus came. Tomas was gone and Morgan was on his own, which he should be used to by now. The bus drew up, engine huffing, and he opened his gritty eyes reluctantly and climbed on.

The journey to Granger's house took him out of the picturesque city centre and through suburban streets that were affluent but bland, rows of semi-detached 1930s homes and the occasional Victorian terrace. The don's house was in one of the latter, brickwork pleasantly crumbled with age but the paint on the doors and window frames fresh and bright. The front garden was carefully tended, a few square feet of gravel with pot plants at each corner.

There was a gilt-framed mirror in the hallway. Morgan paused to look in it, but only his own reflection stared glumly back. His talent allowed him to see death – not life.

Still, Granger's personality remained imprinted on her home. It was there in the neat row of spice bottles on her kitchen counter, in the fridge full of raw ingredients, nothing ready-made, the pots and pans which were heavy-bottomed and expensive. Granger spent a lot of time in this kitchen; she liked to cook. But she lived alone – divorced, the police files said. Morgan thought it was sad, this middle-aged woman cooking gourmet meals only she would eat.

Her sitting room looked pretty similar to her room in the college, bookshelves crowding every wall. But there was a television too, a stack of DVD box-sets beneath it. Morgan was surprised to see a collection of American crime shows: *The Sopranos*, *The Wire*, *The Shield*. It didn't fit with the image he was building of the dead woman.

And then there was her bedroom, the pile of unwashed clothes at the foot of the bed, the bed itself unmade and the pillowcases and duvet cover mismatched. It was as if the neat, house-proud woman who lived downstairs wasn't the same one who retreated to this room.

I am large, Morgan thought, *I contain multitudes.*

It was a line from a poem, though he wasn't sure which one. Every week since Tomas had died, Kate had given him a new compilation and he'd read them doggedly from cover to cover, though he seldom understood them. But he thought he understood that line now, trying to fit together the mismatched puzzle pieces of Granger's life into the picture of a whole person.

He shook his head. It didn't matter who she was. That wasn't why she'd been killed. She'd died because of what she knew – and he could find no evidence of that in her home. He stood in the sitting room, eyes half-lidded as he thought. He couldn't afford to waste time on a dead end. Every second that ticked by saw Lahav free to commit another murder.

It came to him as he was walking back upstairs to take a final look round the bedrooms. He trotted back down the stairs and into the kitchen. And there it was: a long wooden pole with a metal hook on the end of it. He'd recognised it earlier but not really registered it. They'd used something like it in school to open the high windows in the sports hall.

But there were no high windows in Granger's house. So what did the hook open?

He found the trapdoor in the ceiling above the upstairs bathroom. She'd painted the edges to disguise them and the ring was hidden in the light fitting but it was easy enough to see when you were looking for it. He fitted the hook through the ring and tugged.

The trapdoor swung open and a stepladder rattled as it descended, its base landing on the floor with a thud. The wood of the ladder complained loudly as he climbed, each step bowing a little under his weight. When he reached the top he poked his head into darkness and fumbled for the light. It filled the room with a warm orange glow, chasing the shadows from its corners. And here it was at last – the reason Dr Granger had died.

His first thought was that it looked like one of the chemistry labs at school. His second was that it looked even more like an illustration from the book about John Dee he'd been reading when Julie was killed. The picture had been a reproduction of a woodcut, a 17th-century artist's impression of what the alchemist's work room looked like.

A human skeleton hung suspended from the low ceiling, the brittle bones held together with wire. On the wall behind it, there was a poster of – it took Morgan a moment to recognise it – the periodic table. Beside that was another chart, this one looking much older. It was also a list of elements, but even Morgan could tell many were missing, and the symbols beside them were arcane. A triangle-topped cross had been drawn beside sulphur and the sign for mercury looked like a cartoon devil.

A bench in the centre of the room held glass jars full of liquid, their colours ranging from a clear green to a cloudy, urine-coloured yellow. There were lumps of metal too; copper, rusted iron and a small bar of a buttery yellow metal Morgan was almost certain was gold. Beakers were linked together with networks of glass pipes and rubber tubing. A few sat on retorts above unlit Bunsen burners. And there were sheets of paper everywhere covered in scrawled notes and angry crossings-out.

Dr Granger wasn't just studying alchemy – she was practising it. But what had she been trying to do? Morgan looked again at the lump of iron and remembered reading something about turning base metal into gold. Or could Granger have found a way to contact the spirit world as Dee once claimed to have done? Julie had certainly been interested in the subject, and Granger was her tutor. Then there was what Coby had told him, that the old alchemist had been studying immortality, searching for a way to live forever.

Any of those secrets – or all three of them – could have been worth killing for.

Morgan knew he had to tell Kate. He fished his mobile from the pocket of his jeans before remembering that it was compromised. Public call boxes were rare these days, but he thought he'd seen a couple by the parade of shops at the bottom of Granger's road. He'd ask Kate to meet him in the don's attic. He knew she'd want to see what he'd discovered.

Outside the day had brightened and the streets had filled. The faces that passed by were an anonymous blur, but after a second he felt it again: the sensation of eyes observing him from the shadows. His earlier suspicion hardened into certainty. Someone had been following him, and now they were waiting, watching to see what he did next.

His foot hovered for a moment of indecision, then he made himself step forward. He tensed the muscles in his shoulders to stop himself looking around, then forced himself to relax and walk with the same easy stride he always did. He couldn't afford to let the watcher know he'd been spotted.

He heard and saw nothing, but he imagined footsteps behind him. He pictured Lahav holding his knife, the tip burning red as it approached Morgan's unprotected back. Then he remembered that Spalding had taken the knife when he'd arrested Morgan and he pictured the policeman instead, a smug little smile on his face as he raised his hand to kill.

Morgan's face was dripping with sweat, though a brisk wind stirred up the first fallen leaves of autumn on the pavement. A wad of chewing gum pulled at his heel. There was a faint smell of peppermint as his foot jerked free and then he was at the corner. The building ended in a promontory of elderly fruit crates piled outside the corner shop.

He turned as naturally as he could, keeping his stride easy and his arms loose at his side. The second he was out of sight of the main road he dropped and rolled, bringing his body between the rows of crates. The shopkeeper stared at him, raising a bushy eyebrow over a hawk nose.

Morgan could see only a narrow strip of pavement between the crate of browning bananas on one side and the boxes of wilting spring onions on the other. He tensed his legs and leaned his knuckles against the pavement like a runner in the blocks. A moment passed, filled with the pounding of his heart and the muted growl of the traffic. Then, sooner than he'd expected, a shoe dropped into his field of vision, a denim cuff above it. Morgan didn't have time to process the face as he flung himself towards it. The shopkeeper shouted behind him and his target gasped as Morgan hooked an arm around his waist and a foot behind his knee and pushed him to his back.

Frightened hazel eyes blinked into his out of a face he knew – but not the one he'd expected. It was Coby, Granger's other PhD student.

"Get away from him, young man. I'm calling the police," the shopkeeper shouted. He had a cordless phone in one hand and a cricket bat in the other.

Morgan opened his mouth to reply when Coby said, "It's OK, he's a friend. We're just horsing around – sorry."

The shopkeeper frowned, unconvinced, but when Morgan rocked back on the balls of his feet, releasing Coby from his weight, he muttered and headed back into the shop. Morgan closed a hand around Coby's wrist to tug him to his feet then pull him down the street, away from the shopkeeper's watchful eyes.

"Well? Why the fuck are you following me?" Morgan said when he was sure they were out of earshot.

Coby ran a hand through the curly tangle of his hair, pausing with his fingertips caught at the nape of his neck in a gesture that reminded Morgan painfully of Julie. "I know why Dr Granger died," he said. "And if you don't help me, I'm afraid I'm going to be next."

CHAPTER EIGHT

When Alex woke her head felt clogged with exhaustion and her body ached like she'd been beaten. She rolled to the side and found herself lying against the warm obstruction of another body. PD slept with one arm flung above his head and another curled on his stomach. He looked almost childlike and she smiled. When she ran a hand the length of his arm, snaking to avoid the bruises which mottled it, he stirred but didn't wake.

She could tell by the quality of light seeping through the slatted blinds that it was well past sunrise and she knew she wouldn't go back to sleep. After a moment more enjoying the warmth she rolled to her feet and walked to the window. The blinds rattled as she raised them and she heard a mutter of discontent from the bed. She ignored it, leaning her forehead against the cool glass. Her breath fogged the window, blurring the view of downtown and softening the point of the Transamerica Pyramid to a white blob.

"You're drifting," a voice said, and for a second she thought it was in her head. But when she spun around, Raven was there, black feathers glossy in the light. The orange disc of the sun reflected in its eye as it cocked its head.

She squeezed her own eyes closed then blinked them slowly open again, but it was still there. She'd taken the peyote more than 16 hours ago. She couldn't still be tripping.

"A child thinks when she shuts her eyes the world disappears," Raven said. "But the adult knows the world existed before her and will exist after. The world is permanent and the child is temporary."

"You sound like a fortune cookie," she said.

The bird couldn't smile, but its eye twinkled. "Would you like to hear your fortune, Alex?"

"No," she said. "Please, just leave me alone."

"Too late," it said. "Too late."

There was a rustle of wings as it took to the air and she saw that PD was standing behind it. The graze on his face had begun to congeal into a scab. It looked diseased in the pale morning light. His eyes narrowed as he stared at her. "Alex," he said, "who are you talking to?"

Raven settled on her shoulder and its weight felt like an anchor, tethering her to a place she wanted to escape. Her eyes twitched, wanting to look at it, but she kept them focused on PD. Reality is what you want it to be, she thought. The world you live in is the world you choose to see.

"Sorry," she said. "Just thinking aloud."

She reached out a hand towards his cheek, but he flinched away from it, turning his back on her as he scooped his clothes from the floor. "We should grab breakfast," he said. "And decide on our next move."

Heat rose in her cheeks that was part shame and part anger. "So we're just going to ignore last night?"

He laced his shoes as he spoke, leaving her nothing to look at but his mussed black hair. "We're partners, Alex – we shouldn't have. And we can't again."

"You knew it all along," Raven cawed in her ear.

She shook her head, but there was nothing to say, nothing that wouldn't humiliate her further. Her dress was wrinkled and dirty when she picked it up from the floor. She pulled it on, then followed PD out of the door.

Raven flew beside her as she walked the length of the corridor and a figure walked ahead of her, curly brown hair looking almost black in the subdued lighting. In the elevator car, Raven's reflection blinked at her from every surface but the figure who'd preceded her was gone. PD avoided her gaze and left her nothing to concentrate on but the spirit realm, still there no matter how hard she wished it away. Sixteen hours already. How long would she have to endure before it faded and the mundane world returned? Would it return?

Outside it was worse. San Francisco was on fire, orange flames licking at the rubble of a city in ruins. The streets were crowded, but there was something wrong with the image, like a film that had been double-exposed.

Half the people sauntered casually, tourists with nowhere important to go and in no hurry to get there. The other people ran and screamed. Some faces were blackened with soot while others ran red with blood. Alex saw the terrified people pass through the calm – or maybe it was the other way round. Neither group seemed more or less real than the other, and she dodged both, weaving madly across the sidewalk. PD gave her a puzzled stare but his eyes slid away from hers when she tried to meet them. And Raven flew above it all, floating like a burnt-out ember on the wind.

She knew what she was seeing. Years ago, back when this whole nightmare had first begun, Hammond told her that the future and the past had no meaning in the realm of spirit. A hundred years ago, San Francisco had shaken and then burnt to the ground – and in the spirit world, it was burning still.

She stumbled against PD, tripping on a paving slab that both was and wasn't torn from the ground. He grabbed her arm to steady her, then dropped it immediately and turned to go inside a small diner. Here she saw nothing but the burnished chrome counter and tastefully abstract paintings on the walls. She guessed the earthquake had left this building standing and felt a little of the tension leave her as she slid into her seat.

But Raven remained. The bird perched on the edge of their table, beak poised to peck at their food.

"Alex," PD said, finally looking at her. "You've got to get your head in the game. I'm sorry about last night, but let's move on."

"*Sorry?*" she said, voice shaky.

"I know what happened yesterday freaked you out. Last night was... a reaction to that."

Raven laughed in her ear and she felt her spine stiffen. "It's not last night that's bothering me. It's today. It's still here. Or I'm still there. Christ, I don't know!"

"What's still here?"

"The spirit world. I'm..." She gulped a breath. "I'm trapped in it. I can't get out."

"You're not trapped, kid – you're right here."

Her feelings had been teetering all morning between panic and anger. Now they settled firmly on fury. "What the hell would you know about it? You made me take that peyote, and now I'm losing my mind!"

Her words left silence in their wake, and she realised she'd been shouting. People sitting at the tables around them shifted their chairs. One couple near the door slapped down two twenty dollar bills and left with their eggs Benedict and French toast congealing half-eaten on their plates.

PD shifted uncomfortably. "You're not going crazy. You had a big scare yesterday. You've got to expect some after-effects."

"Jesus Christ, you think I'm imagining this? I'm tripping! That damn Raven's still there. He's sitting on the table right by your hand."

PD shot a short startled glance at the table, frowning when he saw nothing.

"I *know* it's not really there," Alex snapped. "Which means even though I've taken no drugs, I'm still hallucinating. Which means I'm clinically fucking insane, no matter what you say."

He opened his mouth, then closed it again, and she could see his mind whirling behind his eyes.

"Didn't expect that, did you?" she said. "What's the matter, your last tame spirit traveller just toed the company line and didn't complain?"

"There *was* no other spirit traveller." He squeezed his lips together, as if realising he'd said something he shouldn't. But after a moment, he continued, "We've got some people who can visit the place when they're dreaming, but that's it. You're the first we've ever managed to recruit who can go there in the waking world. That's what makes you so valuable."

"The first?" She thought back to what Hammond had told her. He'd said something about her being the first traveller of her generation, and let her assume that the CIA had worked with others. She knew why he'd lied. "Which makes me what, your guinea pig? You bastards. You're making me take all this stuff and you don't even know what it's doing to me.

"It's not like that, Alex," PD said. "We wouldn't... *I* wouldn't treat you that way."

"You *are*."

They stared at each other for a moment of silence. PD looked pained and Alex felt a flash of hope. "Please," she said. "If last night meant *anything*, you've got to help me get away from this."

He clenched his hand and when she saw the flash of undisguised rage on his face, she thought for a moment that he was going to hit her. But he brought his fist down to the table with deliberate gentleness. It lay between them like a warning. "Oh, I get it. Nice plan, kid. *Seduce* me into doing what you want. I've got news for you – it was good, but not *that* good. And your poor little rich girl act doesn't cut it with me. You're like the player who gets dealt a pat straight flush, then complains that the deck's stacked. You have no idea, do you, how lucky you are?"

"I used to," she hissed. "I used to have the sort of life other people envied – and then you took it away from me."

"The self pity... Your life was empty. It meant nothing. And now..." Between them on the table, his fist was clenched so tight that his knuckles stood out white against his brown skin. "Did you ever wonder why they recruited *me*? No, of course not, because you never think about anyone except yourself. Well, I'll tell you. They recruited me because I'm a direct male-line descendant of Wovoka – Jack Wilson to your people. If you'd bothered to study what you were meant to study, you'd know who he was."

"I know who Jack Wilson is. He was the prophet who invented the Ghost Dance. He claimed it could bring paradise on earth."

"And drive the white man from our lands." PD's voice was soft but his anger burned behind his eyes. "He was a spirit traveller like you. Our employers hired me because they hoped I'd inherited his powers. Every test they've done on you, they did on me first – only with me it never worked. I know exactly what you're going through because I went through it too. I wasted years of my life. And now some pissy little white bitch has everything I always wanted."

It was the most honest she'd ever heard him, and it made her feel small and cold and hard. "So you're punishing me because you turned out to be such a failure? You only want what I've got because you don't know what it is. It's *killing* me, don't you understand?"

He shrugged. "We're at war and you're a soldier. Soldiers fight and they die. It's what they're for. You're twenty-three now. Grow up."

So that was it, the bottom line. He didn't care about her or what this cost her. He'd make her keep doing it until it destroyed her, and then he'd look for someone else and do exactly the same to them.

The waitress refilled their coffee cups. PD sipped his as if nothing had happened as the bitter smell surrounded them. "We need to find out more about Maria and the man she was with," he said. "I was going to tell you to take more peyote, but I guess that won't be necessary."

"No, I guess not." She stood and PD did too. His hand reached out to stop her and she slapped it away. "I'm going to the bathroom. If that's *permitted*."

He nodded and she squeezed through to the tiled, low-lit room at the back of the diner. The lock gave a satisfying click as she turned it. She'd sat down, dress bunched around her waist, when she saw Raven's eye twinkling at her from the gloom near the door.

"Jesus!" she shouted, springing up. The heat of her anger burnt low in her chest, still simmering from her argument with PD. "If you want to say something, say it. You're supposed to be my spirit guide, aren't you? Well fucking guide me!"

The bird didn't answer, its black eyes blank. After a few seconds staring into them, she began to feel as if she could fall through and into whatever lay beyond. Her head spun with vertigo and she gasped and covered her face with her hands.

When her hands fell away, she gasped again. The Raven was gone and a man stood in his place. For a second she thought it was PD. He was Native American too, young and handsome. But PD would never have worn what he was wearing, the moccasins and the hide breechcloth and most of all the feather headdress.

Then she registered the glossy black feathers that made up the headdress and the black shine of the eyes beneath it, and she knew who this was.

"Raven?" she said.

He cocked his head, the human gesture exactly like the bird's. "Well, no, I'm human."

"But you *were* the Raven?"

"Oh yes. Or he was me. Or maybe both of us are someone else."

She huffed in exasperation.

He looked hurt. His face was far more mobile than PD's, the expressions flicking across it almost comically broad. "Sorry, am I boring you? I don't usually do that. Irritate, yes. I might go so far as infuriate. But I'm seldom actually tedious."

"Could you just..." She sighed. "Could you just go away?"

"But I thought you wanted my help. You were quite explicit about it. 'Fucking guide me'. Those were your exact words." He grinned idiotically.

"Jesus," she said. "I think I preferred you when you were a bird."

"I'm less obliging when I'm a bird."

The bathroom was too hot, condensation sweating from its white walls and coating the lid of the toilet when she lowered it. She sat gingerly and studied her spirit guide. He was as solid and real as anything else in the room.

"Can you make it go away?" she asked him.

"Make *myself* go away?"

She shook her head to deny it and then realised that of course that was exactly what she meant. "Make all of it go away. Make it stop. PD *wants* this – why not give it to him?"

He curled in on himself to sit cross-legged on the floor in front of her. "Oh, PD. The man is an apple – red on the outside, white on the inside."

"So what? I'm white on the inside *and* the outside."

He laughed and when she felt the brush of expelled air against her cheek, she realised his head was at the same level as hers though he was sitting two feet below her. If he stood now, he'd need to bend his neck to fit beneath the ceiling, but she hadn't seen him grow or change. She shivered, wondering if the trick was his, or if she'd simply begun to accept the twisted physics of the spirit world without question.

"And yet," he said, "I chose you. You were picked. Selected. Singled out. Haven't you asked yourself why?"

"Only every day."

"And there's your problem."

She frowned. "Because I don't know the answer?"

"Because you're asking that ridiculous question in the first place!" He jumped up, looming towards her. For an instant he was still a giant and then just an ordinary man, so close she could see nothing but the brown blur of his nose and the sharp blackness of his eyes as he grasped her cheeks in his palms. "That's like asking why tigers have stripes. Why bees sting. Why dogs growl."

"We already *know* the answers to those question." She tried to pull her face out of his grasp.

He held on tighter, fingers digging into her as he shook her head from side to side. "But we don't ask them when the dog is mauling us or the tiger pouncing! Think, girl. Think. You want to escape. So what's the question you should be asking?"

"How to stop the dog attacking. Or how to get away when it does."

He sagged back, as if her answer had cost him great effort. "Yes. Oh yes. So, Alexandra Keve, just how are you going to get away?"

She slumped back too, the cold square outline of the cistern pressing uncomfortably into her back. "I don't know."

"Well," he said, "I guess you'd better start figuring it out."

Alex didn't need to test her boundaries to know they were there. PD wouldn't just let her give him the slip. It was in the way he watched her, the covert glances from the corner of his eye as he drove. And he was still angry with her. She could read that too, in the tense set of his shoulders and the muscle that jumped in his jaw.

The grubby streets of the Tenderloin flicked by on the journey to Alamo Square. She knew that her chances of escape grew slimmer with every block they passed. PD's contact was meeting them in Alamo park, near Jacob Marriot's residence. The contact had intel on Maria's dinner companion as well as plans of his nearby house. Marriot had returned to LA after last night's meal and PD wanted to break into his place while he was gone. He wanted Alex to view it through the lens of the spirit world and tell him what she saw.

And when she'd done that, there'd be something else that he wanted her to do. And so it would go on, week after week and month after month until all the fight had left her and she was just as much a company zombie as he was. She felt a momentary surge of self-pity and fought it. Raven was right. Feeling sorry for herself got her nowhere.

They'd almost passed the bank when she called out sharply to PD to stop. He obeyed immediately, swerving the car to the kerb as his brakes screeched and the normally placid San Franciscan traffic honked behind him.

"What?" he said. "What did you see?"

She forced the anger out of her face so that it was merely blank when she turned to him. "A bank."

"And? Are you saying this place is connected to them?"

"It's connected to me." She released her seat belt and grabbed the door handle.

PD's hand closed over hers, stilling her. "Where do you think you're going?"

"I need to transfer some funds. I spent a fortune on clothes yesterday and now they're all gone. We can't go back to that hotel and I've got to have something to wear. I'd rather get out of this dress – too many unpleasant memories."

The words and their meaning hung in the air between them for a moment. It was PD who looked away first. "You really think this is the right time? We're working."

"Which makes this time different from any other time of the day how exactly? We're always working. I need money, it will only take ten minutes, and you've just wasted three."

"Fine. Get it done." His hand released hers, leaving a moist patina of his sweat on her skin.

She almost fell onto the sidewalk in her haste to get out of the car. The sun was bright but the air cool and she took a deep, steadying lungful of it. Then she couldn't stop herself turning to look at PD. He glared back at her, and she knew that if she took a second longer than ten minutes, he'd come in after her. She could make a run for it, but he'd find her or call someone else who would.

She squared her shoulders and turned back to the bank. It didn't matter – she just had to find a way to slow the pursuit while she escaped. And ten minutes should be plenty of time to set that in motion.

The inside of the building was hushed and gloomy with armed security guards loitering in the shadows. She walked past them and joined the shortest line for a teller, pulling out her iPhone as she took her place behind a gawky teenager wearing a T-shirt a shade redder than his zits.

A quick search of White Pages found the restaurant's telephone number. She could picture their waiter smiling as he'd introduced himself and the less amiable expression on his face as he'd watched her being frog-marched towards the waiting car.

"Hey," she said, when the ring-tone ended. "Listen, I'm a friend of Jeremiah's and he isn't answering his cell. Is he working with you right now?"

"Let me just... Yes, he's–" the woman said, and Alex tapped call end, then stored the number. The pimply boy had finished his transaction and she strode forward confidently, like she owned the place. It wasn't far from the truth. Her mother was a major shareholder.

The teller smiled at her as she asked to see the manager, the smile tightening a little when Alex told her it was urgent. A moment later the man emerged, hand outstretched for a warm handshake.

"My driver's double-parked, so I'll keep this brief," she said as he led her to his office. "I need to make a large cash withdrawal today, and I want to ensure you have the funds available to cover it."

"Large?" He raised an eyebrow.

"Three million."

"Ah. I'm not sure I can accommodate you on that, I'm afraid, Miss...?"

"Keve. Alexandra Keve.

His expression brightened. "I'm sorry, Miss Keve, I didn't realise. I think we can arrange something. Will the end of the day be soon enough?"

"Two hours, maximum."

He only hesitated a second. "Two hours, then. I'll need to make some calls. And you have ID, of course..."

She was still smiling as she climbed back into the car with PD ,nine minutes after she'd left it. "Are you ready now?" he asked.

"Well?" Raven said. She could see him in the rear-view mirror, perched cross-legged on the back seat. "Are you ready, Alex?"

"Yes," she said. "I think I am."

CHAPTER NINE

Morgan used the bus journey back into town to study Coby. Their elbows pressed awkwardly together, cramped side by side in the narrow seat, and he could smell the other man's body, the unpleasant tang of stale sweat. Coby looked nervous, but that was hardly surprising. His teacher and his fellow student were both dead – believing someone was out to get him didn't seem like paranoia.

Still, Morgan thought there was more to it. There was something unnerving about Coby's pale brown eyes. There was an absence in them that Morgan couldn't name but thought he might have seen in his own reflection.

Coby sensed him looking and turned to catch his eye. "I'm not asking you to trust me, you know."

Morgan shrugged, unwilling to have this conversation in public.

Ten minutes later, the bus dropped them off at the same stop he'd first caught it from. He stood at the shelter and scanned the streets, then turned to Coby. "You were watching me here."

"I knew I needed your help," Coby said, walking away. After a few paces, he turned down a narrow, cobbled street.

"But you waited to ask for my help until *after* I'd seen Dr Granger's house," Morgan said as he followed him. "Why?"

Coby's eyes snapped to his face and then away, the movement almost too fast to spot. Morgan found himself picturing a lizard's tongue flicking out to taste the world. "I needed to make sure you weren't actually the person who's hunting me," Coby said.

"How do you know I'm not?"

"He would have burnt down the house if he'd seen what you saw in there."

They lapsed into silence as a jostling group of school children passed them by, and then they were back on a main street again and it was too public to talk. Morgan chewed his lip as he thought about what Coby had said and what it meant. The Israelis wanted to put a stop to Dr Granger's research. After what Morgan had seen in her attic, he didn't find that hard to understand. He couldn't imagine the Hermetic Division would be too keen on it either.

Coby finally stopped in front of a scuffed black door beside a newsagent's window. There were four bells with smudged names in ink alongside them. Coby's was at the top: Bryson. Inside, threadbare carpet led them up three flights of stairs to another door. Coby pushed a key into its lock, but Morgan put a hand on his shoulder to still him. The wood was dark-stained and the marks were hard to see, but when he flicked on the light they leapt into sharp relief. Someone had painted a red cross on the door. The red was too watery to be paint. Morgan was almost certain it was blood. He released Coby's shoulder and stared at him in silence until the other man spoke.

"Protection," he said. "Come in and I'll explain."

The place was a bedsit, smaller than Morgan had expected, cluttered, dark and grubby.

Coby noticed his expression as he looked around. "Yeah, I know. Not exactly the dreaming spires, right?"

Morgan guessed Coby was quoting from something and felt a twinge of pain as he thought of Tomas and his poetry. He shook his head and said, "I live down the Elephant and Castle. Looks all right to me."

Coby's eyes didn't leave him as he crossed the room. "So I guess you know what Dr Granger was researching."

He slid into a sagging armchair and Morgan perched gingerly on the sofa opposite. He didn't like the way the soft springs swallowed him up. They'd delay his response a crucial second if he was attacked, and Coby didn't look like a threat, but he didn't seem entirely safe either.

"You told me already," he said. "You and Julie. Angels, immortality – the philosopher's stone."

"Yeah, but you thought I meant in a theoretical, academic sort of way. Now you know differently. You know it's real"

"I always knew that."

Coby nodded. "Of course you do – you're Hermetic Division."

"How do you know about the Hermetic Division? How do you know about any of it?"

"I'm a historian, a good one – and so was Dr Dee. I just followed the trail he laid down. Before I started, I thought... What we all thought, I guess, before we got sucked into this. That the world was an ordinary sort of place, with maybe the occasional odd thing in it. Like a brightly lit room with just a few shadows. But it's night out there, isn't it?"

Morgan narrowed his eyes. "And you've discovered something that someone wants kept in the dark."

"Dr Granger discovered it. She was dying, you see. Cancer. Slow-acting, but fatal. She never had much interest in Dr Dee or his experiments before her diagnosis. But afterwards..."

"You're saying she discovered the secret of immortality?"

Coby smiled. "Sounds crazy, right?"

Morgan stood, cracking the bones in his neck as he straightened. "My standards of crazy have changed recently. So what was the secret?"

"I don't know." His eyes followed Morgan as he paced the room, watchful and just a little fearful. Morgan wondered what Coby was afraid he might do. Or was it something he was afraid Morgan might find?

"You don't know," Morgan said. "Then why would anyone want to kill you? He's already got rid of Granger and Julie. The secret's safe, right?"

His pacing took him to a battered armoire at the end of the room. He heard Coby shift in his seat as he approached it. When Morgan turned to face him he slouched back just a bit too quickly, faking nonchalance. Whatever it was he didn't want Morgan to find, it was here.

"Well?" Morgan said.

"Dr Granger and Julie don't know the secret either. But they knew – and I know – how to get hold of a man who does."

"I'm listening." Morgan turned back to the armoire. When he slid the draw open there was nothing inside but a dried-up can of deodorant and a packet of disposable razors. The surface itself was loosely scattered with papers but they were all red bills and bank statements. He flicked his eyes to the cracked mirror which hung above it, hoping to catch Coby's reaction to his prying, but the armchair he'd been sitting in was empty.

Morgan turned to find that Coby had moved to the small kitchenette at one end of the room. Water gurgled as he filled a plastic kettle. "I need a drink," he said, glancing over his shoulder.

"You're avoiding the question," Morgan said. "*Who* knows the secret?"

"Dr Dee."

Morgan closed his eyes and clenched his jaw. "I'm this close to just beating the fucking information out of you."

"I'm serious. You spoke to Julie, didn't you? Before she..."

"Yeah."

"Then she must have told you about Dee's spirit communications – that he talked to angels."

"She said Dr Dee claimed he'd found a way to contact them."

Steam from the boiling kettle wreathed Coby's face as he poured water into the mug and the smell of cheap coffee spread through the room. "He *did* find a way. He used scrying mirrors – portals into the realm of spirit. There's one in the British Museum. It's made out of obsidian and it's older than Dee. It's Mexican, actually – a cult object associated with Tezcatlipoca, the god of sorcerers. His name means The Smoking Mirror."

Morgan couldn't help snatching another glance at the mirror behind him. He knew better than anyone what could sometimes be seen in the silvered glass. When he turned back round, he found that Coby had moved again. He was perched on the arm of the sofa, mug cradled in his hands.

"Dr Dee's mirrors let you contact spirits," Morgan said. "You're telling me this – this obsidian mirror – you could use it to talk to Dee?"

"Not that one, no. Dee used the one in the British Museum to summon the angels he talked to and tried to bargain with. But there's another one he valued even more highly. He was afraid to die, you see. Why do you think he was searching for the philosopher's stone? So when he knew the end was coming, he took his most powerful mirror and he looked into it at the moment of his death. He believed his spirit would be caught and preserved in it forever, like a fly trapped in amber. *That's* the mirror you need, if you want to talk to Dee."

"And you've got it. Or you know where it is."

"Yes," Coby said. "That's why my life is in danger."

Morgan nodded. "Except it's all bullshit, isn't it? Because if Dee had the secret, he wouldn't be dead in the first place."

For the first time, Coby didn't seem to have a ready answer. He covered his hesitation by taking a sip of coffee, but Morgan wasn't fooled. "You're sort of right," he said eventually. "Dee did find out how to achieve immortality. But knowing and doing are two different things. And the same people who are trying to stop me now were trying to stop him then."

"The Mossad? Right."

"You're closer than you think. Have you read the Bible? Not all of it, really, just Genesis."

Morgan laughed. "Funnily enough, that hasn't been high on my list of priorities."

Coby didn't smile. "Well it should be, especially for you. Even so, you must know the story of the Garden of Eden, the apple that Eve picked that got us all kicked out of paradise."

"Yeah. So?"

"The popular understanding is that we got kicked out for eating the apple – for disobeying God. But that's not it at all. There was another apple tree in the Garden, you see. Another forbidden fruit, and this one gave you eternal life. God kicked Adam and Eve out so they couldn't eat that second apple too. He couldn't risk it, because that apple would have made them just like him – immortal and omniscient. God didn't kick us out of Eden because he was angry, he did it because he was afraid. And his agents are still afraid and they're willing to do whatever it takes to stop mankind finding a way to rival His power.

"You're saying Dee found the Garden of Eden," Morgan said.

"Finding it isn't the problem – it's getting in. God left a guardian behind, the archangel Uriel. To enter Eden you'd have to defeat him and that's something no mortal man should be able to do."

Morgan took a deep breath. "Listen, you're talking about it like this is literally true: Eden, guardian angels. I've seen a map of the world, and the Garden of Eden isn't on it."

"No, it's not literal truth – it's metaphor. But there's a world beyond this one where metaphor has physical form and the Garden is more than an idea. And Uriel isn't standing outside Eden holding a flaming sword for all eternity. Here's *here*, hunting down anyone who gets too close. Angels and demons can enter this plane if they find a human body to carry them. They're parasites. It's why they're so hard to fight. If you destroy the host body the parasite just finds another."

Morgan remembered Belle and nodded. He supposed it made sense that the same rule applied to both sides in this supernatural conflict. "So you're saying Lahav's an angel? Or that he's got one inside him?"

"Probably. That's why I didn't come to you straight away – there was always a chance the spirit had jumped bodies into yours. The Israelis are definitely working with the forces of heaven. I'd say there's some kind of mutual back-scratching going on. The spirits they're dealing with must be able to tell them where all sorts of interesting things are hidden. And they're powerful allies and dangerous enemies. They're not completely invulnerable, though – not even Uriel, who's one of the most powerful. You've probably seen *The Exorcist*, but that's Catholic tradition. Do you know how Jews perform exorcisms?"

"I guess not with a bell, book and candle."

"No. They use a horn, a ram's horn called a shofar. It's the same horn they blow every New Year and on the Day of Atonement. The sound is said to drive the possessing spirit out of its body."

"And Uriel's just another possessing spirit," Morgan said. "But you'd need a pretty powerful shofar, wouldn't you, to drive out a being that strong?"

"Yes – there's only one shofar in the whole world that could do it, the shofar Hagadol. Legend says it was part of the Temple treasure, lost when the Romans sacked the place two thousand years ago. Interesting, isn't it, that the ancient Israelite priests made it? Almost like they wanted an insurance policy in case God fucked them over the way he fucked over so many other people. Anyway, Dee spent his whole life and fortune tracking the shofar down." Coby studied him, eyes squinted as he tried to puzzle out the expression on his face. "You believe me, don't you?" he said. "You know I'm telling the truth."

Morgan nodded as he strode towards him. "Yeah, I think you might be. But there's something else I want to know."

Coby was still smiling encouragingly when Morgan grabbed him round the waist, pinning him against his body, Coby's back to his front. "I want to know," Morgan hissed in his ear, "why you don't want me to see you in that mirror."

As soon as he spoke, Coby started struggling. There was a wiry strength in his slender limbs, but Morgan was a trained soldier and there wasn't really any question of the outcome. Coby's feet scrabbled against the carpet as Morgan dragged him towards the armoire and the mirror above it.

When they were in front of it, Coby wrenched his head aside, eyes closed. It didn't matter. The spirits were there whether Coby looked at them or not.

Morgan saw a woman with frizzy ginger hair and an older black man with a kind face and tired eyes. But mostly they were children, so many of them that they crowded the glass, leaving nothing of the room behind them. Their mouths moved soundlessly, screaming or shouting, it was hard to tell.

"OK, OK" Coby said. "You can let me go – the cat's out of the bag, right? Before you ask, they're bound to me, though I've never been able to see them. "

Morgan held him a moment longer, then let him struggle free. "Who are they?" he asked. "Did they die here?"

Coby shook his head. "Not here."

"But you killed them."

"Yes." For a long moment, the only sound in the room was Coby's laboured breathing. Then he sighed and looked up. "What you should really have asked is why am *I* so interested in immortality?"

Morgan looked back at the mirror, but the shades were gone, only the after-image of their accusing eyes lingering in the glass. "You're going to hell," he said.

Coby nodded. "When I was a stupid, angry kid, I did a terrible thing. And when I die, I'm going to pay for it. *If* I die."

Suddenly, it was Morgan who couldn't look Coby in the eye. What happened to a man without a soul after he died? It was the question which had haunted him for months. But if Coby was right – if Dr Dee's research was as successful as he claimed – he might never need to find out.

"OK," he said to Coby. "Tell me where the mirror is."

The day had warmed up by the time they reached the river, the sun burning through the thin clouds. The colleges looked golden and the grass still green with the last vitality of summer. It was a peaceful scene but Morgan felt none of it. There was a knot in his stomach that he didn't want to identify. He told himself it was only fear, but it felt like guilt too. He should have phoned Kate to give her a progress report and he hadn't.

Coby scrambled down the riverbank and Morgan followed, trainers squelching in the mud from yesterday's rain. There were two punts tied up there and Coby began to loosen the rope holding the less battered of them.

"You're kidding, right?" Morgan said.

Coby turned to look at him over his shoulder as his fingers kept working at the rope. "It's hidden in the river. Running water foxes magic and stops anyone trying to scry a location. We could hire a motorboat somewhere, I guess, but a punt's the least conspicuous form of transport in these parts."

The boat rocked alarmingly on the water when Morgan climbed in and he sat down hurriedly on the narrow wooden seat. He scowled when he saw Coby smiling at him.

"I'll drive, shall I?" Coby said. He seemed to know what he was doing. The punt sluiced soundlessly through the water, overtaking the other, slower boats which crowded the river.

Morgan leaned back on his elbow and raised his face to the sun.

"Never been punting before?" Coby asked. With his wide pale eyes and loose curls he looked the picture of boyish innocence.

"What did you do to them?" Morgan asked.

Coby looked at him a long moment. It occurred to Morgan that he never did anything without considering it, and that this was both his weakness and what made him dangerous. You'd never know what Coby really wanted, because he didn't act on what he wanted, only on what he thought was best.

"I killed them," Coby said. "That's all that matters. Dead is dead, right?"

Morgan couldn't argue with that. He'd been an assassin once and he hadn't spent much time agonising over how his targets died. People talked about a painless death, but only those who'd never seen someone die. The pain could be brief or drawn-out, but it was always there.

"You knew what I'd see in your mirror," he said instead. "How?"

Coby's lips twisted into something that wasn't quite a smile. "You're a minor celebrity in the occluded world, Morgan – surely you must have realised? You can't do what you did in St Petersburgh and not have people notice. Interested parties have been keeping an eye on you ever since. Granger dying was convenient, in a way – I mean horrible and a waste, obviously, but at least it drew you here. If you hadn't come to investigate, I'd have had to find some other way to get you involved. I need you to finish this. If I could see the spirits that hide in mirrors, I'd know Dee's secret already."

So Coby knew exactly who he was and what he could do, despite his dissembling earlier. Morgan nodded, unsurprised, and watched the water ripple around the pole as Coby plunged it to the bottom of the river. He'd never liked water, not since he'd watched his sister drown as a child, but this river was so tame it was hard to be afraid of it.

So when he felt the prickling in his shoulder blades, he knew it was something else that was prodding his animals instincts awake. He'd lived on his nerves long enough to trust when they told him he was in danger.

The punt rocked as he stood too rapidly. Coby shouted in alarm and the occupants of a nearby boat snapped their heads to watch, laughing as they saw Morgan wobble on his feet. He took in their fresh, happy faces and instantly dismissed them. The river was crowded with punts, tourists leaning on the stone bridges to watch them pass beneath.

Lahav crouched low in a boat twenty feet behind. His face was shaded beneath a cap, but Morgan's eyes were drawn to him in an instant. A wolf couldn't hide among sheep. His aura betrayed him, the signal of a predator.

"He's found us," Morgan said.

"Shit! How? That cross should have protected me from scrying." Coby's voice was too loud. It echoed across the still water and their pursuer's head snapped up.

"Maybe he just followed us," Morgan said. "He's a spy, isn't he? He doesn't need to rely on the supernatural to do his job."

Coby looked shocked, as if this hadn't occurred to him. He punted harder, his strokes less elegant now, as his pale eyes darted nervously back to Lahav.

"I'll watch him – you watch where we're going!" Morgan snapped.

Coby scowled then jumped as the prow of their punt jostled against a boat he hadn't seen ahead of him. The man in blazer and boater smiled lazily at him, but Coby didn't meet his eye, twirling his pole to take their boat between the two ahead. The punts he left in his wake rocked unsteadily and the man in the boater yelled but they were past and now Lahav was five feet further behind.

Morgan blinked when light switched to damp darkness as they passed beneath another bridge. The splash of the pole echoed loudly and he could hear his breathing too, as laboured as if he was the one punting their boat.

He felt useless. There was only one pole and even if they'd had a second he doubted he could have done much to help. Why hadn't it occurred to him that Lahav might find them? That by going straight for the mirror, he'd lead his enemy there too?

But he hadn't been thinking about much of anything, had he? Only getting his hands on the mirror for himself. If he'd told the Hermetic Division and got their back-up, he wouldn't be in this situation now.

He blinked again, blinded, as the punt glided back into daylight.

"We need to get out and get away," Coby said. "We can't risk leading him to the mirror." He held the pole immobile as he talked, only turning it a little to steer them round a rowing boat full of sunburnt tourists.

Morgan closed his hand around the wet wood, jerking it back to the bottom of the river. The punt rocked unsteadily, but Coby got the message and kept pushing them forward.

"It's too late," Morgan said. "We've already led him to the river – he must know why we've come. Do you really want to give him the chance to search until he finds it?"

Coby's already pale face paled further. "But can you take him on? I know what you are, but that knife of his is lethal, even to you."

It was a good question. *I know what you are...* What he'd once been. But he'd given that up, along with most of the power he was heir to. The secret of immortality wouldn't do him any good if he died before he could use it.

He looked behind them, but the gloom beneath the bridge hid their pursuer. "How much further?" he asked Coby.

"Three more bridges, maybe ten minutes," the other man said. "It's under the Mathematical Bridge. Urban legend says Isaac Newton built it, but that's bullshit. William Etheridge designed it to be an occult focus: oak above, water below. The mirror's mystically invisible there."

"But not actually invisible," Morgan said, and Coby grimaced and shook his head.

A second later, they were nosing between two more punts and Lahav was powering from beneath the bridge. He wasn't punting his own boat. A broad-shouldered man leaned on the pole behind him, teeth gritted as he put all the power of his back into each stroke. Was he another Israeli agent, Morgan wondered, or just a hired hand?

He realised it didn't matter as Lahav's eyes hunted and trapped his. This man alone was dangerous enough. There was another boat in front of the Israeli, a punt overloaded with drunk teens. It drifted sideways, the steering left neglected as the pudgy blonde holding the pole took a swig of champagne straight from the bottle. Morgan saw her throat work as she swallowed. And he heard the crunch of broken bone as Lahav drove an elbow into her nose, knocking her out of his path as his boot swung out to shove the boat clear.

The other people in the boat swore and screamed, but Lahav's expression of grim resolve didn't flicker and he was now only fifteen feet behind Morgan. Morgan could see the knife in his hand glowing red. "What the fuck?" he said to Coby. "The police took that off me. How the hell did he get it back?"

"It's not the blade that matters," Coby said. "It's the hand holding it."

Another bridge was approaching, two low stone arches spanning green banks. Stone spheres lined the railing above.

Morgan didn't have time to think as the prow of their punt slid under it. He bent his knees and jumped.

Only his fingertips hooked over the top of the bridge and they took all of his weight. His arms screamed with the strain and his heart pumped too hard. Above him he could hear laughter and he imagined he had an audience. His fingertips dug as hard as they could into the rough stone. His T-shirt rucked up, leaving his stomach exposed as he pulled himself up an inch, then another, but there was no leverage and just no way he could get himself any higher.

All the breath huffed out of his body as it dropped and his nails scraped a millimetre nearer the edge of the stone. His feet swung, searching for purchase, but there was nothing except the empty air of the archway.

When he felt the clasp of a hand around his wrist he flinched away from it, almost falling into the water beneath. Another hand closed around his other wrist, fingers tight against the bone, and he made himself relax. It hurt like hell when they jerked upwards, tearing something in his shoulder that he knew he'd feel for days. Then a hand was under his armpit and the pressure on his arms was gone. There was another heave, his legs helping this time, pushing against the stone of the arch, and he was over. He lay on the bridge and stared up at his rescuers.

They grinned down at him, young and pleased with themselves. "Nice one, mate," the redhead said.

Morgan nodded as he stood. He managed a smile and a mumble they could interpret as thanks, but he didn't have any more time for them. When he looked out over the railing he saw that Lahav was almost at the bridge. The Israeli was staring up at him, frowning. His knife was white hot in his hand, brighter than the sunlight.

Morgan pressed a hand against the nearest stone sphere. It didn't move, didn't even rock, probably cemented in place. He'd been expecting that. The bridge was crowded with tourists and a small group of schoolchildren gave him an ironic round of applause.

He shouldered his way through them and ignored their protests. When he'd given himself a fifteen-foot run-up, he turned back round. The two men who'd rescued him were eyeing him curiously. They must have realised some of what he intended to do, because they started to clear a path for him, shoving the onlookers to one side of the bridge or the other. They grinned at him, like this was all a bit laugh, and he supposed for them it was.

He'd always been a strong runner and his thighs tensed and flexed easily as he pushed himself forward. When he was five feet from the railing he leant back and leapt forward, feet outstretched. He saw a brief flash of his helpers' faces, mouths open in shock. And then the shock jarred through his legs as the soles of his feet hit the stone sphere on the brink of the bridge.

His knees flexed and for a second he thought he'd failed. Then there was a crack, a grating of stone, and his legs straightened again as the sphere flew over the edge of the bridge.

He ended almost as he'd begun, hanging by his arms from the edge of the bridge. This time no one rushed to help him, but it didn't matter. He had a better purchase with his elbows hooked over the top, and it only took a moment to pull himself up.

The crowd which had smiled at him backed away, faces white and shocked. He could see several running away, others with their phones to their ears, probably calling the police. He looked back down at the river. The boat was still there, but Lahav was no longer in it and there was a bright spatter of blood across the punt's wooden side.

He wasn't the only one to notice it. His former rescuer leant against the railing beside him, eyes wide. "Bloody hell," he said. "I think you killed him."

Morgan hoped he had, but he didn't want to rely on it. He took one last look at the water – no bubbles rising to the surface, no body either – then strode to the other side of the bridge. A few hands reached out to stop him only to flinch away when he glared at their owners.

It took him a moment to spot Coby's punt in the pack of boats crowding the water. It was nearer than he'd expected, almost close enough to jump to and he swore as he realised the other man must have stopped to wait for him. When Coby's eyes caught his he raised a hand, pointing onward. Without waiting to see the response, he launched himself over the side in a dive that was nearer to a belly flop.

The rank river water rushed through his nostrils to trickle unpleasantly down the back of his throat. He coughed and swam on, blinking his eyes clear. He could hear a hubbub of voices around him and knew there couldn't be a person left in this section of the river whose attention he hadn't drawn.

Coby's punt was harder to spot once you were in the water. Morgan pulled himself over the side of one boat only to find himself looking into the startled eyes of a middle-aged woman. The next boat was full of students and this time he was pushed roughly away with the punt pole, a bruising impact against already sore ribs. The fourth boat was Coby's. The other man didn't look much more pleased to see him than the strangers, but he paused in his poling long enough to haul Morgan over the side.

Morgan lay in the bottom of the boat, absorbing the sun's heat through his soaking wet clothes.

A second later, the rays were blocked by Coby's shadow. "What the hell were you doing back there?" he said.

Morgan shrugged, sighed, and rolled to his hands and knees. "Lahav's in the river – we can get the mirror."

Coby's brows drew down, suspicious.

"Get moving," Morgan said. "I don't know how long he'll stay under. Fuck, for all I know the bastard can breathe under water."

Coby frowned at him a moment longer, then shrugged and turned back to the river. It was clearer now, the boats around them hustling to get out of their way. To their left, a wide field of grass opened up, ending in a long, low building and another, tall and over-ornate, that was probably a church. At the end of the grass was another bridge, plainer than the one he'd scaled. Morgan alternated between scanning it and scanning the water behind him. He could see neither pursuit nor police, and Coby had said ten minutes. Surely they were going to make it.

"Next one," Coby said tensely as the shadow of the bridge blotted out the sun.

Then they were through and Morgan could see it ahead. Unlike the others this bridge was wooden, a complex puzzle that arced over the water like a kid's toy from the Early Learning Centre.

"Under there?" he said.

"Beneath it," Coby told him. "There's a null zone below the very centre. The struts form a rune whose shape is only visible from a thirty degree angle. No one who wasn't looking for it would see it, although there've always been rumours. It's been rebuilt twice, but it doesn't matter. The power's in the design, not the material."

Morgan studied the bridge as they drew closer, the complex shadows it cast on the water below. "Which side were they working for, the people who built it?"

"Doesn't really matter, does it? Sometimes our acts count for more than our intentions." He twisted the pole, spinning the boat 180 degrees and bringing it to a halt only a few feet from the centre of the bridge. "I'm not sure what they hid under the bridge originally, it's long gone. But it sure came in handy when I needed to stash the mirror."

"*Beneath* the water?" Morgan said. "Great."

Coby smiled. "Well, I guess you're already wet."

Morgan didn't bother to argue. He wanted the mirror in *his* hands, not Coby's. He was using the other man but he didn't trust him.

His soggy T-shirt clung to his body, tangling his arms as he pulled it off. His jeans were worse. Coby raised his eyebrows as he saw Morgan scraping them down his legs, but he didn't want anything dragging him down once he was underwater.

"How am I gonna find it?" he asked Coby when his jeans were round his ankles. He lifted them above his head, rocking back inelegantly on his hips to tug them off.

"It's in an oak box, about half a foot square," Coby said. "I only hid it three weeks ago, so it shouldn't be buried in silt. I guess you'll just have to feel around."

"Great." Morgan knew if he gave himself time to consider it, he'd reconsider. He *hated* the water. He had only dark memories of what lay beneath it. But he slid himself to the side of the boat, took one deep breath and tumbled over.

He didn't keep his eyes open. There was no point. He kicked with his feet, hands still and spread out in front of him. The bottom came sooner than he'd expected, a slimy brush of mud and weed against his fingertips that made him cringe away before he forced himself forward.

His eyes opened on instinct, but he could see nothing. There was no light beneath the muddy water and he had to fight hard not to panic. He felt his heart pounding as his fingers trailed through the mud. He stayed down as long as he could, until the air was burning in his lungs, but his fingers found nothing except pebbles and eventually he had to kick up to the surface again.

When his head struck wood, he felt a fierce moment of fear before he realised he'd come up beneath the boat. Coby was leaning over to look at him when he'd worked his way to the side.

His face fell when he read Morgan's. "No?" he said. "Nothing?"

Morgan didn't answer, just took another big gulp of air and jackknifed in the water to dive back down. This time his fingers found something solid within seconds, but when he tried to grasp it a piercing agony shot up his arm and he let out a great gulp of air in a silent scream. His feet felt weak as they kicked him to the surface and when he neared it he could see the cloudy trail of blood flowing behind him.

"Jesus," Coby said when Morgan grabbed the side of the punt, only to snatch his hand back with a hiss of pain as the cut on his palm opened wide and oozed blood.

Morgan shook his head, teeth gritted, annoyed with himself. "It's nothing. Just some junk on the bottom of the river. Piece of scrap metal, I th   "

"I'm sorry," Coby said, but he didn't look it. His hazel eyes were flat and Morgan thought the only thing he regretted was that Morgan hadn't yet found the mirror.

Morgan didn't much like the idea of diving again with an open wound in his palm. The water was filthy and god knew what sort of infection he could pick up from it. Childish memories of watching *Jaws* crowded his mind, creatures hidden beneath the water which were drawn to blood.

"Fuck," he said, then dove back down into the water.

He used his knuckles to brush the surface this time. The wound ached deeply and he had visions of finding the jagged metal again. He imaged it catching against a finger this time, cutting it through. When he felt something hard beneath the mud he flinched back from it instinctively. But it was smooth and warm: wood, not metal. He'd been down a minute at least and he already felt the burn of oxygen deprivation in his lungs, but if he surfaced for air he'd never find this same spot again.

The box was buried deep in the riverbed, sucked down by the hungry mud. Morgan's fingers were clumsy as they scrabbled to find its edges, digging for purchase. His lungs hurt and his palm throbbed in time with his heartbeat.

When he finally fought it free of the mud's grasp the release of tension opened his mouth and he drew in a lungful of water. After that, it was pure, unreasoning panic. He hugged the box against his chest and kicked his legs and it seemed like nothing more than chance when he finally made it to the surface.

He was further away from the punt his time, and it was hard to tread water with the box pressed to his chest. The blood from his palm seeped into the wood to leave a growing red stain. Coby cursed and poled towards him. As soon as he was within arm's reach, he dropped the pole and fell to his knees, reaching out to grasp the wooden box.

Morgan held on to it stubbornly, kicking with his legs until he was outside the other man's reach.

Coby huffed in irritation. "I can't use it without yo—," he said. "I'm not going to let you drown."

Morgan hesitated a moment longer, then released his hold on the box and let Coby lift it into the boat. The other man eyed it for a moment, and Morgan knew he was itching to open it, but instead he turned back and helped drag Morgan over the side of the punt for the second time.

He knelt on his discarded jeans and T-shirt, the sun warm on his bare back. "Well?" he said to Coby. "That's it, right?"

Coby nodded, and Morgan could see that his hand was shaking as he reached around his neck and drew out a thick silver chain from beneath his shirt. There was a key hanging from it and Coby leaned forward to fit it into the box's lock.

The mirror was smaller than Morgan had expected, but very beautiful. The frame was too pale to be gold, but it didn't look like silver either. Morgan guessed it might be platinum, a metal more precious than almost anything else on earth. It was engraved with designs that reminded him unpleasantly of the runic alphabet in his father's diary and there were rubies embedded in its back.

He wondered how much it was worth, then realised that no monetary sum could equal its value, if it really contained what Coby claimed. He looked at the other man, and saw that his face was pale, sweat coating it. His eyes looked feverish as they bored into Morgan's.

"What do I do?" Morgan asked. "How do I use it?"

"Just look into it." Coby's voice was husky and he coughed to clear it. "It's like any other mirror, but the gateway should be broader. Dee's waiting in there. He wants to be contacted. Just look through the glass, Morgan, and tell me what you see."

The handle was bone and felt slick and warm in Morgan's hand. It was soothing against the still bleeding cut on his palm. The mirror wasn't glass, he realised, but crystal. It shimmered, facets scattering the daylight, and he wondered how he was expected to see anything in its broken surface. And then he wasn't looking at the crystal but through it and Dee was right there.

Morgan almost smiled at the image, exactly like something out of one of those BBC costume dramas he'd seen advertised but never watched. Dee's neck was ringed with a wide ruffle of lace that made the head above it look like it was detachable from the body below. His beard was long, grey and pointed and his gaunt face was lined with pain. Coby had said that Dee looked into the mirror in the moment of death. Morgan didn't find it hard to believe this was a dying man.

"A blackamoor," Dee said. "A *savage* has possession of my mirror."

His voice was hard to understand, the words rounded in an accent Morgan didn't recognise. It took their actual meaning a moment to register and then Morgan scowled at the man in the mirror.

"What?" Coby said. "What did he say?" His voice was shaking and his cheeks were tense with strain.

"Nothing yet," Morgan told him.

Coby's breath left him in a rush. "Ask him where it is."

Morgan turned back to the crystal mirror.

Dee was still there, mouth pinched tight. "Well, savage?" he said. "Speak."

Morgan kept his voice calm as he said, "Where's the shofar? Where did you put it?"

The ancient alchemist's head tilted, as if he found Morgan as hard to understand as Morgan found him. "You seek the shofar?" he said. "So it remains hidden, in whatever future is your dwelling place. But perhaps you will find what I could not. The shofar is lost in the forests of the New World."

"Lost in the forests of the New World," Morgan repeated for Coby's benefit and also because he wasn't sure he understood.

Dee took in a harsh breath and flinched as if it hurt him. It occurred to Morgan that a man's spirit trapped in the moment of death would be dying forever.

"They stole it from me," Dee said. "The hordes of the ignorant took my treasures. They took them to our Queen's colony across the great ocean. Yet when I sent my agents in pursuit, they too disappeared."

Coby shook Morgan when he didn't speak, but he was too intent on the mirror to respond.

"So you don't know?" Morgan said. "You've lost it."

"Only one message remained," Dee said. "Croatoan."

"Croatoan?" Morgan repeated.

Coby's hand clawed suddenly into his arm. The other man's wide brown eyes were bright and Morgan knew that whatever Dee's message was, Coby at least had understood it.

He turned back to the mirror to ask more. He didn't want to have to rely on Coby to explain. But when he looked at Dee, the old man's eyes were focused over his shoulder. His pale skin paled still further until he looked exactly like the corpse he was.

"He is here," Dee hissed. "You have brought my death to me!"

And then Coby too was shouting in inarticulate alarm and Morgan lowered the mirror and spun.

Lahav stood on the river bank, dripping water. The Israeli's face was less handsome with the bloody bruise which had almost closed his left eye. His other glared with fury. The same red light shone within it that glowed from the knife in his hand.

Lahav moved his arm back then forward, and the knife spun end over end through the air towards Coby. A wave of heat preceded it and Morgan felt a moment's pity for the other man. And then Coby reached for Morgan, swinging his body into the path of the knife.

He struggled in Coby's arms, but it was already too late. The knife shot towards him and he knew it would scorch as it skewered him. In a futile, instinctive gesture he raised the mirror. The knife burned into it and through it, and the force of the blow drove him back into the muddy river waters for the last time.

CHAPTER TEN

Alex counted her heartbeats all the way to Alamo Square. PD seemed content with the silence and she was happy not to speak. She knew the tension in her voice would betray her. The bank would have her money in two hours. She needed to be ready to leave by then.

PD's contact was waiting in the small park at the centre of the square. They were to meet on the bench at the highest point of the hill which offered a view over downtown San Francisco that seemed to transform the city into a toy-town version of itself, the distant Bay just a painted backdrop.

PD walked to her left and Raven to her right as they climbed to the top of the park, but she ignored them both. When she swept her eyes over the view below she saw the same double image, a modern city basking in sunlight and an older one consumed by flame and earthquake. She was learning to ignore that too.

PD's contact turned out to be a woman not much older than Alex. She had short brown hair, narrow brown eyes and was dressed like she'd wandered over from one of the bars in the Castro. PD obviously knew her already. He smiled and hugged her, making circles in the small of her back with his palm. Alex felt a hot flare of jealousy and ruthlessly suppressed it.

"Curtis, this is Keve," PD said.

The other woman's handshake was firm to the point of pain. Alex broke it as soon as she could, looking at the view rather than her companions. She was afraid of what they might see in her eyes.

"Not smooth sailing, then," Curtis said, eyeing their bruises.

PD shrugged. "Nothing we couldn't handle. What have you got for us?"

Curtis handed him a thin manila folder. He tucked it beneath his jacket without looking at it.

"It's not much," Curtis said. "Jacob Marriott's either damn good at flying below the radar or he hasn't been involved in anything that might interest us until recently. He's stinking rich, but there's no mystery where it came from. It's family money. He's East Coast stock but his father moved out here when he married himself a failed actress and semi-successful model a third his age."

"Interesting," PD said. "Maybe he's repeating family history with Maria. Might explain where all her money comes from."

Curtis shook her head. "Unlikely. Marriott was married to the same woman for fifty-two years and by all accounts he was devoted to her – not even a whisper of a rumour of any infidelity. She died of bone cancer just two months ago. And it looks like it was the wife who actually introduced him to the cult. Her financials indicate several very sizeable payments to an off-shore shell company. We haven't confirmed yet, but we're 99 per cent sure it's a front for the Croatoans."

PD frowned. "So not every Croatoan's getting rich out of this – some are paying top dollar to get in. Maybe Maria isn't in trouble at all. Maybe she's part of the group running this shell game, taking people like Marriott for a ride. It explains what you saw in the restaurant – if she's given herself to the devil's side."

It was very possible, Alex thought. Maria had certainly seemed to be the one with the power, whose presence was like a scar on the spirit world. But she wanted PD interested in Marriott – she needed him to break into the man's house as he'd suggested.

"It's possible," she said. "But I don't think Marriott's an

innocent in all this. There was definitely something odd about him too."

Curtis quirked an eyebrow. "Odd?"

"We can trust her instincts," PD said quickly. "If she says he's odd, we need to investigate."

Curtis looked at her untrustingly and Alex wondered what PD had told her. Not very much, she guessed. She was Hammond's dirty little secret – and her partner's too.

"We need to get Alex inside the house," he said. "Is that possible?"

Curtis shrugged. "Marriott's got some pretty impressive security measures in place, but I think I can override them. It's a risk, but not a huge one."

Though PD's face was impassive, Alex knew he was weighing up pros and cons. She needed to contribute to the pro side, but she knew he'd get suspicious if she seemed too keen on the mission. There was no trust left between them.

"No way," she said. "They know us now – it's much too dangerous. And I've seen all I'm going to see."

As predictable as Pavlov's dog, PD shook his head. "They're representing one hand and playing another. We need to see their hole cards, but they *are* wise to us now and infiltration's out. Marriott's house is our best bet." He turned to Curtis. "You've got a surveillance van set up, right? Can you co-ordinate from outside the perimeter?"

"Sure. I've given you blueprints of the interior and details of the security system. If you keep a com link open once you're inside, I should be able to disable the parts of the system you're passing through while leaving the others intact. Should prevent any meta-alarms being triggered."

PD grimaced. "You *should* be able to disable the system and you *should* be able to halt the alarms?"

Curtis smiled thinly. "In this line of work, there are no guarantees."

* * *

Marriott's home was on the south-west of the square, kitty-corner to the ornate houses known as the Painted Ladies. Its design echoed theirs, light-green wooden slats finished with elaborate carvings round the windows and doors. Just a dollhouse, Alex thought, a pretty façade with nothing real inside. A fake home for make-believe people.

"We"ll have to try the front door," PD said. "Curtis can disable the surveillance, loop the last minute's input so they don't know anything's wrong."

Alex frowned. "But unless she's telekinetic, she can't unlock it, can she?"

"Then we use the basement entrance round the back. We can climb the fence – I can boost you – but if anyone sees us from the street..."

He was right. But they had to get inside. If they didn't, her two million dollars would sit unclaimed and she'd be sent somewhere else on some other godforsaken mission and her chance to escape would be gone for good.

"Honestly," Raven said. "Do I have to do everything myself? Evolution gave you a brain – try using it."

She fought not to react, keeping her gaze fixed on PD.

"What does it matter if he knows I'm here? Is he going to think you're crazy?" Raven asked. His black eyes looked guileless in his unlined face, but there was a spark of mischief buried inside them. "Mr Teepee Tom over there *wants* you to hear voices. I'm giving you some good advice – the least you could do is pass it on."

Alex sighed and turned to face him, ignoring PD's sharp glance. "You realise you haven't actually given me any advice yet, don't you?"

His eyebrows rose into his hairline in an exaggerated expression of disbelief. "I haven't? Oh no, you're right, I haven't. Well, obviously you need to look more closely at the fence. Look through your other eyes, Alex. It's hardly there."

PD's hand closed around her forearm, turning her to face him. "What is it, kid? Who are you talking to?"

She smiled sourly. "My spirit guide. I think he just told me I can walk through walls. Or fences, anyway."

PD looked like he wanted to argue, but this was the one area where she was the expert and he was forced to defer to her. It gave her a perverse sort of satisfaction.

"Fine," he said finally. He reached into his jacket and handed her the floor plan of the house. "If you get inside, go to the front door and let me in. Curtis can guide you. You don't need to speak aloud, just subvocalise and the throat mic will pick it up."

They were both wearing them, as well as pea-sized earpieces. Curtis would hear everything that happened and Alex thought she could use that to her advantage. But only if Raven was right – and she could somehow use the spirit realm to enter Marriott's house.

"Be careful, kid," PD said, not quite meeting her eye. And then he was gone, slipping back across the road to the park.

The double-vision had been tormenting her all day. Her head was pounding and she had to look at her feet as she walked to stop herself dodging obstacles that weren't really there. But as soon as she *wanted* to see the spirit realm, it faded like mist burnt away by the sun. The world was suddenly real and sharp and the fence she needed to somehow walk through was as solid as her own body.

"Shit," she said.

Raven laughed in her ear. "It's like one of those magic eye puzzles, isn't it? If you look too hard, you stop being able to see them."

She turned to face him, but he wasn't there either, faded away along with the rest of the spirit realm.

For a moment she felt a blank, grey despair. But she'd *heard* Raven. The spirit world was still there. It was always there. What had he told her earlier that day? Something about only children believing things disappeared when they could no longer see them.

She looked again, squinted, tried looking out of the corner of her eye. Nothing. The world was still the real world and the spirit realm was gone.

Except the realm of spirit wasn't any less real, she realised. In some ways it was more: a place where people's true selves were on display. How could she hope to find it by denying its reality?

As abruptly as it had disappeared, the spirit world was back. Clouds of black smoke churned in the sky and she heard the distant sound of screams. And Raven was right. The fence was barely there, just a green blur in the air. She closed her eyes and walked towards it, remembering the way it appeared in the spirit realm, not the wood and metal of the waking world.

Her face hit the wood, the impact on her nose bringing tears to her eyes. "Christ," she said, turning to Raven. "I thought you told me it wasn't there?"

"It *isn't* there," he said. "But you're not there either. You're here."

She bit back a tart retort. Raven was infuriating, but nothing he'd told her was a lie. He must mean that she herself wasn't in the spirit realm. So how could she make herself travel there?

"Travel? Travel indeed!" Raven said. "And where exactly is this distant place you're going to be travelling to?"

She sighed. "It's right here." So travelling was the wrong metaphor. And, she realised, metaphor was as powerful as truth in that world.

"I don't need to go there," she said. "I need to see myself there."

He grinned. "Give the woman a prize!"

Now she'd said it, she understood why she'd been reluctant to understand it. Because to see herself in the spirit realm, she'd have the see the *real* her. She'd been born pretty and her parents had been rich enough to help her get prettier: tooth whitening, regular manicures and pedicures and facial scrubs; a nose job when she was sixteen. But that was nothing, just a disguise overlaying the truth of her. To enter the spirit realm, she'd have to see herself stripped bare.

She thought instantly of PD, who'd seen her bare – and not just physically. She'd been an easy mark for him. She'd so wanted to believe he really cared for her, that anyone did. Just like he'd said, poor little rich girl, mom and dad giving her everything except love. He and Hammond had stolen so much from her – her freedom, every future she'd every imagined for herself. And what he hadn't taken by theft, she'd just *given* him. No wonder he treated her with contempt. She was pitiful.

In the spirit world, all those truths would be evident. She had to see herself, but she was afraid that what she'd see would be too painful to face.

"I never promised it would be easy," Raven said. "If it was easy, everyone would do it."

"I need a mirror," she said. "Something to see myself."

"But you already have. The way's open."

He was right. She looked around on a different world. Only the burning city remained, the part of San Francisco's past that the spirit world remembered and preserved. She felt a sudden stinging on her shoulder and slapped her hand against it, only to feel a fluttering beneath her palm. When she raised it, there was a butterfly underneath – a living creature where before there'd only been a tattoo. She watched it drift away on the breeze, mesmerised.

"Hurry," Raven said. "You won't be able to stay here long – not your first time."

She felt only a faint stirring of air across her eyeballs as they passed through where the fence both was and wasn't. For a moment the world was painted the same green as the wood, and then she was through. There was a jolt when her foot hit the ground and she felt a less physical jarring as she fell back into the mundane world.

She glanced at her shoulder, expecting the tattoo to be a tattoo again, but it was still gone. Her skin was raw where the butterfly had torn away from it.

"What happens there is real," Raven said. "It can hurt you. Truth does."

She nodded as she studied the yard she'd found herself in. It was decorated with crumbling, fake-antique statues and artfully overgrown potted plants. Above them she saw a camera swivelling towards her and hurriedly tapped the mic on her throat. "Curtis – I'm through the back. Surveillance camera will be on me in seconds unless you do something."

There was a tense space of silence during which she could feel her pulse throbbing in her ears. Finally Curtis said, "You're covered, Keve. Guards are one floor down and the door's unlocked. Go on in."

She felt horribly visible as she walked the length of the patio to the basement entrance. The camera's red eye winked at her but no alarm sounded and when she put a tentative hand on the door handle it opened easily.

The room beyond looked like a child's playroom, long-abandoned. The ping-pong table was thick with dust and the rubber surface of the paddles was decaying, coming away from the wood in diseased-looking lumps. A spider scurried away from her as she moved across the floor and she hopped back.

Raven laughed softly beside her. "No harm in him, he's an old friend of mine. Or am I another version of him?"

"Oh god, will you shut up?" Alex muttered.

"Say again?" Curtis said.

Alex flushed. "Nothing. Just – thinking aloud. Sorry. I'm in the basement, it's pretty much empty. There's a door at the far end that I'm guessing leads up."

"Copy that. I'll clear ahead of you. Stop for instructions when you reach the top of the stairs. There's a security guard up there. I can blind the cameras, but if he sees you it's game over."

There was a narrow corridor beyond the basement room then, as Curtis had said, a staircase leading up. The steps were stone, grey and a little damp. Alex felt the cold of them seep through the thin soles of her sandals as she climbed.

Another door barred the exit at the top. "I'm there," she told Curtis. "What now?"

"Through, left, left again," Curtis said. "And hurry it up, Keve. You've got less than a minute till the guard comes past.

Alex cursed and wrenched the door open. It squealed alarmingly and she cringed as she eased it shut behind her, reducing the sound to a soft groan. She was moving as it faded, left and left again as instructed. The house up here was far grander, with wooden floorboards below and chandeliers above. Works of art flashed by on the walls as she hurried past them. She thought she recognised some – a minor impressionist, what might have been a Hopper – but she didn't linger to check.

The second left turn took her into a small study. There was a polished wooden desk with a blotter, a modern filing cabinet looking crass and out of keeping next to the upholstered leather armchair and bookcases filled with what she was sure were first editions.

There was also a key in the door, solid and brass. Her hand shook as she pocketed it.

"Keve?" Curtis barked in her ear. "Report!"

"I'm in the study," Alex said. "I don't think I've been seen."

"You're safe there. Give the guard thirty seconds to move back to the kitchen, and then your path's clear to the front door. You'll need to continue down the corridor, first right then second left. I've picked the electronic lock already. You just need to handle the chain and the bolts and PD's in. I'll tell him when he can approach."

Alex's whole body shook as she followed the path Curtis had laid out. She wanted to throw up and she was sure her fear was visible on her face, but she hoped PD would put it down to the mission itself. She ended up in a large entrance hall with a marble staircase curving from the centre of the floor to the upper storeys. Slick with sweat, her fingers fumbled with the bolts as she opened the door.

"Nicely done," PD whispered as he entered.

She nodded, swallowing guilt, and closed the door behind him.

"You need to get upstairs, stat," Curtis said.

PD strode across the black and white chequered floor of the lobby, pressing Alex ahead of him. His hand rested in the small of her back, an oddly courtly gesture. Their footsteps rang on the marble and Alex winced as Curtis said, "Guard's less than 30 seconds away. Hurry it up, guys,"

The security guard appeared as Alex put her foot on the first step. Only the fact that he had his head down saved her. She sucked back her gasp of surprise, but the man must have heard something because his head jerked up and any second now he was going to see her. His face swung towards her, nose flaring like a bloodhound on scent.

She gasped again as PD grabbed her collar, the sound stifled behind the hand he clamped over her mouth. Her shirt bunched painfully around her neck as he dragged her up the stairs. As soon as they were round the first curve, he pressed her body to the stairs beneath his.

The sharp corners of the marble dug into her back and hip hard enough to bruise. She felt PD's heart thundering against hers, their breaths mingling in the air between them as they waited. There was no sound below, and the guard was as invisible to them as they were to him. But if he followed his instincts. If he climbed the stairs...

If he did, at least the discomfort of this unsought embrace would end. Something in her ached to pull PD closer, to surrender to the illusion of caring he offered. His face was only inches from hers and his expression was deceptively vulnerable.

Then she heard the sound of footsteps – moving *away* from them.

When a door slammed at the far side of the entrance hall, PD took his hand from her mouth.

"FYI, Keve," Curtis said. "I can hear you cursing under your breath when you're wearing a throat mic. Are you guys OK?"

PD helped Alex to her feet, releasing her as soon as she was able to stand unassisted. "Still undetected," he said.

"You'd better keep going up," Curtis said. "The cook's heading your way too. Maybe she and the guard are getting together for a nooner."

The landing was less grand than the hall, wooden floorboards replacing the marble once again. The smell of polish flavoured the air with a hint of lemon.

"Well?" PD whispered to her. "What do you see? Which way should we go?"

Alex had forgotten she had a genuine job to do. And she'd almost forgotten the spirit world – or ceased to notice it. Raven had gone, but she sensed him hovering over her shoulder, a whisper of wings and human laughter. The house itself seemed solid, a single not a double image. She took a second to think what that might mean.

"This has always been a home," she told PD as she led him down the left-hand branch of the corridor, following nothing more concrete than a whim.

He gave her a *so fucking what?* look and she shrugged. "You wanted to know what I see. I can tell you this place didn't burn down in the earthquake. And I think it might always have belonged to one family. It feels... stable."

The corridor ended at an open door. Alex poked her head around and saw that it was a bathroom. The smell of lavender displaced the scent of wax as she inspected the claw-foot tub.

"Anything?" PD asked.

Alex turned away. "Well, they don't shop at Ikea. Let's try the bedrooms."

The first two were guest rooms, neatly made-up but characterless. Alex shook her head at PD when he raised an enquiring eyebrow in each. Then she opened the door to the third and stopped, breath caught in her lungs.

PD put a hand on her shoulder. "Bad?" he asked.

She didn't want to think there was sympathy in his voice. She didn't want to recognise that he might be trying to apologise. She shrugged off his hand and went in, forcing her legs to take her towards the bed. It was impossible to look at the figure on it for long. It flickered and shifted, leaving no clear picture, only a blur of pink flesh and an impression of terrible, unremitting suffering. She closed her eyes and looked away, but it didn't really matter. She knew this was an image she would never forget.

"Tell me what you see," PD said.

"It's..." She closed her mouth, swallowing bile convulsively before she was able to carry on. "I think it's someone dying. Whatever killed them was slow and very, very painful."

PD nodded. She focused intently on the well-known planes of his face, while in the periphery of her vision the figure on the bed flickered and changed and suffered and screamed.

"It could be Marriott's wife," PD said. "This looks like the master bedroom, and Curtis said bone cancer. That's not a good way to go."

Alex looked quickly at the apparition then away again. "I think you're right. Whoever that was, they *mattered* to this house. That must be why it's held on to them, to what happened to them."

PD strode to the mantelpiece and ran his hands over a series of framed photos, each showing the same couple at different stages of their life. "Look at this. It must be the pair of them."

Alex stared at them. "They look happy. Normal, too. But there must have been something missing for them, or why would they join a cult?"

PD's sharp brown eyes met hers. "Same reason anyone does. They wanted the things money can't buy."

"Or in their case, that a great deal of money *can* buy," she said, intrigued despite herself. "Wonder what it was and why they couldn't get it elsewhere. And look – over there in the corner. There's a bunch of medical equipment, heart monitor, the whole nine yards. People like the Marriotts could afford 24-hour care. They must have brought her back here once they knew it was terminal so she could die in her own home. Except I don't think she died here. If she had there'd be an end to the suffering. But all this room remembers is the pain."

"There could have been complications or she might have needed surgery. It doesn't have to mean anything – not every twitch is a tell."

"I know. The spirit world doesn't always show you what's important, just what's true." She looked at the machines more closely and realised that she recognised the dress tossed casually over one of them. "Wait a minute – that's an Oscar de la Renta."

"If you say so."

"It's a one of a kind. Maria was wearing it last night."

He frowned. "So she is screwing him. If she's part of a scam, it's a way to get his trust."

"Yeah," she said. "Sleeping with him in the room where the wife he loved spent her last, painful days. Whatever Maria's selling must be pretty damn special." Their eyes met and held and Alex felt a moment of... *something*. An image of the partnership they might have had – could still have, if she made a different choice.

"You reading me, guys?" Curtis's voice said sharply in her ear.

"Yeah," PD said. "What's up?"

"The guard and the cook have gone out to the yard. Downstairs is clear for the moment – you probably won't get a better opportunity."

Alex grimaced at the unmeant truth. This was it, her chance to break free. She thought about the way PD had touched and spoken to her and almost didn't do it. But then she thought about this morning, the way he's pulled away from her as if she was an embarrassment to him. And she thought about the figure on the bed, the form she could still see writhing and which she knew was destined to haunt her dreams. If she didn't escape, there'd be more sights like that, day after day, until she became so hardened to them she stopped caring. Or until they broke her mind entirely.

That's what PD was condemning her to.

"Let's go," she said to him. "The study's near the lobby. I didn't get a chance to search it before, but I... sensed something."

He nodded and led the way back to the first floor. She watched his back as he walked, trying to think about nothing, concentrating on her breathing.

"Which way?" he asked.

"Next door on the left," she said.

He went in ahead of her as she loitered in the doorway, gathering her nerve.

"We need to be careful, kid," he said. "When you look at stuff make sure you don't move it. They can't know we've been here."

She nodded, not trusting her voice. He turned his back on her to open the filing cabinet and she knew she needed to do it right then.

The door creaked as it swung shut and he must have spun to face her. She thought she caught a brief glimpse of his startled face. And then the door was shut and the key felt awkward in her hand as she turned it in the lock. The doorknob rattled and she heard PD calling out to her.

"Christ!" she said into her mic. "What the hell's going on, Curtis? They've trapped PD, they're after me. Jesus – I thought you were going to keep us safe!" She made her breathing ragged as she walked calmly down the corridor towards the basement.

"What?" Curtis said. "I see nothing – surveillance footage is all clear."

"The surveillance footage is bullshit!" Alex said. "Oh Christ, they're coming. They're–" She tore the mic from her throat and stamped on it, then did the same with her earpiece. When she was confident she couldn't be heard, she pulled out her phone and redialled the last number. Her hand was shaking so hard she had to try twice before it connected.

"Bayview Bistro," said a female voice. "How may I help you?"

"I'm trying to get hold of Jeremiah," Alex said. "There's a family emergency. Can he come to the phone?"

"Of course," the woman said. "May I tell him who's calling."

"Tell him it's Maria Vargas."

She heard the clunk of the phone being put on a wooden surface and then the ambient sounds of a busy restaurant for several long, tense seconds. She could hear PD too, banging on the door at the end of the corridor, and she debated just leaving him there. The cook or the guard might find him.

But PD was a trained agent. Two civilians would be unlikely to hold him for long, and she needed him out of action for at least a day. Long enough for her to collect the money and cross the border into Mexico.

Then she heard the clatter of the phone being picked back up, and a male voice saying. "Maria?"

Alex hesitated only a moment. "Actually, it's not. It's the woman you tried to kidnap last night, but you're going to want to hear this anyway. There's an intruder in Jacob Marriott's house on Alamo Square. A CIA agent. He's locked in the study right now, but if you don't send someone to deal with him, he's going to be escaping with some fabulous intel to share with his bosses. Just thought you might like to know."

Jeremiah inhaled a shocked breath. "Wait a minute! Why the hell should I believe–"

"Your choice," she said. "But what have you got to lose by checking?"

She ended the call. Either he'd act on her words or he wouldn't. There was nothing more she could say to convince him.

She didn't have Curtis to guide her through this time. Without the other woman to switch off the surveillance she was bound to be seen. She needed the alarm raised, but she wanted to be clear first. The cook and the guard were no match for PD. They might be a match for her.

The basement steps seemed very far away. Her pace picked up to a half jog and her shoulders twitched with the urge to look behind her, but she didn't give in. There was only one way out and she had to take it. If someone was following her, that just added to the urgency.

The shout came as she wrenched open the basement door, deep and male. She flung herself down the stairs, almost tripping as she took them two at a time. The guard's heavier tread pounded behind her, gaining. Then it slowed, and she felt a moment of relief – until the sharp crack of a gunshot deafened her.

For a moment she was only shocked. Then she felt a trickle of blood down her left cheek and a moment later a stinging pain.

Someone's shooting at me, she thought, the idea almost inconceivable. *I've been shot.*

The sting deepened to a burning throb as she fled down the stairs. She stumbled at the bottom, falling to her knees on the concrete floor. The impact jarred her knees, but it saved her life. The second bullet passed above her. She saw the wood of the door ahead splinter as it hit.

The thought of standing and running terrified her. She knew there would be more bullets. How could the guard miss again?

But he'd kill her for certain if she stayed where she was. Her knees screamed as she pushed herself to her feet and there was another shot and another liquid gush and flare of pain in her side. And then she was running and her heartbeat was pounding so loudly in her ears it was all she could hear.

A bullet ploughed into the door as she reached for it. Splinters arced out, scoring scratches in her hand and arm. She gritted her teeth and turned the knob. The door opened and she threw herself out as a fist-shaped hole punched through it inches from her hand.

She sprinted towards the back fence, legs catching on and upending a planter. The rich smell of peat enveloped her as she heard footsteps behind her. The fence was only feet away. It was solid wood, thinner in the spirit world but still there.

She shut her eyes, lowered her head and ran on. In the second before she reached the fence she felt a light touch between her shoulder blades, and though she couldn't see him, she knew that it was Raven guiding her. And then she felt an impact that was more psychic than physical. The shock of it made her open her eyes and she saw that she was through. A different, smaller garden lay ahead of her and an unlocked side entrance that would take her to the street.

She spun, gasping for breath, to look at the fence behind her. She wasn't sure what she expected. Maybe the outline of her body, like in a cartoon. But the fence was whole. There was no sign that she'd passed right through it. And from the other side, she could hear the confused, fearful yells of the man who'd been shooting at her.

He didn't know where she'd gone. Neither did Curtis – or Hammond. She was free.

CHAPTER ELEVEN

Morgan knew he was drowning. He felt sleepy, almost happy, as he drifted down to rest on the muddy river bottom. His lungs were filled with water and there must be a knife deep in his chest, though he couldn't feel the pain of it.

His vision was distorting. The water seemed to swirl with hidden shapes and forms. He thought he saw a little girl's face, his sister's. She smiled at him and he tried to smile back. He saw her hand move, the small, blunt fingers reaching for him, and he thought he felt the brush of them against his arm. She was frowning, as if there was something she wanted him to understand. But his mind was drifting with the current and he couldn't fathom what she wanted.

Then the sight of her face was fading, lost behind red flames. And suddenly there *was* pain, blooming in every cell of his body until he opened his mouth wide in a scream. He knew that it must be water rushing to fill it – in some corner of his mind he still understood that he was drowning – but the water felt like burning pitch pouring down his throat and into his lungs.

When he felt another, firmer grasp on his forearm, he thought for a second that it was his sister, come to rescue him from this agony. But the grip was harsh and unforgiving and as it tugged him to the surface he caught a glimpse of a hard, dark face. Then everything faded to black.

* * *

He came to coughing as something pressed too hard against his chest and a gush of river water and saliva slicked down his chin and onto his neck. He rolled to his side, retching, bringing up nothing but bile.

After a moment, he became aware of a warm hand on his back and another supporting his head. He squirmed away from them both and pushed himself to a sitting position, though his body felt boneless and badly put together.

His rescuer stared back at him through one fierce red-brown eye and another swollen almost shut. The Israeli looked like an ordinary man, but if Coby hadn't lied he could be a lot more.

"Lahav." Morgan scrabbled at his waist for a weapon he didn't have. He wasn't even clothed, still wearing only his boxers.

"I saved your life," Lahav said. "I'm not going to kill you now."

Morgan blinked his eyes clear of the water dripping from his hair and looked around. They were still outdoors. He could smell the crushed grass beneath where he lay, and the sky above was almost obscured by a canopy of leaves. They were hidden from sight, but Lahav couldn't have moved him far. He'd been near death when he was pulled from the river. The Mossad agent had only had a few minutes in which he could revive him.

Except Morgan shouldn't have been alive at all. He groped at his chest, feeling for the knife wound that should have pierced it, mentally groping for the pain that should have accompanied it, but there was no wound and no pain.

"Why?" Morgan asked. "Why kill me then save me?"

Lahav grimaced. "I wasn't aiming for you. I wanted to kill the other, the American. He put you in the path of my dagger."

It was true. And Lahav had run away rather than fight him before – but it didn't matter. Lahav might not want to hurt Morgan but Morgan sure as hell wanted to hurt him.

"Tell me why I shouldn't turn you in to the police," Morgan said.

"Because you're weak right at this moment, and I will kill you before you run five feet."

"You said you didn't want to kill me."

Lahav shrugged. "But I will if I have to."

"The police will be here soon anyway," Morgan said.

"Yes, and your Hermetic Division with them. You haven't been inconspicuous, Morgan. So we have not so much time to decide what to do."

Morgan tried to push himself upright, only to collapse back to the ground as another coughing fit shook him. His lungs felt like they were full of razor blades and he wondered what diseases he'd caught from the unclean water.

It didn't matter. He'd failed. Coby had turned on him, as he'd guessed he might. Morgan had been prepared to risk that to get the information he wanted, but now he had it, it meant nothing to him. And the only people who might have helped him understand it were the ones he'd betrayed to gain it.

Still, they didn't know that. He could claim to have done what he did in order to find the mirror for the Division before Lahav laid his hands on it. And if Lahav came as part of the package – captured or dead – it would be even better.

The other man wasn't expecting the attack. His hard face looked briefly shocked, and then Morgan was over him, legs pinning his to the ground, one arm holding Lahav's above his head and the other over his throat, pressing the life out of it.

"If you kill me," Lahav rasped, "you'll never know."

Morgan knew he should just press harder until the other man couldn't speak at all. But he found himself releasing the pressure. "Know what?" he said.

Lahav's smile looked ghastly in his battered face. "How to find what it is that you're missing. How to be whole."

Morgan's breath left his body in a whoosh, as if he was the one being strangled. He remembered the sensation of drowning, which had felt like burning. "What do you mean?" he asked, hating how weak his voice sounded.

Lahav knew he'd won. Morgan could see it in his face. "There is no soul in you, my friend. It's why the dead are drawn to you. There is a void inside, and nature abhors a vacuum. People tell you and tell you but you don't want to believe. Believe now. And believe this. The One I work for can give you what you want."

Morgan released him. He half expected Lahav to attack immediately, but the other man just rolled to his feet, groaning. "Why, though?" Morgan said. "You say you can give me what I want, but why would you?"

Lahav crouched and Morgan saw that he was rifling through a small military rucksack. He must have dropped it when Morgan attacked him. "You spoke to Dee," he said. "It's important for me to know what he told to you – what you told to the American." He stopped talking as he pulled the carved crystal mirror from his bag. It glinted in the sunlight that sneaked between the leaves of the trees.

"If you've got that, why do you need me?" Morgan said.

Lahav threw the mirror at his feet. It took Morgan a moment to recognise the leather-bound rod protruding from the front of the mirror. It was the pommel of Lahav's knife. He guessed the blade must have sheered off when it struck the glass – that this was what had saved him. Then he looked closer and realised he was wrong.

The blade had passed *through* the mirror. The crystal was crazed around it, reflecting back only a fractured vision of the world. Morgan couldn't help himself – he flipped the mirror over, like a child trying to figure out how a magic trick worked, but there was nothing there. The blade had gone *inside* the mirror.

"My blade has the power to kill anything, flesh or spirit," Lahav said. "Thanks to you, Dee is dead now, dead for real and for ever. What he knew, now only you and the American know. The American, he will use it to become what you chose not to: immortal and invulnerable. But we can stop him – with your help. We can give you a soul, but you must earn it. It's up to you, Morgan."

The sound of sirens had been building under his words. "No more time to think," he said. "If you're joining me, we must go."

Morgan found he couldn't move, frozen by indecision. If Lahav was what Coby hinted and the Israeli himself implied, the offer might be real. He really could give Morgan what he so desperately wanted. Or Lahav might be nothing more than a man and the offer nothing more than a ruse to tempt Morgan into betrayal.

He heard the rustle of undergrowth and when a voice called out and another answered, his body seemed to make his decision for him. He scrambled to his feet.

Lahav nodded once. He grasped the hilt of his knife, pulling it out of the world behind the mirror. "Follow me, then."

It only took Morgan a moment to realise Lahav was leading them *towards* the sirens. He opened his mouth to protest, then closed it again. The Mossad agent had managed to elude both the police and the Hermetic Division for several days. He probably knew what he was doing.

As the sound of sirens grew louder along with the rumble of traffic, Lahav dropped to his stomach. Morgan did the same, though there were brambles beneath the grass which snagged his boxers and scratched at the exposed skin of his belly. The smell of earth rose up, rich and comforting.

When they reached the road, he appreciated the other man's caution. Police cars were parked only twenty feet away, sirens off now but lights still flashing as the cops milled around them. He wondered what they thought they were investigating. Had they been called after Morgan's attack on Lahav, or Lahav's attack on him? Or did they know the real truth now, that they were on the trail of a double murderer? If Lahav was right and the Hermetic Division had been called, they probably knew everything.

Morgan put his mouth was against Lahav's ear and mouthed, "Back?"

The Israeli shook his head, never taking his eyes from the road. "They will have people on all the exits from the river. There's no clear path."

After a few seconds, the random jumble of cops shook itself out into some kind of organisation. They peeled off in pairs, some heading down the road, others across the grass towards the river. It seemed for a moment they might all leave, but three remained idling by the cars as one of them sparked up a cigarette. At the bend of the road, Morgan could see another congregation of uniformed figures.

"Shit!" he said.

Lahav clamped a hand on his arm to silence him, then nodded in the opposite direction. There was a pedestrian approaching, a young man around his own age. The newcomer was staring at the cops with the casual curiosity of someone who had absolutely nothing to hide.

The cops themselves hadn't noticed him yet. They were huddled together laughing, maybe sharing a joke at the expense of the colleagues who'd walked away. They were distracted, and Morgan didn't think they'd have a better chance to make their move. He raised himself to a half-crouch, ready to spring across the road, but Lahav moved first. The Israeli sprang out to the pavement with startling suddenness. Morgan stood to follow, then stumbled back as he realised Lahav's intention. He had one arm round the waist of the passing tourist, the other hand clamped across his mouth. Another second and he was back in the bushes beside Morgan, the tourist trapped beneath his body.

Morgan lowered himself back to his knees. He kept his eyes on the cops, half-seen through the screening bushes, but they hadn't moved. They hadn't seen anything.

When he looked back at Lahav, the other man had his knife to the tourist's throat. It was glowing the orange of a summer sunset.

Morgan grabbed his wrist and the tourist's eyes flicked to him, then back to Lahav. They were wide and terrified. Morgan tried to smile at him, the expression falling off his face as he looked back at Lahav. "No," he said. "No collateral damage."

"I only kill those who have transgressed," Lahav said. His expression was so bland Morgan found it impossible to tell if he was lying. He loosened his fingers all the same, then almost cried out as Lahav's arm lashed out the instant it was free. But it was the pommel of the knife which struck the tourist, and the man's eyes rolled up into his head as he slumped into unconsciousness.

"Get dressed," Lahav said. "He's your size, I think."

Morgan wanted to argue, but the Mossad agent was right. He was far too conspicuous wearing only his boxers and the day was drawing to a close, chilling his damp skin unpleasantly. He sighed, taking the time to check that the tourist was still breathing, his skull intact. Then he began unbuttoning the man's jeans, tugging them down his legs before pulling off his hoodie and brown T-shirt.

The fit wasn't perfect on Morgan. The jeans were too loose at the waist and tight around his muscular thighs, and the T-shirt pulled around his shoulders. But no one who wasn't looking for it would notice. He could walk down the street without attracting curious glances.

First they had to get to the street, though. And the cops were still there, gazes once again scanning the road right and left.

"Not here," Lahav said. "Pull back, then left – we need to be near the colleges."

"I thought you said they were watching everywhere?"

"They are." Lahav moved before Morgan could ask anything else, crawling on hands and knees through the undergrowth. Morgan sighed and followed, annoyed that he made far more noise at it than the Israeli.

They broke from the trees into an open, over-grown meadow. The deep green of the grass was dusted with the white of cowslips, their long stems bobbing a little in the breeze. It was very beautiful, but the Mossad agent hardly seemed to notice, only grunting in irritation as he dropped to his stomach to slither through the more open terrain. It was slow going, but ten minutes took them to another road as Lahav had predicted. And there were policemen at each end of it, he'd been right about that too.

But the pavements were more crowded, the rush of tourists making the cops' job that much harder. Morgan saw one of them, a young man with sandy hair, frowning as he scanned the passers-by. And then he saw what Lahav must have been waiting for and couldn't help smiling. The other man was cold as iron, but he knew his job.

The tour group was at least 30 strong, Italian by the look of their olive skin and dark hair. Lahav would fit right in, though Morgan would need to keep to the centre of the group if he wasn't to stand out. But the police were barely paying them any attention as they followed the red umbrella of their tour leader.

A couple of the tourists gave Morgan puzzled glances as he pushed his way through them, but their protests were drowned in the general hubbub and when he raised his head to watch the tour guide give her speech they quickly did the same.

The group was drifting left, towards the centre of town. Morgan could see a cop on each side of the pavement, eyes scanning the crowd. His attention wanted to stay on the cops, to watch them watching for him. He made himself focus on the tour guide instead, as the woman's musical Italian washed over him. And he concentrated on steadying his breathing as they approached the policemen flanking the road.

Just for an instant, Morgan felt eyes on him and knew he'd been spotted. Then the eyes passed and he realised, with a physical rush of relief, that he'd been seen but not perceived. He felt Lahav stiffen then relax beside him, and guessed the other man had felt the same careless regard.

"We should check Coby's bedsit," Morgan said. "I know where it is."

"A waste of time. The American won't return there."

Morgan smiled. "Exactly. Which means he'll have left it without having a chance to clear it out. If we want to find out what he's up to, that place is our best hope."

Lahav nodded, but he didn't look pleased. Morgan's smile widened as he led the way towards Coby's building. He knew his job too.

Lahav stopped outside Coby's door, rearing back as if struck – and Morgan saw the red cross still smeared on the wood.

'Protection' Coby had called it, and now he knew what it was meant to protect the American from. He felt a shock of both fear and hope.

"If I open the door, can you get past it?" he asked the Israeli.

The other man nodded and Morgan turned the knob. Locked. He kicked out fast and hard against the weakest point and the wood gave with barely a groan of protest. The noise might have alerted the other residents in the house, but Morgan doubted they'd act on it. He'd lived in this kind of place himself and he knew how very little neighbours knew or cared about each other.

Lahav brushed past him to enter first, but Morgan was interested to see that the other man was very careful not to touch the door, as if even the faintest contact could hurt him. He knew there might come a time when he too needed some protection from the Mossad agent.

Coby's room was as cramped and messy as Morgan remembered it. But nothing looked like it had been packed and he thought his guess had been right: the student hadn't wanted to risk returning when he'd fled the river.

"What should we be looking for?" Morgan asked.

Lahav raised an eyebrow. "This was your idea, my friend. What do *you* think we should expect to find?"

It was a good question. Morgan hadn't trusted Coby, but he'd underestimated him. He'd assumed the other man was working on his own, and that his need for Morgan would bind them together, at least temporarily. But what if he had other allies?

"Is he working for the other side?" he asked Lahav. "For Belle and her people?"

Lahav scanned the room. "Let's try to find out."

There was a surprising amount of junk in such a small space. There were stacks of papers, but they all seemed to relate to Coby's PhD, likewise the stacks of books in, on and around the bookshelves. When he finally found something, it was in Coby's sock draw, buried between twelve identical pairs of socks. He heard them clink as he slid the draw open, an almost musical metallic sound. Brass fragments shone through the black material.

They were shell casings of at least three different kinds, some from a small-calibre handgun, others clearly the product of a large semi-automatic. Morgan pulled them out and lay them on top of the chest of drawers, herding them with his hands when they would have rolled off. He counted twenty-seven in total. Coby had hidden them and they must have been important – he could feel that they were – but he didn't understand why.

"Trophies of his kills," Lahav said. "Did you know he was a murderer when you agreed to help him?"

Morgan forced himself to look the other man in the eye as he nodded. "I knew he'd killed, when he was younger. I thought... I guess I just assumed he regretted it."

"As you regret the things you've done," Lahav said. To Morgan's surprise there was no judgement in his eyes. "Coby has no regret, Morgan. If he could feel remorse, then there would be hope for him when the end comes. But he can't feel it. He is a sociopath, without conscience – the only thing he can feel about his crimes is pleasure. That is why he must seek immortality. Because if he won't repent, he must go to hell."

Morgan wiped his hands against his stolen jeans, though he knew there'd been no blood on the shell casings. They weren't what had killed Coby's victims, only a memento of the murders. "Who did he kill?" he asked, a question he knew he should have asked Coby.

"Two teachers and a lot of other children at his school in Iowa," Lahav said. "He murdered them when he was 17."

Morgan returned the casings to the drawer and slammed it shut. "Hang on – I remember that one. The boy in the George Bush mask. But he shot himself after he shot all the others, didn't he?"

"The police, they found a body on the scene wearing the mask and carrying the murder weapons. They had the school locked down and no one had crossed their perimeter, so they said he must be the killer. But the people in the town who knew that boy, and knew Coby Bryson, to them it wasn't so clear. Coby was outside the building, he could not have done it – and yet...

And so he finished his time at high school surrounded by people who suspected what he'd done and hated him for it. I've seen his photo in the yearbook. He's smiling. This is the man you've helped nearer to the secret of immortality."

Morgan felt himself flush, but he stood his ground. "And you want me to help you instead. But you killed Granger and Julie in cold blood too. Do *you* regret it?"

Lahav grimaced. "I took no *pleasure* in it. But it was necessary. They were dangerous. I removed the danger. This is my job."

Morgan found himself getting angry all over again. "Julie wasn't dangerous. I didn't see any evidence she was involved in Granger and Coby's research. And even if she was, what's so wrong with that? So she wanted to find the secret of immortality. So fucking what? Wouldn't we all want that?"

"It's forbidden," Lahav said. "The Almighty has forbidden it."

He seemed to think that was the end of the argument. And maybe it was. What did Morgan know?

"There's nothing else here," Lahav said. "We won't find where he's gone, because he didn't decide where that was until you told him Dee's secret."

Morgan gritted his teeth, but he knew the other man was right. He had one puzzle piece and Lahav had a lot of the others. They needed each other. But after Morgan had handed over his intel, Lahav wouldn't need him anymore. And he trusted the Mossad agent no more than he'd trusted Coby, despite what might be living inside him – or maybe because of it.

"What do you want from me?" Lahav asked, reading Morgan's doubts in his face. "I will swear an oath to work with you, if you want. And if you don't trust my word, think of this. While you're with me, you're not with the Hermetic Division, telling them what you know. It's to my benefit to have you stay with me."

"Or you could just kill me as soon as I've told you."

Lahav fingered the bloody lump on his forehead and smiled wryly. "You're not so easy to kill. And you have... value. You can help me to catch Coby. An alliance, Morgan. I swear by Hashem that I'll work with you, until Coby is stopped."

Morgan hesitated, and in that moment of hesitation, the door opened.

Kate looked alarmed when she saw Lahav and Morgan standing side by side. Afraid for him, Morgan realised. Her expression slid into something harsher when she realised he and Lahav were only talking. He opened his mouth to tell Kate this wasn't what it looked like, then realised how much like a man caught having an affair that would sound.

She shut the door gently behind her. "For god's sake, Morgan. He killed two people."

"Yeah, and I killed a lot more, and you still took me on."

"That was your job," she said.

He raised an eyebrow and she sighed, understanding his point if not quite conceding it.

"Morgan is working with me now," Lahav said.

Kate's head snapped round, almost as if she'd forgotten he was there. Morgan understood that this was just between him and her.

Lahav didn't seem to. "Our countries are allies," he continued. "There's no reason we can't pursue the same aim. I can promise you what I do is no threat to Britain, or the Hermetic Division."

"That's for me to decide," she said. "Why don't you tell me what you're up to, and maybe I'll even agree with you."

Lahav's mouth clamped shut. Kate brushed her greying hair from her eyes as she turned to look at Morgan.

His eyes flicked between her and the Israeli, undecided. They finally settled on the Israeli. "Why can't we tell her?" Morgan asked. "Why can't the Hermetic Division and the – whatever the hell your lot are called – work together on this?"

The Mossad agent shook his head. "You have such faith in human nature, my friend. But it was your people who wanted the Ragnarok artefacts, objects with the power to end the world. They seek out secrets not to keep them, but to use them. And this secret mustn't be known."

"What secret?" Kate asked.

Morgan hesitated, then said, "Immortality."

"Immortality? That's what this is about?" There was something in her eyes, a spark of interest, and Morgan felt his stomach clench because he saw that Lahav was right. The Hermetic Division would want this.

"And why not?" he asked Lahav. "So what if the secret gets out? People stop dying. That's a good thing, isn't it?"

Lahav had manoeuvred so that his back was to the door, blocking any escape. Morgan saw Kate take note of it. The pulse in her neck flickered faster but she gave no other sign of distress. "You wouldn't hurt me," she said. "Morgan would never work with you then."

"No I wouldn't," Morgan said. He was certain about that, at least.

Lahav sighed. "A world without death – not a utopia, but *this* world without death. People still living and loving and making more people, and more, and then more, and none of them dying. A world without enough food for six billion people, with ten billion, twenty, a hundred billion. Starving skeletons walking a ravaged earth, praying for a death they have forever denied themselves. And ruling over this hell is Coby, a killer without conscience or pity. Surely you see why this secret has to be kept?"

Morgan did, but he didn't trust himself to be thinking straight. He *wanted* to believe the Mossad agent, because he wanted the chance to earn the reward the other man was offering. And if this explanation gave him a fig leaf to cover what would otherwise be naked treachery...

He looked at Kate and she looked back. She already knew what he intended. She barely struggled when he pushed her up against the wall, one forearm against her throat. She only began to twist in panic as unconsciousness approached.

"Shh," he told her, "it's OK, it's just for a little while, shhh."

Her eyes glazed and he felt all resistance melt out of her body as he lowered her to the floor. "Get something to tie her up and gag her," he snapped over his shoulder at Lahav.

The other man didn't move. "They'll find her soon. We will have very little time to get away."

"Tough," Morgan said. "It's this or nothing."

There was a moment's more hesitation, then Lahav did as he'd said. When he'd finished, he looked expectantly at Morgan and he understood the message in his eyes. Lahav had spared Kate, against his instincts. Now it was time for Morgan to fulfil his side of the bargain.

"John Dee talked about the shofar."

Lahav nodded and Morgan saw the sudden tension in his eyes. "And did he say where it could be found?"

"He said it was stolen from him and taken over the ocean, to the Queen's colony. He told me it was lost in the forests of the New World. And he said the people who took it disappeared, but they left a message behind."

"Croatoan," Lahav said.

Morgan narrowed his eyes. "You knew already?"

"No. But I understand now why I could never find it."

"And do you know where it is?"

Lahav smiled. "I know where we should look."

CHAPTER TWELVE

Alex walked ten blocks without stopping. She forced herself not to scan the crowd or look behind her for signs of pursuit. Her plan had worked, it must have. PD was trapped in Marriott's house with the Croatoans and the Agency believed she was imprisoned there too.

When she hit Market she finally stopped. She was beside a small row of shabby fast-food joints and cafes, the metal tracks of the MUNI scarring the road ahead of her. The sidewalk was crowded, mostly tourists waiting for the trains or crossing to explore the more picturesque streets of the Castro. Alex hesitated a moment, then joined the cluster at the MUNI stop. It was faster than walking, slower than a taxi. But it was anonymous, no driver who might remember her and report her destination to anyone with a badge who asked.

When the train came it was crowded and Alex was glad to lose herself in the sweating anonymity of the passengers. Raven stood beside her, his insubstantial body half over-lapping with a fat German woman. The sight made Alex feel sick and she shut her eyes.

Her heart was pounding and she felt a bitter taste in the back of her throat which she thought might be adrenaline. This was it; she was committed now. There was no going back, not just to the Agency but to the ordinary life she'd once yearned to return to. Her father was cold and distant, her mother self-obsessed and neglectful. But when she thought of never seeing them again, her chest ached and she felt the prickle of tears building in the corners of her eyes.

Her only option was to take the money and flee over the border. She vaguely recalled that Venezuela had no extradition treaty with the USA. She couldn't begin to image what her life there might be like, but... Live free or die trying, wasn't that what they said?

Her eyes jolted open when the mechanical voice announced Civic Centre. She pushed through a crowd of towering jocks and squeezed out of the door moments before it shut. Outside the station the crowds were thinner, dispersed through the wide, unwelcoming spaces between the buildings. Alex headed west, over grass littered with homeless men drinking beer from cans wrapped in brown paper bags.

The bank was beyond the Opera House, in the grimmer streets that sprawled around the government buildings. She felt her heart speed as she drew closer. Her mouth was so dry it hurt to swallow. Her footsteps echoed on the marble floor when she entered and she felt as if everyone was watching her. There must be cameras here, though she couldn't spot them. She could only hope no one who mattered was watching them.

There was no line this time and she found herself in front of the same teller she'd faced earlier. "Miss Keve," she said.

"Sarah," Alex said, reading from her name tag. "Is it ready?"

Sarah nodded a little jerkily. Alex felt the first stirrings of unease in her gut. But the spirit world showed her nothing dangerous. The woman's face was overlaid with her other self: a Labrador, gentle and loyal. She was no threat to Alex.

"If you could wait out here a second," Sarah said, "I'll need to go through a few formalities and the money's all yours."

Alex watched her walk to the back of the bank. Her blonde hair swayed with each stride, but her hips were stiff. Alex's stomach roiled. Something was wrong. She didn't need the spirit world to tell her that, only her instincts. They were screaming at her to run. But if she ran, it would be with nothing. And without the money to buy a new life over the border, where could she go?

She looked around instead, using both her inner vision and her outer. The security guard was just a lazy, fat old tom cat, whiskers twitching behind his crooked smile. There was a woman and her child, sulky and whining behind her. The woman was a robin, perky and quick, the child nothing at all, barely a whisper of life in the spirit world, too young to have learned who he was.

The other tellers were no more threatening than Sarah, all bent over their own work. But damn it, they were concentrating *too* hard on what they were doing. Not one of them looked up and caught her eye. It was as if they were afraid to.

There was no one else. Outside, the traffic grumbled and the sky was clear and blue and this had to work, it *had* to.

"You're a strange one," Raven said at her shoulder.

He was shaking his head, his mouth pulled down at the corners. She bit her lip to stop herself responding. The last thing she needed was to draw attention to herself by talking to thin air.

"I mean," he said, "you've worked out how to walk through walls, but you can't figure out how to *see* through them? That's like being able to run a four-minute mile but being incapable of walking to the bottom of the road. Preparing blow-fish flawlessly but being unable to boil an egg. A qualified pilot of the space shuttle, but when it comes to push bikes–"

"Jesus – I get it!" Alex snapped. The tellers to either side of her jerked quick looks up and away and she blushed, dropping her eyes to the floor. But Raven was right. This bank looked like it had been built in the last decade. No one lived here, no one loved here – and she had to assume no one had died here. In the other world, the place should barely exist.

She'd grown used to seeing both worlds, overlapping and bleeding into each other. To see through the walls she needed to blot out the real world, and the thought sent a jolt of fear through her. She'd be blinding herself to the mundane, and what if she could never get that vision back? No amount of money would help her then. She might as well return to the Agency.

She looked at her watch. Sarah had been gone two minutes and not a single other customer had entered the bank. The young man who'd been cashing a cheque to her left had already left and it looked at if the woman and her child were finishing up. When they were gone, Alex would be the only customer in the place.

Was that what they were waiting for? She gritted her teeth and prepared to let the mundane world fade away entirely.

Entering the spirit world was a release, a letting go of assumptions. It was almost a rush, and she let herself feel it. A euphoric sort of calm flowed through her as she looked at the marble walls of the bank and allowed herself to recognise that they weren't truly there, not in any way that really mattered. In the eyes of eternity, there was nothing in front of her but air.

She'd expected the walls to fade gradually, but it was like a blink – one moment solid, the next moment gone. And then she could see exactly what waited for her outside the bank, both in the spirit world and in the mundane.

The wolves were crouched ready to spring, scores to the front of the bank and more at every exit. In the spirit world she couldn't see their weapons, but she saw the glint of their teeth and the feral gleam in their eyes. They were hunters and they had cornered their prey.

There was no point pretending any more. She turned to Raven to ask for help and gasped as she saw him. His face was at once beautiful and subtly and terribly wrong. When he smiled it was more frightening than the leer of the wolves who waited for her outside the bank. And she understood that he was many things, but he would never be her friend.

His smile widened. It looked as if it could swallow her whole. "I never claimed to be other than I am," he said. "You can't blame me if you preferred to believe a comforting lie than see the dangerous truth."

"What *are* you?" she said.

He looked at the agents waiting for her beyond the transparent walls of the bank. "Do you really think this is the time to be asking?"

"No," she said. "I should have asked you the first time you gave me advice and before I was stupid enough to take it. But I'm asking now."

Outside, she could see that the CIA's wolves were moving closer. Any second now they'd move in. Raven held out his hand towards her, fingers loose as he wriggled them in a 'come here' gesture.

She stared at them and didn't move. "What are you?" she asked him again.

"Oh," he said. "I'm this and that. I'm neither one thing nor the other. I'm the joker in the deck, the one card that doesn't belong to any suit. I'm your only hope of getting out of here, Alex. Take my hand."

She took it, letting his warm fingers curl around hers.

"Now what?" she said.

He shrugged. "Now we walk out of here. To see the spirit world so clearly, you have to be in it. The wolves can see you but the men can't, and the men haven't learnt to listen to the wolves inside."

"But I'd already done that. I didn't need you." She tried to wrench her hand out of his.

"Too late now," he said and pulled her through the transparent walls of the bank.

He dropped her hand when they'd gone a block. She walked a little faster, letting him slip behind her until she couldn't see him even in her peripheral vision. But the prickle between her shoulder blades told her he was still there, and watching her.

The city burned and shook apart around her. Fully in the spirit world now, she could see only fragments of the modern city superimposed on the old. A splash of blood stained a concrete wall as a man slashed another man's throat and the writhing flesh in the house to her left shone through the flames. She wondered how long the place had been a brothel, and if it was the pleasure or the degradation that the spirit world remembered so clearly.

While she stayed in the spirit world, she was invisible to the agents pursuing her, but how long could she stay here? Could she eat here? She thought suddenly of the old Greek myth. Persephone had eaten seven pomegranate seeds while in the underworld and been condemned to spend the winter of every year in darkness.

Maybe she could stay in the spirit realm until she'd crossed the border, at least. That would be less than a day's travel by road, more if she had to walk, and she thought maybe she would. And then she'd need money. It all came back to that. If she wanted to live in the real world she'd need some real cash.

She waited until she was on Nob Hill, the city undulating towards the sea all around her, before she took out her iPhone. She hadn't known if it would travel into the spirit world with her, but it seemed solid enough in her hand as she switched the power back on. She wasn't sure what she was going to tell her father, but she would talk him into helping her. He was her *dad*. That was his job.

The welcome screen flashed on – and a second later, the phone rang. For a disoriented second she thought it was him, somehow anticipating her need. But the number was unfamiliar.

She hesitated, finger poised over 'end call'.

"You should probably hear what he has to say," Raven said, and though she'd determined not to take his advice again, she pressed 'answer' and put the phone to her ear.

"Alexandra," Hammond said, "stay on the line, do you hear me? Stay on the damn line."

She hadn't spoken to Hammond since Eastern Europe, but his voice instantly took her back to that time, in the grim prison in a nameless forest, when she'd realised there would be no escape for her.

"We can mend this," Hammond said. "It's one hell of a mess, but it's not irreparable."

"What, we're just going to kiss and make up?" she choked.

There was a small but telling pause before Hammond said, "You've got amends to make, no question. But maybe I pushed you too hard and too fast. I know I'm not blameless."

He was talking like a hostage negotiator, she realised. Making promises that were meant to be comforting, not kept. But there were things she could learn from him, too.

"All right," she said. "Tell me what I can do."

"Good. Good. That's the right attitude, Alexandra. Well, I guess telling you to give yourself up isn't going to fly."

"You guessed right."

"Then let's talk about PD."

"I am sorry about that. But no harm no foul, right?"

This time, the pause at the other end of the line was longer. "You think he's with us," Hammond said eventually.

Alex felt the first twinge of unease. "Well, yeah. Curtis knew where we were. She must have called in reinforcements."

"She did. By the time they arrived, you were gone – and so was PD."

"Well get him back then! You know who's got him and where they're based."

"Really? That never occurred to us. As it turns out, he's not *at* their office on Haight. And we were lucky they let us look. Because how exactly, Alexandra, do you think we can go about getting a search warrant? We can't go public with the fact we've been spying on a domestic religion. The first amendment nuts will have their usual hysterics. They'll say it's Waco all over again, and this time the shit will rain down on us, not the feds."

Alex felt a knot of something she didn't want to recognise as guilt in her stomach. "You're a covert fucking agency – do something covert and get him out."

"Perhaps we could, if we knew where they'd taken him."

"If anyone can find him, you can."

She could imagine Hammond's thin-lipped smile on the other end of the line. "You've seen the Croatoans, Alexandra. PD told me what you saw. Who do you think is better placed to find PD – us or you?"

The knot of guilt tightened unpleasantly. She fidgeted a moment, not sure how to reply. She'd stopped to talk in one of the quieter cross streets, foot braced against the steep gradient.

She'd been keeping her voice down as she spoke, but she realised that in the last few minutes, no one had passed.

It was a quiet street, but it was the middle of the day. And now she thought about it, there hadn't been a single car, either.

"Alexandra," Hammond said. "Damn it, are you still there?" There was a note in his voice, something off – too anxious.

She dropped the phone and stamped on it. It cracked beneath her heel but the screen remained lit, like a beacon, which she realised far too late was exactly what it was. As soon as she'd switched it on they'd been able to track it.

She leapt to the side seconds before the hooks of the taser scraped against the pavement where she'd been standing. She smelt the ozone tang of the electric charge which had been meant to pass through her body and, for a second, came face-to-face with her attacker. He was an SFPD beat officer, but his eyes were blanks, hidden behind the heavy black of night-vision goggles. A wolf's snout stuck out beneath them, teeth bared in a snarl.

They'd found a way to see her, even hidden behind the veil of the spirit world.

She ran, gasping for breath after only a few paces, her chest too tight with panic to take in the oxygen she needed. She heard the pounding of other footsteps behind her and when she pelted past a cross-street she could see more men waiting for her there. They were only just jerking into motion. Perhaps they hadn't expected her to spot the trap before she'd sprung it.

She descending the hill, each step a mini plummet and each landing an impact that jarred from her foot to her spine, but her pursuers drew nearer no matter how fast she ran. And then she saw the road block ahead of her, more SFPD uniforms behind it, wolf tongues lolling below black night-vision goggles.

She was boxed in. There were cops at each end of the street, and a solid wall of buildings at either side.

But of course she was being a fool. The buildings were solid to them – not to her. And they might be able to see her in the spirit realm, but they couldn't travel into it.

She was running so fast that stopping tumbled her to the pavement with all the momentum of her flight. The bullet graze on her side opened and bled. The men behind her were so close she could smell their sweat, and then they were over her, leaping to avoid her prone body. She heard them curse and one of them fired, but the taser went wide and in the minute it took them to come to their own, more controlled, halt she rose to her feet and ran straight at the nearest house.

It was only as her shoulder struck the wooden slat and she felt the grain of the wood against her bare arm that she realised what she should have noticed far earlier. The spirit realm was fading – or rather she was, fading back into the mundane world. She'd seen the policemen as men rather than wolves. Reality was reasserting itself.

She heard the click of multiple weapons being cocked behind her and she closed her eyes and pushed against the wall with both her mind and her body. She felt resistance, the painful press of wood against bruised skin and then, finally, something gave – and slow as molasses her body seeped through and into the house beyond.

She'd entered a white-painted living room. Bland, motel-print posters flicked past as she sprinted into the corridor beyond. The house was empty but her pursuers would be through the door soon. Though Hammond might not want to cause an incident by raiding the Croatoan headquarters, she was sure he'd risk almost anything to get her back.

The corridor led to a kitchen, floor-to-ceiling windows looking out onto the overgrown yard beyond. She tugged at the doors, but they were locked tight, and when she leaned against the glass it was just glass, cold and impenetrable against her shoulder.

The spirit world was gone entirely now. But she'd been living in the real one for twenty-three year, damn it. She wasn't helpless. She felt along the shelf above the door then yanked open kitchen draws, scattering silverware on the floor before she found the key in a small bowl beside the sink. Her fingers fumbled with it as she heard a booming impact behind her, the sound of something metal hitting the front door.

The key scratched shrilly across the glass before it slid into the keyhole. It turned easily and she had her hand flexed to push open the door when she saw what waited for her outside. The brick walls of the yard were swarming with uniformed men, night-vision goggles beetle-black over their eyes.

She snapped a look over her shoulder, expecting to find Raven standing there, ready to give advice she shouldn't follow and would anyway. But Raven was lost to her in the world he inhabited and she had only visited.

The men outside were over the wall. She stepped back from the window as they crept closer. They were being cautious, still unsure of her powers, but that bought her five minutes at most. And the men at the front would be through the door before then. The only escape was sideways – through the rows of houses.

Her hand drifted to her pocket and she didn't know why until she pulled out the packet half full of brown flakes. It was the remains of the peyote PD had given her in the restaurant.

She opened the bag and tipped the contents onto her palm. It was a large dose. If she took it right now, she might slip into the spirit world fast enough to make her escape. But the last dose she'd taken had been smaller and the effects had lasted for nearly a day. Each time she travelled, she travelled further and for longer. If she took the drug this time, she might travel so far that she could never return. That was the fate she'd fled the Bureau to escape.

Outside the window, the men crept nearer, faces intent as they hunted her. The sounds coming from the front door had changed, softer now as the wood splintered and gave.

She could return to the Bureau. They wouldn't kill her – but she'd never be free again. Or she could take the drug and take her chances in the world it opened to her.

Her hand shook as she lifted it to her lips. The peyote stuck to her tongue and the roof of her mouth, all the saliva having dried at the prospect of taking it. She ducked her head under the tap to sluice it down with water, wincing at the taste.

As soon as it was in her throat, something insubstantial but powerful forced its way past and through her. More suddenly than she could have imagined, the spirit world was back and Raven with it. He looked like the man she'd first seen, harmless and a little absurd. She wondered if it was his choice to seem that way, or if her mind had simply refused to face up to the truth of him again.

"Well, about bloody time," he said, grinning as he held out his hand.

She didn't hesitate before taking it this time, but she shut her eyes as he pulled, letting him lead her where he wanted.

She didn't know how long the journey had taken, but when they stopped she found herself on a narrow wooden pier with the Bay to either side of her, a sailing ship that looked two centuries old tossing and tearing apart in a storm that moved only the sea directly beneath it.

Ahead of her, a figure walked away across the water, curly hair hanging lank in the salt spray. Though she'd grown used to seeing him every time she travelled here, she still found him disturbing. He was linked to her in some way she couldn't understand and she felt his presence even when she turned away from him. Behind her the city burned, but the streets were empty of wolves. She'd escaped, she just didn't know the price.

She squinted her eyes and tightened something less tangible inside her mind, trying to return to the mundane world, at least a little.

"Word of warning," Raven said. "Time doesn't pass here, it lingers. In the spirit realm you're both now and then. If you're careless – and I have known you to be careless – you could step into the past rather than the present. And then where would you be?"

She shivered, understanding what he meant. To the spirit world, San Francisco had been most vivid when it was torn apart by earthquake and fire. If she let it, it would spit her out into that moment of history. She thought very hard about her own time instead, its speed and cruelty as well as its comforts and conveniences.

The ancient sailing ship paled to a phantom, the modern tugs and pleasure boats hardening into visibility around her.

"So," Raven said, slouching against a railing. "Your daring – if somewhat last-minute – escape has freed you from the clutches of the CIA. What now?"

Yes. What now? "I need to get away. I need money."

He smiled. "And how do you intend to get it?"

"I don't know. I thought you could tell me."

His smile dropped. "Oh. Well, no. The acquisition of wealth has never been one of my top priorities."

"I don't want to be wealthy. I just want to have enough money to live." There was something else she wanted, too, but she was very carefully not thinking about it. She didn't *want* to want it. She didn't want to care.

"That's a laudable goal," Raven said. "Good luck with that."

She didn't know whether he was answering the words she'd spoken or the ones locked inside her head. She was sure he could get her the money if he wanted. She was pretty certain he could do whatever he damn well pleased. But it was equally obvious he wouldn't.

"Fine," she said. "Then can you make Hammond go away? Or make it so he can't find me?"

His brow furrowed. "Why would I do that?"

"To help me out?"

"And why would I want to do that?" For a moment, the black eyes staring back at her were in a different face, less friendly and more frightening. Then he shook his head and was just a man again.

"Please," she said. "I need your help."

"You can have whatever you want," he told her. "You just have to tell me the truth about what that is."

She wanted to go back to her old life, but she knew that wasn't possible. Not just because of what she'd done, but because of what she'd seen. She couldn't live that life and pretend she didn't know what lay beneath it.

And, of course, she wanted to take back what she'd done to PD. She wanted to undo her betrayal, which had turned out to be more profound than she'd intended.

"Fuck you," she said. "And fuck him. He deserved what I did. He never cared about me. Christ, *you* showed me that. You told me it was the truth."

Raven smiled. "The truth isn't singular, Alex. Only angels and demons believe that it is, and I'm a conscientious objector in their war. The spirit world showed you that you craved love so much, you'd see it even when it wasn't there. PD might actually care for you, and that would still be true."

"And does he?" Alex asked.

"That's not your truth to know. Maybe he feels nothing at all. Maybe you were just an easy lay. So tell me, Alex, what do you want?"

She sighed. "I don't want PD to suffer because of what I've done. I want to find him."

"Now that," he said, "I can help you with."

CHAPTER THIRTEEN

PD woke reaching for a weapon which was no longer there. His head felt too heavy for his shoulders and his thoughts were sluggish, as if the gears of his mind were gummed up. He opened his eyes, only to squeeze them shut again as the bright light started a painful throbbing at the base of his skull. He felt around his head, probing for lumps, but there was nothing. He'd been drugged then.

He lay still a moment, listening. There was no whisper of breath, only the distant brush of wind through leaves. No point in faking unconsciousness if there was no audience to appreciate it.

When he opened his eyes again, half-veiling them with his lids, he thought for a moment that he was in a tent. There was red and gold fabric all around, thick and muffling. But when he pushed it aside, he saw that it was suspended from the ceiling of a white-painted room to form a rough tepee over the bed. There were geometric patterns on the fabric that PD guessed were meant to imitate Indian work. But it was fake, all of it.

There was a sink in the room. PD used it to splash water on his face, trying to clear the last of the drug-induced fuzziness from his mind. He felt in his ear and at his throat for the com links he'd been wearing and wasn't surprised to find both gone. His memory was beginning to return. He recalled being trapped in the house on Alamo Square, locked in Marriott's study while the Croatoans closed in.

Alex, he thought in sudden panic.

Hammond would end PD's career and maybe his life if anything had happened to her. And... he remembered the way she'd smiled after he'd rolled from on top of her, breath coming in heaving gasps. Her smile had made him look away, too unguarded. The instant he'd seen it, he'd known he should have kept his hands off her. But when she'd stroked a finger from his throat to his cock, he'd felt it twitch back into life and he'd lifted her on top of him and started all over again.

A part of him had felt she *owed* him this, for all the shit he'd taken protecting her from Hammond over the years. And the bigger part of him had just wanted her. Almost as if by taking this from her, he could take the other thing she possessed that he so badly wanted. And then the Croatoans had come and the door had locked, shutting him away from any possibility of making things right with her.

Except he'd been locked in *before* the cultists came.

She'd set him up. Jesus, he was an idiot. She'd been planning it all day. That's why she'd insisted on going to the bank. And she was a god-awful useless liar. He'd have known she was deceiving him the instant he looked in her eyes. But he hadn't, had he? He'd fucked her and then let her fuck him over because he hadn't been able to face up to what he'd done. His chest burned with a toxic combination of rage at Alex and self-disgust.

His room had a window hidden behind a gauzy curtain. When he pulled it back, sunlight streamed in, the pure white of the deep desert. He didn't know how long he'd been unconscious so he couldn't guess how far he'd been taken. Had he left the country altogether? But the shape of the distant mountains looked familiar, and he thought he might be in the Mojave, somewhere south and east of San Francisco. There was a fence a hundred or so feet away, separating the dusty desert plants from the irrigated greenery which surrounded the building.

The window wasn't barred. He opened it to let in a gust of hot,

Rebecca Levene

dry air. The fence was high and topped with razor wire and his room was on the third floor. Besides, his mission objective was to discover more about the Croatoans. He'd fucked up everything else, but he could still do this.

For the first time he noticed what he was wearing. Someone had dressed him in buckskin pants and a tunic cinched at the waist with a beaded belt. He looked like a Red Indian extra from a 1950s Western. He saw a camera peering at him from one corner of the ceiling. They were watching him. He searched the room anyway, but aside from a bar of cinnamon-scented soap there was nothing and no sign of his own clothes.

He didn't really expect the door to open, but the handle turned smoothly. He slipped into the corridor without anyone trying to stop him.

There was a man outside, leaning against the far wall and PD's muscles tensed as he took a step back. The man barely seemed to notice. He smiled vacantly then walked away in an unsteady zig-zag. Drugged too, PD guessed. Another prisoner? He was dressed in the same absurd tunic and pants, though he was white, his long hair swinging around a blandly handsome face.

PD followed the man down the featureless white corridor until they entered a larger, more crowded space. The hundred or so people inside sat in loose circles, eating from communal bowls. Some of the circles passed a peace pipe around along with the food. From the pungent smell in the air, PD could tell it was filled with something other than tobacco. There was music coming from hidden speakers, an inoffensive New Age tinkling.

These people were a joke. PD had been searching his whole life for the thing that should have been his birthright. Then he'd found Alex and he'd seen it in her eyes, the crazy reflection of the spirit world which had always eluded him. It was so near when he was with her, and yet frustratingly still out of his reach. And these people... they didn't even understand the thing they pretended to want.

Were they a threat? Alex had said they were, but then Alex might have been lying for days. The Croatoans had seemed

173

harmless until that confrontation in the restaurant – *after* Alex had been inside their base. Had she made her deal with them then? He'd thought they were trying to kidnap her from the restaurant, but maybe he'd actually foiled an escape attempt. Shit. It all made sense. He should have guessed it then, but he'd let her lead him along by the cock. She'd played him like a pro.

He needed to get back to base and start the search for her. He couldn't let her get away. With her powers she was more of a danger than the Croatoans could ever be. The embers of rage burned inside him as he walked through the room.

One long wall was glass, looking out on the compound and the arid desert beyond. PD walked beside it, unremarked by the people in the room, until he came to an archway and the entrance hall beyond.

The door to the outside wasn't locked either. PD took a deep breath of the desert air as he swung it open. There were cars outside. He might have to jack one of them if he wanted to complete his escape. He thought they wouldn't try too hard to stop him. Alex had probably paid them to keep him out of the way while she ran for it, but could she have paid them enough to risk killing him?

"Leaving already?" a man said behind him. "Don't you want to see what you came for?"

PD tensed, considering running, but he was outnumbered and unarmed. He released the door handle and turned round slowly, hands held away from his body.

The man who'd addressed him looked in his thirties, curly haired and unremarkable except for his wide hazel eyes. They made his expression seem startled, but the eyes themselves were just blank.

"We brought you here for a reason," the man said. "We have no intention of harming you." His gaze travelling over PD's body made him twitch with unease. It wasn't quite sexual, but it was oddly appraising.

"Kidnapping is a federal crime," PD said. "You're all in on a busted flush. Let me go and I might just drop it."

The man shrugged. "You're free to go."

PD stared at him. He didn't sense a lie. But he didn't move and after a moment the man smiled, as if he'd known that was how PD would react. "I lead the Croatoans," he said. "I'm Laughing Wolf."

"I'm PD, but I guess you know that. What do you want with me? If you're not working with Alex, what are you doing? No more bullshit."

Laughing Wolf opened his arms wide, a studied and theatrical gesture. PD saw that he was dressed as a Mojave shaman, the costume not a pastiche like those of the other Croatoans but the real deal. "I want you to spirit walk with me," he said. "Let me show you what we can really do."

PD sensed the trap, of course he did. But they already had him in their power. They could have killed him before he woke. And every scrap of information he brought back to the Agency was worth the risk to his life.

Especially if they really could teach him to spirit walk. Especially then.

"OK," he said. "I'll call that raise."

A timid young woman led PD back to his room, where an even more absurd outfit had been laid out on the bed for him. He raised a sceptical eyebrow at her, but she looked back blankly.

"The ceremony isn't until sunset," she said. "Laughing Wolf said you can relax till then."

She left and this time PD heard a key turning in the lock. He grimaced and looked down at the beaded jacket on the bed, then shrugged and began to change into it. He had a flash of childhood memory, his grandfather helping him dress for his cousin's naming ceremony back when they'd still lived on the rez. He'd complained bitterly, hating the meaningless tradition, a vestigial remnant of a long-gone time as useless as an appendix.

Then the casino had changed everything, bringing money and an escape route into the white man's world. And now here he was, among the white people he'd always despised most – the wannabes who wished they were red.

He lay on the bed, staring up at the fake tepee until the girl returned for him.

"You're lucky," she said as she closed the door behind him. "I've been here three months, and they tell me I'm still not ready to take the spirit road."

"Take my advice, kid," he said. "Stay away from that place. It isn't Disneyland."

She looked offended, as if she thought he was patronising her. Maybe he was. The one with the real knowledge was Alex – the bitch who didn't want or deserve it.

The girl led him through a maze of white corridors to the opposite side of the compound. She opened a door to let in a waft of hot air and a view of the desert beyond, the sun reddening as it approached the far horizon. There was only the fence between him and freedom.

At least thirty cultists sat in a loose double circle around a central fire. The outer ring faced inward and the inner ring faced outward, pairs of white faces gazing at each other. The flames were almost transparent in the sunlight, shivering the image of the world behind them.

Laughing Wolf stood near the fire, no longer dressed as a shaman. It took a moment for PD to identify the fringed white cloth over his shoulders as a tallit, a Jewish prayer shawl. It was out of place here, a genuine piece of one culture in this fake recreation of another. And he recognised the curved horn hanging from Laughing Wolf's belt, too. It was a shofar. He'd heard its sound throughout his childhood every Rosh Hashanah and Yom Kippur, welcoming in the new year and marking the end of the Day of Atonement's twenty-five hour fast. But this horn looked... weighty. PD thought he could see the air shimmering around it, just as the air around the fire did, as if the shofar too was burning.

Laughing Wolf nodded as he approached. The people in the ring were silent as they sat cross-legged, wood smoke the only scent in the air and the crackle of the fire the only sound. Laughing Wolf's wide hazel eyes looked flat in the firelight. "Sit," he said. "Join our circle. Be welcome."

PD could see no weapons among the Croatoans, but he found himself moving to obey. He needed to know. It was the point of his mission – it was the central question of his life.

He had an unwelcome memory of Alex telling him he only wanted what he didn't have because he didn't understand what it was. He shook his head to deny her claim as he settled on the hard ground.

In front of him, the inner ring looked back. For the first time, PD realised that the outer ring of cultists were all young and pretty. The inner ring were older, some leaning awkwardly sideways as if kneeling hurt arthritic joints. PD was opposite a man so wizened that he looked mummified. His rheumy eyes raked over PD's body and he didn't like the expression in them.

The sun seemed to be rushing towards the horizon. It looked like the red giant it was too small to ever become, a glimpse of a future that couldn't be. It was an odd thought, and PD tried to shake it away, but his head felt muzzy. He glanced at the fire, at the smoke rising from the green wood, but he smelt nothing herbal and he'd eaten or drunk nothing since he'd been in the Croatoan compound.

He looked at Laughing Wolf and saw he'd raised the shofar to his lips. His cheeks were puffed as if he was blowing it, but no sound emerged. PD felt something, though, a vibration in his chest that matched the traditional notes of the horn. *Tekia*, he thought, as a long deep soundless blast seemed to echo through him. And then *teruah*, a treble trill the human ear wasn't built to hear. It seemed to tug against a part of him that wasn't quite physical and he felt the first flash of pure terror. Inside him, something was breaking loose which had been firmly anchored for the whole of his life.

There was another noise, a desperate howling PD thought came from this strange congregation. He looked around, the movement of his head a supreme effort. But their faces showed only the same fear he felt. Had any of them done this before, or was this the first time for all of them? Was it possible to undergo this terrible spiritual parting more than once?

PD turned to peer into the darkening desert behind him. When he saw the yellow flash of eyes, low to the ground, he tried to rear back. But his body was no longer his to command. Though he still occupied his physical form, he no longer controlled it.

The eyes drew closer. They blinked and when the howling came again PD saw that they were coyotes. They slunk closer, bellies low to the ground, teeth bared in a snarl. PD knew, though he couldn't explain how, that they'd been drawn by the same force that was tugging at something inside him, worrying at it with invisible teeth until it remained connected only by a thread.

PD wanted to see what Laughing Wolf was doing. But he remained motionless, gaze fixed on the nearest coyote as it crept closer. Its tongue looked black in the darkness and its fur sparked with flecks of gold as the firelight caught it. Its flat yellow eyes remained locked on his as it took another step closer. He could smell its rank musk and feel its breath hot against his face.

PD felt eyes behind him, too. He sensed them travelling over his body, possessing it. And then the shofar spoke again, soundless and powerful. *Tekia. Tekia. Sheravim-teruah.* The vibrations went on and on, shaking everything inside him, shaking it all loose.

He felt it deep in his chest when it snapped, the cord connecting something that was him to something else that was only his physical housing.

For a moment he was drifting free, untethered to anything in the world. He felt the stars burning in the dome of the sky and knew that he could reach them if he tried. His spirit soared high above the desert and higher still, until he could see the curve of the earth and the perilously thin blanket of atmosphere around it. The moon was above him, barren and pitted, and he flew towards it, wanting to tread on its grey dust.

But the earth's gravity was still beneath him, a pull that was no longer a force and more like a yearning. He belonged in the world below not the world above and he felt himself tumbling back towards it, the desert rushing up to meet him, the fire and the man beside it, still blowing on the shofar as if he had endless breath inside him.

PD could see his body, legs crossed and torso listing to one side. His eyes were closed, but as he drew nearer he saw them blink open and focus, though it wasn't his will that moved them or his mind that looked out from behind them.

He moved until he was within reach of his body, though there was nothing to reach with. For a moment he looked into his own eyes and saw someone else look back. And then he heard the shofar again, the low, commanding note of *tekiah*, and he was moving sideways, away from himself.

A moment later he felt the snap of a connection remade as something anchored him back to the physical realm. He blinked open his eyes, and he could see, but it was all wrong. The colours had faded while the view had sharpened. And the *smells*, so clear and sharp they seemed to form a map of the world.

He opened his mouth and felt his tongue loll over his teeth, drool slicking between the sharp fangs. And as he finally understood, he lifted his head and howled.

CHAPTER FOURTEEN

Lahav didn't say a word for the entire flight. Morgan was reminded of his first meeting with Tomas and the trip they'd taken to Budapest. Tomas had been silent too, lost in his own thoughts. But there had been something soothing about his former partner's silences. Lahav was stiff with tension.

The Israeli had procured them fake passports from somewhere. No one except the flight attendants spared them a second glance on the plane and when they landed the journey through security was slow but problem-free.

Morgan relaxed a little as they passed through customs and into the sterile cleanliness of the arrivals lounge. He turned to Lahav. "You going to tell me why I'm in Las Vegas now?"

"No," Lahav said. "I will tell you when we've hired a car. When we're alone."

Half an hour later, he gestured Morgan outside, where a big black Jeep flashed its lights at them as they approached.

"Aren't those supposed to be bad for the environment?" Morgan said.

Lahav snorted as he climbed in, the most human reaction Morgan had yet seen from him. The city outside the tinted windows was featureless but definitely foreign. The houses were too regular, too new, too widely spaced. "I've never been to America before," Morgan told Lahav.

The Israeli shrugged.

"Why am I in America now?" he asked. "What makes you think Coby would come back here?"

Lahav kept his eyes on the road as nondescript suburbs gave way to scrubby desert around them. The interior of the car was air-conditioned and chilly. It made the view outside seem almost like a mirage. Morgan found it hard to believe he'd come so far so quickly.

"You don't know what Croatoan is, do you?" Lahav asked.

Morgan scowled, sensitive to the suggestion that a better-educated man would. "No. I don't know."

Lahav nodded. "If you were American, perhaps you would. It's an American legend – the lost colony of Roanoke, England's first settlement in the New World. Roanoke is an island off the coast of North Carolina, but your country called it Virginia then, after its virgin Queen. There were several attempts to found a colony, all failing – the last in 1587."

"Hang on," Morgan said, feeling the first stirrings of excitement. "That's the same time John Dee was alive, isn't it?"

"Yes. And very shortly after his house was burgled, many of his most precious possessions stolen."

"You think the colonists took some of his stuff with them when they went."

"I think that now, yes."

Morgan shifted so that his shoulder was leaning against the car door and he could study the other man. There was something in his expression he couldn't read, a tightness to his jaw that suggested frustration. He seemed angry, but maybe with himself. "So where did the colonists take the shofar?" he asked.

Lahav grimaced. "Croatoan."

"It's a place?"

"It was a message. The colony disappeared, you understand. When a ship returned for them in 1590, not a single person was left – only the word 'Croatoan' carved into the trunk of a tree. They call it a great mystery."

"Yeah," Morgan said, "but I'm guessing you know the solution."

"Everyone who thinks for two seconds knows the solution.

There was a native tribe on an island close by, the Croatoans. They'd been friendly to the English colonists when others had not. And many years later, when the Croatoans were contacted again, some were found to be blue-eyed or fair-haired."

Morgan smiled. "So the colonists just moved in with the local tribe and married them, and they took the shofar with them. But where are they now?"

"Gone. Lost to history."

Morgan slumped back against his seat, watching the road unroll ahead of them, heat haze shimmering and blurring its margins. "Bullshit. As soon as you heard that word, you knew. You brought us *here*, didn't you?"

"Yes. The Croatoans *did* disappear from history, but recently a new group appeared using their name. A cult for the young and foolish."

They were in full desert now, the sky above washed out by the heat so that it was almost the same colour as the sand below. The only features were the cacti, squat and bulbous against the horizon. Morgan watched a small bird land on one and wondered how its feet bore the sharp spines.

"It's a pretty big leap," he said, twisting his head to watch the bird until it was out of view. "I mean, if it's like you say, and everyone's heard the story about the lost colony, couldn't they just have picked the name because it sounded cool?"

"It's more than that. We have already been investigating the Croatoans. There are claims about them, and they've grown in power far too quickly. They have it. They must."

"So that's where we're going now – to find these Croatoans?"

Lahav nodded. "But first, we'll meet some friends of mine."

"What sort of friends?"

"Friends with guns. If the shofar is here, we'll need them."

Morgan jolted out of a light sleep, hand reaching for a shapeless something he'd been pursuing in his dreams. He clenched it into a fist instead and looked across at the man driving, but Lahav had his eyes on the road and didn't seem to be paying him any attention.

The change in speed was probably what had woken him. They were slowing down, though they didn't seem to have arrived anywhere. There was desert all around, closer now they'd moved to a more minor route, then more minor still as Lahav yanked the steering round to pull them onto a dirt track. The Jeep rattled as the view disappeared behind a cloud of dust churned up by its wheels.

"We're here?" Morgan asked then, after Lahav nodded curtly, "Which is where, exactly?"

"The northern edge of the Mojave Desert. A small town called Cima."

The Jeep slid to a halt on the rough ground. The dust cloud grew then settled, and Morgan saw that they were *somewhere*, though it wasn't much different from nowhere. A few buildings dotted the bleak landscape around them, the same colour as the sand and many looking as if they'd been half worn away by it. He noticed a straight black line bisecting the landscape halfway to the horizon and guessed it might be a railway line. It was hard to imagine why a train would ever visit a place like this.

"This is a ghost town," Lahav said. "Built for the railway, abandoned when the trains were."

Morgan grunted as he swung open the car door. "Welcome to Cima, population nil."

He stepped out and stopped, feet grating against stone, as he saw the five SIG Sauer semi-automatics trained on him. The men holding them were big, heavily tattooed and massively muscled. They held the guns as though they knew how to use them and were eager to start.

"Not nil," Lahav said from the other side of the car. "Leave him, Jimmy, he's with me."

"*Him*?" said one of the men, scrawnier and angrier looking then the rest. But the blond giant in the centre of the group lowered his SIG Sauer and after a moment all the others did the same.

They crowded round to embrace Lahav, slapping him so roughly on the back even the Israeli was rocked on his feet.

Morgan saw that their eyes were still on him, though, and he felt others unseen in the abandoned buildings all around.

One of the men handed a semi-automatic to Lahav along with the holster to hold it. Morgan raised an eyebrow when the Israeli caught his eye and Lahav nodded. "Give him a weapon too," he said to the one he'd called Jimmy.

Jimmy shot Morgan an unloving look. "You sure about that?"

"He knows how to use it," Lahav said.

Jimmy nodded curtly and pressed the handgrip into Morgan's palm. He was surprised at how alien it felt to him. The years he'd spent as a soldier seemed like a long time ago.

The building they led him to was little more than a shell, the roof decayed and sagging and the walls stripped bare by winds and time. It was hard to tell what the place had originally been – a shop maybe, or a meeting hall. On the far wall, two planks of wood had been nailed to form a crude cross and someone with more enthusiasm than talent had painted a picture of Mary holding the baby Jesus below it.

A man with a straggly beard and tattoos of swastikas on his muscled forearms was kneeling in front of the makeshift altar. His shoulders were shaking and Morgan thought at first that he was laughing. But when he lifted his face to the broken ceiling, tear tracks glittered in the harsh midday sun.

Jimmy scowled when he read Morgan's expression. His own face was seamed with scars, one cheek lumpier than the other as if the bone beneath had once been broken and never properly set. "What are you staring at, boy?" he said.

Morgan was very aware of the men around him, the weapons in holsters at their sides and over their backs. His own semi-automatic wouldn't do him much good against so much concentrated firepower. "Nothing," he said. He looked at Lahav. "I suppose I'm just wondering what we're doing here."

"Oh, you *suppose*," the man beside Jimmy said in a nasal accent that Morgan guessed was meant to be British. "What in hell *is* he doing here, Jimmy? We need real men to fight the good fight, not this foreign faggot."

Jimmy grabbed the man before Morgan could, backhanding him across the face and knocking him to his knees. "Watch your mouth, Ben! We're all God's children here."

"Not all of us," Lahav said, his eyes cold on Morgan. "But we need him."

"For what?" Ben glowered at Morgan as he wiped blood from his mouth and climbed back to his feet. "Them Croatoans ain't no threat to no one. Jimmy's been keeping track of 'em for months, checking they ain't up to no ungodly business. They're nothing but rich assholes dressing up like Sitting Bull. That's a joke, not a mission." He shrugged off Jimmy's hand and pushed past Morgan to exit the derelict church.

The man kneeling before the cross looked over his shoulder at them. The tear tracks had dried on his cheeks, leaving a smear like the trail of a slug.

Jimmy shook his head. "Don't mind Ben. He's new here, hasn't learnt our ways."

Lahav smiled and suddenly Morgan was sick of it all. He'd betrayed his own people – betrayed Kate and Tomas's memory – and for what? An agent of another power who'd never claimed to be doing anything other than using him.

"You know what," he said, "I *do* mind him. I'm not here to help you and–" he looked at Lahav "–I'm not just a weapon you can holster and forget about when you don't need it."

Jimmy smiled. "That's exactly what you are to him, boy. And you're less than that to us."

Something in Morgan snapped. Jimmy was too big and heavy to topple head on. Morgan got behind him instead, one hand under his chin and another pressing back against his nose so that the pressure and the pain flipped the bigger man onto his back. The breath burst out of Jimmy in a rank cloud, stinking of cigarettes.

Morgan barely registered the shouts around him or the cocking of guns. He pressed his arm across Jimmy's throat, hard enough to hurt, not hard enough to kill. Not yet. "You've got no idea what I am, you ignorant fuck. You think you're dangerous? I'm a fucking nuclear bomb. You think you're better than me? You are. I'm the worst person in the whole fucking world!"

He felt Lahav's hand on his shoulder and froze. The other man's flesh felt too hot against him but he wondered if it wasn't him who was too cold. He was shivering, even the arm pressed against Jimmy's throat, and after a minute he lifted it up, rocking back on his heels and running a hand over his face. Sweat slicked off him and other moisture which might have been tears. He didn't know what he was doing any more.

He expected Jimmy to push him away, maybe to punch him. He half expected a bullet in the back of his head. But the other man just nodded at him and for the first time his eyes looked something other than contemptuous. "Don't give up hope, brother," he said. "No one is beyond redemption. Not even us. And not even you."

Jimmy showed him the town, his tread heavy beside Morgan's, combat boots crunching the skeletal plants. The men in the church had remained behind, their eyes sliding over Morgan as if they'd suddenly ceased to notice him.

There were more men scattered throughout the ghost town. Some were shooting at targets using anything from old-fashioned revolvers to machine pistols. Others were wrestling or boxing, faces streaked with blood and dust. A group of ten jogged in from the desert with heavy packs on their backs and dry tongues licking cracked lips.

Morgan felt wrung-out after his outburst and strangely weightless. "This is a training camp," he said.

Jimmy nodded. "You got that right. Bad times are coming, brother."

Morgan had been with the Hermetic Division long enough to guess what the other man meant. "You're talking about the apocalypse."

"The end of days. The signs are there for those that know how to read 'em. Satan's forces are growing strong and we intend to oppose them." Jimmy's hand clenched around his brass belt buckle and Morgan saw that he had HATE tattooed on his knuckles. Beneath the collar of his loose khaki T-shirt, another tattoo poked out. It looked like the tip of a bat wing.

"Mate," Morgan said, "don't take this the wrong way, but you look like you ought to be fighting on the other side."

Jimmy laughed, a hacking sound not much different from a cough. It left flecks of saliva in his wild blond beard. "Was a time I woulda been – we all would. Lahav tell you anything about us?"

Morgan shrugged. "He told me you had guns and that you could help us with the Croatoans. I don't know how you know him or why you're working with him. You do know who he is, right?"

"An Israeli agent," Jimmy said, pronouncing 'Israeli' as if it had about seven syllables. "You reckon it's unpatriotic, but there's a higher loyalty than love of country, even this one."

"You mean in the other conflict. The one between heaven and hell."

"The only war that counts, and I was on the wrong side of it for a helluva long time. I got in my first fight when I was 13, beating on some kid just 'cause I didn't like the colour of his skin. By the time I was eighteen I was cooking meth, and when I knifed a man so bad he nearly bled out, I finally got where I belonged – behind bars."

Morgan looked over the dusty desert and the men running and crawling across it under a maze of barbed wire. "And then you what – saw the error of your ways?"

"Not hardly." Unselfconscious, Jimmy yanked his T-shirt over his head, using it to swab the sweat under his armpits. When he turned his back, Morgan saw that a demon spread its wings across the whole expanse of flesh, tail curling round to point its tip at his belly button. It was a crude prison tattoo, and it must have taken hundreds of hours of pain to complete.

"Need all the friends you can get in that place," Jimmy said, "even the bad ones. You're white and you want to survive inside, you join a gang that puts swastikas on your body and tells you you're the master race. That's just the way it is. And it wasn't like I objected to sticking a shiv in some black bastard when occasion required. It was only when I got a shard of glass in my own gut things changed. They say I died on the operating table and I... I saw the flames – I saw where I was going. When they brought me back round I got me a Bible and I read it cover to cover. Then I preached it to anyone in there who'd listen."

Morgan's eyes scanned the private army around him. "These people–"

"The Tribulation Militia. Used to be what I was, till I showed them how to be something better"

"You really think this is what God wants? What happened to peace and love and all that shit?"

Jimmy turned to face him, T-shirt clutched in one meaty fist. "Scripture tells us when the last battle comes, the good will be Raptured right up into heaven to sit at the Lord's right hand. That ain't gonna happen to us. We're so heavy with sin, no way we could lift ourselves into the clouds. But those who remain behind have a task too, to fight the Devil's forces here on earth. That's the battle we're training for, and when we win that war, we'll have earned our places in paradise."

A fire of absolute conviction burned in his eyes, and Morgan found that he wanted to believe him. "But how can you be sure that Lahav really is on God's side?" he asked. *And how,* he wondered, *can I?*

Jimmy just smiled. "We're having a prayer meeting later. Join us and you'll understand."

The sun set quickly in the desert, leaving a surprising chill in its wake. Morgan watched it all the way down, standing on the borders of the ghost town and looking out on the nothing beyond.

He could hear the militiamen moving behind him, gathering in what might once have been the town square. He hadn't seen

Lahav since he first arrived and he wondered why he'd been so quick to follow him. Seeing Jimmy's blind faith in the Israeli and the God he claimed to represent had forced him to face his own. Lahav had some powers beyond human, but what did that mean? So did Morgan.

When he felt the hand settle on his shoulder, he knew it was Lahav. He turned to face the other man and found his face shadowed, the sliver of new moon not enough to illuminate him. He hadn't realised how dark it had grown, lost in his own thoughts.

"You want answers," Lahav said.

Morgan nodded. "I reckon I'm owed some, don't you?"

"No one is owed anything. But you will get them. Come – it's starting."

Morgan followed him, trainers catching in the loose rocks that littered the sand. There was light up ahead and as he drew closer he saw they'd lit a bonfire. He wondered if they'd pulled down more of the houses to feed it. The flames flickered a playful yellow and the militiamen sat in a ring around it, bottles of beer in one hand, crosses in the other.

He expected Lahav to find a seat on the edge of the circle, but the other man kept walking towards the fire. Morgan followed as far as he could, until the heat was too much and he had to stop, hand held in front of his face to shield it. Sparks floated around him and the flames rose high overhead, and Lahav kept on walking.

Morgan took one step back, then another, as Lahav stepped forward. The flames licked at the Israeli, tongues lapping against his brown cheeks as the fire seemed to seep inside and then blaze out of his eyes. They met Morgan's and Morgan felt the heat of them.

A hand grasped his elbow and he realised that Jimmy was pulling him back, away from the sparks that threatened to set his clothes alight. He didn't resist as the other man drew him down to his knees.

From that angle, Lahav looked huge. Or maybe he really had grown as tall as the flames which surrounded him. He drew what must have been his knife, the blade which in his hands could cut through anything. Morgan was numbly unsurprised to see that it too had grown until it was almost as long as Lahav himself. The Israeli held it in two hands, pointed it upwards, and the militiamen roared their approval as their shadows danced in the desert all around.

Behind Lahav's back, the flames seemed to gather and rise, bunching around his shoulders and flaring out. They looked like wings and Morgan was reminded of Belle, whose shadow had once appeared winged too.

"Do you understand now, brother?" Jimmy said. "Do you see why we follow him?"

Morgan nodded dumbly, watching the figure of the angel against the night sky.

Lahav left, striding into the desert as the flames faded into a red glow around him, but the ceremony went on. The men circling the fire clasped their hands to form a ring. Morgan let his own hands be taken. He felt the other men's calluses rough against his palms and realised his own skin had softened in the months since he'd left the Middle East to work for the Hermetic Division.

He couldn't join in the prayers; he didn't know the words, but he tried to feel something as he listened to them.

"When Satan seeks to rise against me," Jimmy said, "the Saviour rises in my defence."

But Satan had risen against Morgan and through him and there had been no one to save him except Tomas and his own fallible conscience.

"These are the days for reversal, overturning and demolishing," the militiamen said. "These are the days for noise and fighting, when the demolition dust will blind many eyes."

That, at least, Morgan believed. The world was crumbling and he felt powerless to preserve it.

"Do thy friends forsake, despise thee?" they sang. "Take it to the Lord in prayer. In his arms he'll take and shield thee – thou wilt find a solace there."

Morgan scrambled to his feet, releasing the hands of the men to either side of him and avoiding their eyes as he retreated away from the fire and into the empty desert. He could feel Jimmy's gaze follow him, but the man himself didn't and Morgan was soon hidden from their eyes in the darkness.

He saw Lahav when he was still twenty feet away. The light of the fire seemed to cling to the other man, illuminating the sand around him so that every rock and pebble had a small, sharp shadow.

"I know what Belle is," Morgan said. "I don't know why it's harder to believe in you than in her."

"They're stronger in this world," Lahav said. "Evil acts are there for everyone to see. We try so hard and fail so often... It takes faith to believe in what I serve." He looked worn out and more human with it.

"You're possessed by it too," Morgan said. "It's inside you, the way the demon's inside Belle."

"Yes."

"You invited it in."

"Yes. The Shomer Hamikdash thought they could use the *malachim* the way the CIA uses Belle and her *dybukk*. I volunteered to open myself to it, but when Lahav came he wouldn't serve. How could he? It's our place to serve him." The other man looked across the desert, eyes black in the night.

"So what happened?" Morgan asked.

Lahav shrugged. "A truce. The Shomer have always had an interest in the lost Temple treasures. My search for the shofar didn't displease them."

"*Your* search?" Morgan said. "Or *his* search, the thing inside you? Because I'm not talking to him now, am I?"

"No, he rests now. His power is in the world of spirit. To do what he just did in the world of flesh drains him."

"So I'm talking to the real you now. Whoever you are."

"I'm Meir Porat." He drew in a deep, shuddering breath. "Yes. I'm still Meir."

"Are you... do you *want* him inside you?"

The Israeli's eyes slid shut, and when they opened again they were blank. Morgan wasn't sure if the angel had returned or if the other man was simply unwilling to reveal any more than he already had.

"What I want is irrelevant," Lahav said. "You know what I am now, so you know what I say is true. Join *my* side in this conflict, and you can be saved."

Morgan knew he ought to have felt relieved. He hadn't been played for a fool and he really could get what he wanted. But instead all he could remember was Julie's smiling face before Lahav had slit her throat. Maybe she had needed to die – if she'd been involved in Dr Granger's work, she might not have been a total innocent. It was just that he'd expected the other side to be different, an opposite to Belle and her kind, not a reflection of them.

Still, this was war. That was one thing both sides agreed on. And Morgan was a soldier; he knew the acts that war demanded.

"I *have* joined your side," Morgan said. "Just tell me what to do, and I'll do it."

CHAPTER FIFTEEN

The plane juddered as it landed and Coby gritted his teeth. He'd always hated flying. He liked to be the one in control. When he stepped out onto the tarmac the brightness of the Californian sun hurt his eyes and he felt the clamminess of his skin gluing his shirt to his back and beneath his arms. After six years in Europe he'd forgotten how hot his homeland could be in the Fall.

He examined his own feelings about being back. He'd felt no nostalgia for America in all the years he'd been away, but he was surprised to find a kind of comfort in the familiar signs and signifiers of the place: the shape of the magazines in the newsagents, the fonts on their covers, the brands of candy for sale beside them. An automated voice announced flights and departure gates and for a moment he heard it as accented and foreign. Then something inside him clicked back into an old, accustomed position and the accent was gone. He heard it instead in his own voice, an exile's distortion of his vowels as he told the immigration officer that he was here on holiday and no, he didn't intend to stay long. He couldn't stop himself darting a glance behind him as he walked through customs, but there was no one behind him.

Coby had last seen Lahav standing on the river bank as the knife he'd meant for him had plunged into Morgan instead. Coby had run and hadn't looked back, and every second until he was on the plane to America his shoulders had tensed with fear of the hot blade they expected to feel between them. But Lahav hadn't caught him and soon it wouldn't matter if he did.

The exit from the airport led straight to the BART station, minimalist and unwelcoming. He let one train go by, checking to see that everyone boarded it before taking the next. If he *was* being followed, they were being subtle about it.

Sound inside the train was muffled by the incongruous carpet, an oddly suburban gesture on this city transport. It was grubby and he could see a black scar where an illicit cigarette had been stubbed out on the material. It was nothing like London's Tube with its over-bright lighting and claustrophobic curves.

Coby had sometimes caught the train from Cambridge and then travelled the Tube late at night, hunting. He was careful not to indulge himself too often, but if one or two of London's rough sleepers went missing, who was there to notice or care? The grim network of subways around Elephant and Castle had been his favourite stalking ground. He couldn't imagine a much worse place to spend your last moments on earth.

He didn't like his urge to kill. It was a weakness and it made him vulnerable. But he recognised that it was an addiction he couldn't kick. If he was careful, the only court he'd have to answer to was the one he'd face after he died. And now...

He'd heard of the Croatoans and their claims that they could spirit travel. He'd even intended to check them out, after he'd recovered the shofar. Ironic that they'd had it all along. It was odd they hadn't used it yet, but maybe they didn't understand its true power. If that was the case, he could swap information for the chance to enter Eden alongside the cult's leaders – and they could all pick the apples from the Tree of Life. He'd never have to face that final judgement and neither heaven nor hell would have any hold on him.

He left the BART at Civic Centre to take the N-Train to Buena Vista Park. The view from its peak swept out towards the mottled green of the Presidio and the Golden Gate Bridge beyond. The sky was a very clear blue, the sea too, and he drew in a satisfied breath of the pine-scented air through his nose. Paradise, he thought, or a pale imitation thereof. If he did this right, he'd see the real thing. A literal Eden – or as literal as anything could be in the metaphorical realm of spirit.

It didn't take him long to find the Croatoan centre in Haight-Ashbury, though he was surprised not to see recruiters loitering outside. There was no bell either, and after a moment's hesitation he turned the handle and pushed the door open.

It was dark inside, shutters over the windows blotting out the sun. And it was silent. When Coby flicked on the light switches he saw that the place was almost empty – just a dark, cavernous space, no tables or chairs. The bulbs which illuminated it were bare, even the shades taken. The place had been abandoned, but not in any kind of hurry.

Damn it. This was the only link he had to the cult. There were recruitment centres in other US cities, but if this one was abandoned those probably were too. And he couldn't waste time rambling all over the country – not with the Mossad agent on his tail.

He had to hope they'd left something behind. He gave the entrance hall a cursory glance – nothing but paint and a few spiders – before heading deeper into the building. It was bigger than it had seemed from the outside, and he realised that the neighbouring houses must be a part of the Croatoan centre too, their apparent individuality only a façade.

The first corridor was lined with rooms, each as empty as the initial hall. They weren't much larger than cupboards and he guessed they'd been used for one-on-one sessions with potential recruits.

The next corridor was featureless, but a smell grew, stale and unpleasant, as he approached its end. It was the scent of an unwashed body – a living smell, not a residue. He heard shuffling from the room beyond and the smell strengthened.

The old man was huddled at the far end of the room, sitting in the centre of a pale rectangle on the dark blue carpet. Coby guessed that something heavy must once have sat there, but the old man's weight barely flattened the fibres beneath him. He looked lost inside his baggy combat jacket and his face was emaciated beneath his worn baseball cap. The smell was coming from him, so strong now it seemed to thicken the air. There was the stink of alcohol too, cheap booze soaked into the old man's clothing and oozing from his pores. He was just a bum who'd made the same discovery Coby had – that the Croatoan centre was vacant property.

Coby smiled. They were alone, and this was a man no one would miss. He shouldn't, he knew he shouldn't, he had more important things to do, but it had been too long since his last. He felt the urge as a tightening in his groin and a hot flush along his neck. He had to do this. He needed it.

The old man's eyes were a little glazed, but there was still an intelligence that the drink hadn't entirely eradicated. He would know enough to fear death. Coby saw that fear in his eyes now as he read the expression on Coby's face with animal instincts that living on the streets must have honed. Animals knew when they were hunted.

"Hey, buddy," the old man rasped. "We're all friends here. Right, pal?"

"I'm nobody's friend," Coby said. He took a step closer and the old man scrambled to his feet, but he could only retreat a pace before his back was to the wall.

"It's the occupational hazard of being a sociopath," Coby said. "We can't form attachments like you ordinary people do. I just don't have it in me to care." He took another step closer, arms stretched to either side in case the old man decided to bolt. "It's not that I don't feel *anything*. They say we sociopaths don't have empathy, but that's not quite right. I understand perfectly what you're feeling. There's fear, and later there'll be pain. If I didn't understand it, I couldn't take such pleasure in it."

He wasn't sure the old man had understood everything, but he'd understood enough. A thin trickle of urine seeped from beneath the man's pant leg and the sharp smell cut through the musk of his body odour.

Coby didn't have a weapon with him, but that was OK. He liked to use his hands. The skin of the old man's neck was unpleasantly greasy and his fingers caught in the tangled ends of his beard. Beneath that Coby could feel his pulse, fast and frantic.

"Please," the old man said. "Please don't."

Then Coby's hands were too tight for him to speak and he watched that lovely red flush of blood colour the man's sickly flesh and heard the helpless sucking of his lungs for breath that wouldn't come.

At the very end, the old man began to fight. Coby always wondered at the strength of the will to live, even among those who had so little to live for. He tightened his hands, using his weight to press the old man against the wall. The frail fingers clawed at his and he knew that he'd have scratches when this was done, but what did it matter? He'd be beyond the reach of any human law very soon.

The old man's lips turned blue and Coby knew it wouldn't last much longer as the fingers clawing at his hand slackened. He felt the usual mingling of excitement and disappointment as he saw the light in the old man's eyes die. He let him go as soon as he felt the body slacken, and it flopped to the floor, drool leaking from one corner of the bloodless lips. Corpses didn't interest Coby. It was death he enjoyed, not the dead.

"Well," a voice said behind him, "You've certainly kept yourself busy, son."

He spun round, almost tripping over the old man's sprawled legs.

The speaker stood a few paces back, one arm loose at this side and the other pointing a gun at Coby's heart. It took him a moment to place the seamed face beneath the yellow-grey hair and then his gut clenched with fear. But what the hell was the detective inspector from Granger's case doing in San Francisco?

Spalding looked down at the dead old man. "I see repentance isn't high on your agenda." Coby glanced at the corpse then back at the policeman. There was no point denying it. He shrugged. "Like the song says – I am what I am."

"You should have taken us up on our offer," Spalding said. "You didn't have to suffer in hell if you served our master on earth. We haven't intervened so far because we trusted the opposition to keep their own house in order. But we can't let you do this, son."

When Coby frowned in confusion Spalding laughed and used his free hand to flick open the buttons on his cheap white shirt. There was a pentagram tattooed on his chest, the lines of it a little fuzzy beneath the wiry hair. Coby grimaced. "Of course. But why should you care? I've been doing your work quite nicely for you so far, and believe me, once I've eaten the apple, you're not going to be seeing a softer, kinder Coby."

"Not good enough. You'll be doing our master's work, but you won't be *his*. Hell doesn't want allies – only slaves."

Which was exactly why he'd turned down their offer in the first place. He felt his heart race but he made himself smile confidently as he said, "What if I've found the emancipation papers? Do you want to be a slave to them – in this life and the next? Work with me and we can both be free."

Spalding hesitated, and Coby felt a moment of hope, then the other man shook his head. "I picked my side. You haven't found the apples yet, son. I'm gonna make sure you never will."

Coby saw Spalding's eyes narrow as his finger tightened on the trigger and couldn't quite believe it was going to end like this. When he heard the volley of shots he waited for the pain, but it never came. A second later, Spalding's body tumbled to the floor, a halo of dark blood spreading around it. Coby stared at it, uncomprehending. Then he saw the curl of smoke in the corner of the room and for the first time noticed the gun turret hidden there and the camera above it which must have guided its movements. Someone had been watching. They'd seen Coby murder the old man, but they'd chosen to kill Spalding.

The flood of adrenaline left him as quickly as it had come and his legs gave out. The carpet cushioned his knees and hands as he leaned forward and emptied the contents of his stomach onto it.

When he was sure his legs would hold him, he stood and made a circuit of the room – the search he should have conducted before, if he hadn't been distracted by the lure of the helpless old man. There was nothing but one rickety table with a CD player in its centre. It was plugged in, a red light blinking beside the play button.

It was such an obvious invitation that he hesitated. But if it was a trap, his head was already inside its jaws. He pressed play.

"Hello, Coby," the recording said. The voice was distorted, clearly disguised, but he thought it was male. "We haven't been properly introduced yet, so you can call me Laughing Wolf. You've got no reason to trust me, I know, but I *did* just save your life. And I've got the thing you're looking for. Of course, neither you nor I can wield it the way we really want – and you almost got the one man who can use it killed back in Cambridge."

There was a pause, and Coby thought, *Morgan.*

"Yes," the recording said, as if it could read his thoughts. "But don't worry, the knife missed, and he's already here. And there's one other player. I'm not sure if you've considered this – no, I know you have – but possessing the power to kill the guardian and eat the apples of life is no use if you can't get into Eden in the first place. So we need a spirit traveller, someone to open the way. And she's been drawn in too. All the pieces are in place, everyone except you. Now I'm going to tell you exactly what you need to do."

CHAPTER SIXTEEN

The metal of the boxcar burned beneath the fabric of Alex's jeans, but the wind was cool on her face as the engine powered through the desert. She could see the pure straight line of the tracks ahead of her, lost in heat haze before they reached the horizon. The train's form kept shifting beneath her, one moment red and rusted crates, the next wooden and rotting. The engine sometimes ran on diesel, other times puffed out clouds of steam which dissipated into nothing as they floated past her. Sometimes the ghosts of horses galloped alongside them. The railway had been a constant in this empty landscape, and the spirit world remembered it.

Raven sat cross-legged in front of her, his back to their destination. He'd told her he'd know when they reached it and she didn't doubt him, though the desert seemed featureless to her, the cacti and scrubby bushes repeating tediously through the hour-long journey from Roseville.

The wind had dried her eyes, drawing tears that evaporated before they could ease the discomfort. "Well, this is fun," she said.

Raven's bright black eyes fixed on her and she had to look away. She couldn't pretend any longer that she didn't know what he was. She'd missed as many of her Native American History classes as she could, but she could hardly avoid learning about the trickster god who flew through so many of the stories. Legends said Raven stole the sun, moon and stars to provide people with light in their darkness, that he gave fire to mankind, his white feathers dyed black by the soot from the ember in his beak. But it was also Raven who denied humans the second life they'd once enjoyed. His motives were his own and his help was perilous.

"Why did you choose me?" she asked him.

He smiled and nodded as if he'd been expecting the question. "Why must there be a reason?"

"Because you want something from me, I know that. And the things I can do, they're powerful. It's too risky to give them to some random person and hope they'll use them right. It's crazy."

He scratched at the hair around his ear, looking troubled. "You weren't chosen, Alex. You aren't special. Well, no, of course you are. Everyone's special, aren't they?"

"You sound like my therapist."

He laughed. "Evolution designed you humans to be pattern-detecting creatures. You're made to seek out meaning, reason, sense. But the world is senseless and nothing happens for a reason."

She watched the desert for a while, the close blur of yellow sand beneath the train's wheels. The train changed but the sand remained the same. "That's bullshit. Everything happens for a reason. It's cause and effect, isn't it?"

"Ah," he said. "Determinism. Then I suppose the reason I chose you is because millennia ago the molecules of the universe happened to be arranged one way and not another."

She poked his crossed legs with her toe. "You're a pain in my ass, you know that?"

He grinned and she realised that for a moment she'd been treating him as if he was just another person – an irritating one. And maybe that was what he wanted. But she refused to forget what he really was. And she knew he still hadn't answered her question.

"That's a shame," he said. "No more time to chat. We're here."

She scanned the landscape and saw nothing except more sand and yet more cacti. He nodded to her left and when she squinted into the distance she thought she could make out the dark blots of buildings. If it was a town it wasn't a very large one. The train showed no signs of slowing and there was no station along the ruler-straight track ahead.

"Jump," Raven said, pulling her to her feet.

She leaned against the sudden push of the wind. "Are you insane?"

He grinned at her and she guessed that in some sense he was. She resisted only a little as he tugged on her hand. And then they were both flying through the air and for a moment it was exhilarating. She closed her eyes and braced for the shock of impact.

It came far more softly than she'd expected. Her legs folded under her and for a moment she found herself looking into a beak as long as her body and the bright black eye larger than her head. Then she blinked and it was just Raven, smiling and offering her a hand to get up.

Her fingers shook in his and she let go as soon as she was standing. The rumble of the train faded into nothing as it raced to the horizon. In its absence she heard the sounds of the desert, short sharp chirps of birdsong and the distant howling of some larger animal. And there was another sound she'd only recently learned to recognise: the abrupt *pop* of gunfire.

She glanced at Raven. "They're not shooting at me, right?"

He grinned. "Well, not yet."

It didn't surprise her when he guided them towards the sound of the guns. He walked a little ahead of her and she entertained herself by walking in his footsteps, her own smaller imprints lost within his. She had a sudden, vivid memory of a day on the beach when she was six or seven and she'd done the same thing walking in the sand behind her father.

As they drew nearer, she saw that the dark blots were houses, though they looked derelict. There was movement around them, she estimated at least fifty people, but she didn't think they'd been spotted. It was possible she was still cloaked within the spirit world. She was finding it harder and harder to tell.

When they were close enough to the town to see individual faces, Alex slowed to a stop. "If PD's here, is he a prisoner?"

Raven wobbled a hand in the air. "Yes and no." At her glare, he added, "Not in the way you mean."

As if they were as dissatisfied with his answer as Alex, she heard the animals howl again, high-pitched and desperate. A curt volley of barks followed, nearer this time. Her eyes swept the desert, but they passed over the creature twice before she picked out its shape from the loose rocks around it. It was mottled brown, dog-like but not a dog.

"Brother coyote," Raven said.

The creature slunk closer, belly low to the ground. The hairs on its ruff stood on end and she could see a subvocal growl shaking its jowls. A second later, another coyote appeared behind it, and then a third and fourth.

Distantly, Alex registered that the gunfire had stopped, but she couldn't tear her gaze away from the creatures. There were more of them now, a semi-circle of fur and bared teeth around her. She raised her hands in a gesture of surrender that she knew they wouldn't understand.

"Raven?" she said.

There was no reply. The thought of looking away from the threat of the coyotes made her breath catch in her throat but she braced herself and turned.

Raven was gone. And when she turned back to the animals, they were another pace nearer. She thought she could feel their breath on her skin, hotter than the desert wind. She could certainly smell it, rank with decayed meat. She took a step back and their eyes followed. She guessed the nearest was the pack leader. He was a little larger than the others and there was intelligence in his expression as he studied her.

"Are you really here?" she asked him, her voice husky with fear. "Or am I there?"

The coyote's head cocked as if he was listening. His eyes locked with hers as she remembered once reading that an animal's never would. Though they were the amber-yellow of a beast's, she felt a shock of recognition as she looked into them. She *knew* this creature.

The coyote's head suddenly turned, hearing keener than hers, responding to the footsteps she registered a moment later. The man running towards her had a gun drawn and she flinched before she realised it wasn't aimed at her.

She moved before she made the conscious decision to do it, flinging herself towards the man and in front of the coyotes. For a second she found herself staring down the muzzle of his weapon and he cursed and jerked his arm as his finger tightened on the trigger. A puff of dirt and sharp fragments of rock exploded to her left as her ears rang with the gunshot.

"Please don't shoot them," she said.

Other men joined the first. She could smell their sweat, ranker than the coyote's breath. She kept her eyes focused on the young black man who'd fired the shot as he frowned down at her. There was a softness about his face that suggested baby fat only recently shed. She thought he was probably younger than her.

"What the hell do you think you're doing?" he said. His accent was British, not at all what she'd expected.

"And who the heck are you?" the man at his left shoulder asked. He was opposite to the shooter in every way: massive, white, bearded, forty-something. He wore only combat trousers and a sleeveless khaki T-shirt and she could see swastikas tattooed on his arms. It was hard to imagine he and the younger man were friends, but they stood shoulder to shoulder and looked at her with the same hostile expressions. The big white man had a fox's spirit in him, but behind the younger black man's face she saw nothing at all. It made her uneasy and she realised that she was beginning to depend on the insights the other world gave her.

The coyotes had fallen back, away from the men and their guns, but their eyes were still on her. And their leader... The face that overlaid his long muzzle and sharp ears was human. It was impossible, but it was PD's.

The young man lowered his gun. "I'm sorry, I thought they were attacking you. I didn't realise they were your pets."

She choked out a laugh at that, which made him frown. "They're not pets. They're..." But what could she say that these people would believe?

"Lady, you still haven't told us what you're doing here," the bigger man said. "Where's your car? Ain't no way you walked."

She laughed again. "I took the train."

He stepped closer, enveloping her in his stale body odour. There was a hesitancy about his movements, the sense of something held back. She suspected that if she'd been a man, she'd already be on the ground.

"I'm sorry," she said. "I don't mean to jerk you around. I really did ride the train – the freight train. It went by about half an hour back."

"I saw it," the other man said. He held out his hand and after a second she reached out and shook it. "I'm Morgan."

She nodded. "Alex."

The older man stared at her for a long, unfriendly moment before saying, "Jimmy."

She tugged her hand to release it from Morgan's, but his grip didn't loosen and he shifted his fingers until they circled her wrist. "No one jumps a train in the middle of the desert for no reason. Tell us what you're doing here. Last chance." He hadn't holstered his gun, though he wasn't yet pointing it at her.

She didn't know who these people were, but they were too well armed and too twitchy to be up to any good. And though they didn't seem to be Croatoans, she had no guarantee they weren't allied to the cult. She could leave, slip into the spirit world and disappear like mist. But Raven had brought her here for a reason. Whatever had happened to PD, she suspected these people were somehow connected. Leaving now would be taking the coward's way out, and she'd done that once already.

She looked at Morgan, into his eyes, searching for the spirit truth behind his mundane face.

There was nothing, only a guarded expression and a light sheen of sweat on his smooth skin. "How about you tell me who *you* are first?" she said.

He quirked a smile, eyes cutting down to the gun in his hand. "Yeah, but you're not going to shoot me in cold blood, are you?"

He flinched, as if she'd hit some kind of nerve. "I wouldn't bet my life on it."

She took a breath and took a gamble. "Look, I don't know what you guys are up to and I really don't care. I'm here for the coyotes, that's all."

"OK," Morgan said. "Why?"

She wished she could ask Raven for the advice she usually scorned. But he wasn't there and all she could do was what he might have done – answer with a truth that could be understood as a lie. "Because they're friends of mine."

Morgan nodded. "You're part of this, aren't you? I don't know how, or which side you're on, but you're a soldier in the war."

She meant to tell him she had no idea what he was talking about, until she remembered something Raven had told her. "Actually, I think I'm a conscientious objector."

"Impossible," a new voice said. The man was olive-skinned and dark-eyed with a hawkish nose and an unfriendly expression. Then she saw what lay behind the human mask: fire and wings.

She stumbled away from him and to her knees, holding a hand in front of her face to shield her from the light. It shone through her fingers, a red glow around the black shadow of her bones.

Abruptly, the light blinked out and when she lowered her hand she was looking at an ordinary Middle Eastern man.

Morgan reached down to help her to her feet as he looked at the newcomer. "Lahav, she saw you, didn't she? The real you, I mean. What's going on?"

"She's a CIA agent," Lahav said. "And she's a spirit traveller." The men behind and around him tensed and suddenly a lot more guns were pointing in her direction. Lahav scowled at the men, and the weapons dropped – all except Morgan's. "Is she on our side?" he asked.

"Maybe if I knew what your side was, I could tell you," Alex said.

They brought her to the least derelict of the buildings in the ruined town. It had been turned into a church, a crude wooden cross nailed to the back wall. *Angels and demons*, Raven said, and she'd thought he was speaking metaphorically. But if these people were to be believed – this soldier of the Hermetic Division and the Mossad agent with the winged spirit living inside him – it was literal truth too. There *was* a war being fought, and she'd stumbled into the middle of it.

"I'm not on any side," she told them. "My... bosses at the CIA didn't talk about any of this. I'm not even sure they know."

Morgan eased back on the creaky pew beside her. "They employ Belle. They've got to have an idea."

Lahav shook his head. "They choose ignorance, as they once chose not to ask very much about Saddam Hussein's prisons or his palaces or the unmarked Kurdish graves while he kept the Ayatollah in check. They use what's useful to them and they never ask what it means or what is the true price."

"So why *are* you here?" Morgan asked her. "What's the CIA's interest in this?"

Alex looked up, through the gaps in the roof to the pure blue sky above. These people weren't her enemies and they could be allies. "I'm not with the CIA, not any more. The Croatoans kidnapped my partner and I need to get him back."

"Then our interests align," Lahav said. "They have something of ours, too."

Morgan darted a surprised look at the other man but Lahav's inexpressive face gave nothing away.

"I showed you mine..." Alex said.

Morgan hesitated a moment, then sighed. "It's called a shofar," he said.

*   *   *

When he'd finished, Alex felt a nauseous churning in her stomach. The coyotes howled a question in the desert and she finally had all the information she needed to answer it, but she didn't know if the answer would do them any good. She stood, rattling the wooden pew.

"I think we're both after the same thing," she said. "It divides spirits from bodies, right? Jesus. Jesus, they're clever."

"The Croatoans?" Lahav asked.

She nodded. "The bastards. They tell all their young, pretty members they can teach them to spirit travel – and I guess it's even true. But they tell the old, rich members something else entirely. No wonder the cult got so much money and power so quickly. Who wouldn't pay everything they had to live forever?" She thought about Maria, who from one day to the next seemed to become a different person. And then she thought about James Marriott, who'd loved his dying wife so much, the wife whose suffering had infused the bones of their house. Suffering, but not death. Because she hadn't died. Of course she hadn't. She'd just... moved.

Lahav frowned. "The shofar can clear the path to Eden, but it hasn't happened. I would know."

Alex laughed, giddy with a sort of horrified excitement. "That's because you're thinking of bodily immortality, aren't you? But the body isn't really what matters – it's the spirit. The spirit can live forever if it can find new young bodies to house it. The only thing you need to do is make sure they're vacant."

"Christ, I get it," Morgan said. "They use the shofar to drive out the spirits of their young recruits and then the new spirits get to move in."

"And the old cultists leave their money to the young, because they've leaving it to themselves. It's perfect. Murder with no bodies, a crime that'll never be investigated."

Morgan chewed his lip, eyes downcast as he thought. "But why use the shofar to get that sort of immortality, when you can use it to get the actual apples from Eden, the real thing?"

Lahav nodded. "A good question, but if we get the shofar it won't matter. I can hide it, and there will be no more immortality of any sort."

"*After* we've used it," Alex said.

Lahav glared at her, and for a moment she saw the fire in his eyes, bright and uncompromising. But she stared him out. "The souls they drive out aren't destroyed," she said. "I guess... I don't know. They're drawn to the nearest thing they can inhabit."

"The coyotes," Morgan said. "Your partner as well, right?"

She nodded as Lahav shook his head. "No," he said. "These people are lost. Sad, but not important. The shofar is far too dangerous to leave in the world a moment longer than we must. The murderer, Coby, is still out there, hunting it. He must not get it."

Her neck prickled with the knowledge of all the guns around her, and the hostility of the men holding them. "A few moments won't hurt. There's a reason we were brought together – like you said, Morgan, it can't be coincidence. Help me and I'll help you."

Lahav looked round at the men with their ragged beards and khaki T-shirts and the hair-trigger violence in their eyes. "I don't think we need your help."

Alex smiled. "Did I mention that I can walk through walls?"

"I don't like it," Jimmy said. His hands moved fluidly over his weapon as he spoke, disassembling, checking, reassembling; the practised, instinctive motions of a soldier before battle. His men were doing the same, strapping ammo belts around their chests, sheathing knives at their waists and ankles.

Morgan patted the SIG Sauer in its holster on his hip, but didn't take it out. He didn't think steel would win the battle they were heading for.

"She's government," Jimmy said. "And she's..." He shook his head, denying what he wanted to say.

"Irritating as fuck?" Morgan suggested.

Jimmy shot him a quelling look. "She ain't on our side. Said so herself – there ain't no damn conscientious objectors in this war."

"If you're not with us you're against us," Morgan said.

Jimmy nodded and clapped a hand on Morgan's back. Morgan felt a warm swell of something in his chest at the other man's casual inclusion of him in an *us* that would stand against all of them. But he didn't share Jimmy's distrust of the blonde. He felt... a kinship with her, he supposed. It was clear she'd broken ranks with the CIA. She was another stray piece on the chess board, neither black nor white.

A reverent silence descended on the room as Lahav entered it. He carried no gun, but then he hardly needed to. *The white bishop*, Morgan thought. The other man's eyes met his, assessing and cold. There was no fellowship in them. Lahav knew Morgan wasn't on his side, but maybe if Morgan did this thing for him, he could change that. He could earn a place in the light.

"What do you say?" Jimmy asked the Israeli. "Can we trust her?"

"We can use her," Lahav said. "Maybe she opens a way through without fighting, but we must be ready to fight. We must allow Morgan to reach the shofar. Don't try to take it for yourself – leave it to him."

"Me? Why?"

Lahav's eyes bored through him. "The shofar protects itself. If you are too close when it's used, it drives your soul from your body. But you, Morgan... You have nothing to lose. For you alone the Shofar Hagadol is safe."

Because I have no soul, Morgan thought. *That's* why Lahav needed him, and also why he let Lahav use him. How very convenient for the Israeli. "OK," he said. "Let's do it."

Alex felt eyes on her as she walked from the ghost town into the desert. The sun was heading towards its zenith and it burned intolerably above her, scorching the vulnerable skin of her shoulders even through her blouse. Her face had already reddened. She could feel the tight glow in her cheeks.

When she'd walked far enough away that the buildings' outlines were blurred by heat haze, the coyotes surrounded her, tongues lolling and too-human eyes fixed on her. They weren't quite hostile, but they weren't friendly either. She wondered how much they understood, how much of the people they used to be remained. In the spirit world their faces had always been animal, but that was metaphor, not reality. There had been a human intelligence shining from their eyes. Now the light behind them was wilder and more bestial. *We're shaped by the bodies we inhabit,* she thought, *and they're being changed by theirs.*

She dropped to her knees and one of the creatures sloped forward to stand nose to nose with her. It was PD, but his face was altered too. His teeth were a little too long, his nose a little too sharp and his eyes seemed dazed. She understood that if she couldn't find the body he belonged in soon, he'd become the beast he now only resembled.

"I don't know if you can understand me," she said. "But I think I can help you. I know something that can put you back in your body. I just have to find it – and your body. Jesus, this is the freakiest conversation I've ever had. Look, PD, I need you to follow me. You have to be close if we find the shofar. I don't think these guys are going to let me use it for long. Just... be ready, and stay safe."

The coyote sat as she stood and she couldn't be sure he'd understood her. She had little expectation any of this would work. She didn't trust the people she found herself working with, and the Croatoans outnumbered them and must be expecting them – or her, at least. But she'd try, and that would be enough to ease her guilt. It would have to be.

She turned away and didn't look back as she returned to the ghost town. The men were ready when she reached them. Morgan pressed a holstered gun into her hand. Her fingers fumbled to fasten the leather straps across her shoulder as she eased into the jeep beside him, and then the engine turned and caught and it was too late to wonder if she was doing the right thing.

Jimmy drove them, arm hanging through the open window. Dust settled on his skin and blurred the black tattoos that crawled across it. Beside her, Morgan was still and silent as he gazed at the empty desert. His mouth was tight and she wondered if it was the coming combat he was afraid of.

It scared the shit out of her, she knew that. She looked at her gun and fiddled with the safety, flicking it on and off. She wondered if she'd actually be able to fire it – if she could really point it at another human being.

She looked back up to find Morgan staring at her. "You know how to use that?" he asked.

"I've been taught."

He nodded and looked back out of the window. She studied his face, his one face, and wondered what it meant that the spirit world could show her nothing about him. It didn't surprise her the British had an equivalent of the CIA's Bureau of Counter-Rational Warfare, this Hermetic Division. But the CIA had recruited her and PD for very specific reasons. What was it about Morgan that made him useful to MI6?

They were still in empty desert when the jeeps halted. Morgan vaulted over the side, then walked round to open her door for her.

"I can do that myself," she said. "I've got hands."

"They're shaking," he told her.

She was surprised to see it was true. Fine tremors shivered her skin.

"Stay behind me," he said. "You're not here to fight. Just... do whatever it is you do."

"Yeah. Whatever it is." She knew she could leave them behind here and walk through the world of spirit. But the CIA had found a way to see her even in that place, and she couldn't be sure the Croatoans didn't know it too. She needed these people and their guns to keep the cultists occupied.

"I'm coming with you," Morgan said.

She frowned at him. "Into the spirit world? You can't – I don't know how to take someone else through."

"Then you'd better figure it out. You can't take the shofar without me."

"Don't you trust me?"

He shrugged. "Listen, the shofar's in the real world. So I'm guessing you'll need to come into the real world to get it. As soon as you do, someone can use it against you. You're not safe from it."

She studied him. "And you are?"

"Yeah. I am."

They walked a little further over the sand and rocks, the fierce sunlight pushing down on their heads. After a while, Alex realised the other men had disappeared, faded into the desert like mirages.

"They're circling," Morgan told her. "They'll create a diversion while you take me in."

A few more paces and he dropped to his knees and then his stomach, his upper body supported on his forearms. He looked at her until she dropped to the ground beside him. Small stones pressed into her skin through her thin blouse and she felt the prickle of cacti. When Morgan began easing himself forward on his stomach, using his elbows for leverage, she sighed and did the same.

Her blouse tore after only a few yards and she couldn't tell if the liquid she could feel trickling into her belly button was blood or sweat. It was definitely sweat trickling into her eyes, the salt stinging them till she could barely see anything beyond the beige blur of the sand and Morgan's darker form ahead of her.

"Should have paid attention to all those courses we sent you on, kid," she imagined PD saying. *"Should have been ready."*

But she wasn't and she didn't know how long she could keep this up. She heaved herself forward and grabbed hold of Morgan's leg. It tensed against her with a strength she hadn't expected.

"I can't do this," she told him. "I'll be dead before I get there."

"I thought you were CIA."

"There was a reason I left."

He sighed. "It's not much further, and–" He lifted his head as the distant sound of gunfire floated through the clear desert air. "OK, once the guards have moved we make a run for it."

"But what if they don't all go?"

"They won't. That's why we've got guns."

He wriggled back to her athletically. She could smell his sweat, clean and sharp unlike the stale odour of the other men. And she could see the hard muscles in his arms, but there was a softness in his eyes when he looked at her. "It's good to be afraid," he said. "Keeps you safe."

"Running straight at an encampment of armed fanatics is safe?"

His grin was unexpected and charming. "Well... saf*er*."

Then he was jerking her to her feet and forward before she'd had time to process that it had begun.

The fence was closer than she'd realised, ten feet or more of steel mesh topped by razor wire. She could see no guards on it, only a startlingly green lawn surrounding a sprawling building a hundred feet behind. Her legs burned as she ran and the air grated against her lungs as she gasped for breath.

Any minute now, she thought, they'll come back with their guns and we're right out in the open. Beside her, Morgan seemed barely winded. They'd be at the fence in five seconds, four, and he showed no signs of slowing and she had no idea if she could slip herself back into the spirit world, let alone whether she could take Morgan with her.

Two seconds and she squinted her eyes and grabbed for the spirit world with her mind and for Morgan's hand with hers. His skin was momentarily warm against hers and then he'd wrenched it loose and he was swarming over the fence with a speed and strength that made it look effortless. She could only run straight on, hoping she'd held onto at least one of the things she'd grasped for.

For a terrible moment she felt the wire as it cut across her eyelids. But the searing pain was an illusion and it was gone when she broke through to the other side, running a few more paces until momentum and exhaustion tumbled her to her knees on the grass of the Croatoan compound.

She looked over her shoulder to see Morgan clambering down the fence. He was moving a little more slowly as he dropped the last five feet and blood dripped down his face and arms from a collection of deep scratches.

He paused a moment when he saw her, then held out a hand and hauled her to her feet. "You weren't kidding. Reckon you can take me with you next time?"

She looked at his blunt fingernails resting against the pulse point in her wrist and then at his stubbornly singular face. "I don't know. I'll try."

"OK. Odds are they've got cameras pointing out here even if the guards are gone. We need to get into the building before they send reinforcements."

He released her hand as he jogged towards the building. She could hear the gunfire more clearly now and voices shouting. Screaming, too. "Do we know where this shofar thing is?" she gasped as she ran beside him.

He shrugged.

"Do we even know for sure it's here?"

"Lahav seemed pretty certain."

"And you trust him?" she asked.

"You saw what he is, didn't you?"

Angels and demons, Raven had said disparagingly, as if he didn't see very much difference between them. "That's not an answer," she said.

"I *have* to trust him."

Spurts of gunfire continued to sound as they reached the building but no Croatoans appeared. The place was modern; she doubted it had been built more than a decade ago. It was gossamer-thin in the spirit world, just a spiderweb of stucco. When she pressed her hand against the wall it moved through – but only a short way. There was... *something* blocking her, curlicues of air that seemed to have substance. And beneath them she could see wooden cross slats that were more than just supports for the stuccoed surface.

Morgan raised an eyebrow when she looked at him. "Not happening?"

"I can't break through. I think this place was built by someone who knew about people like me – and knew how to stop us."

She glanced down in surprise when Morgan touched her hip, but he was just reaching for her holster. He eased the gun out and pressed it into her hand, curling her fingers around the grip. "Then we're gonna have to do this the old-fashioned way."

The gun felt too loose in her hand, its textured grip slipping against her sweaty palm. "I, uh, can't really shoot straight."

He gave her another of his quick smiles. "I guessed. I'll be using single aimed shots, you keep up suppressing fire if we need it. It keeps them from running towards us – doesn't need to be accurate. Got it?"

"Yeah."

"Just try not to shoot me in the back."

He meant it as a joke and she managed a smile, but she thought of PD, whom she'd certainly stabbed in the back.

"Lahav's intel says there's a side door to our left," he said. "We'll make for that. Once we're inside... I suppose we'll head for the path of most resistance."

"*Most* resistance?"

"The shofar's what this is all about. Stands to reason it'll be heavily guarded, right?"

"Right," she croaked.

He nodded, then put his back to the building and crab-walked left. Alex followed him, feeling the press against her own back of something that wasn't quite material. It prickled her shoulder blades and she had to fight to keep from stepping away.

They were twenty feet from the corner when she heard the crunch of feet against gravel and Morgan dropped to one knee in front of her. She was still gawping stupidly at him as the guard appeared. His face, young and not too bright, was turned a little to their left. And then her ears rang with a single shot and there was a hole where his nose had been and a shower of red spray that fell to the ground seconds after his body.

She looked at Morgan, hands rock-steady on the gun he'd just fired – and fired again as a second figure careened round the corner and straight into the path of his bullet.

"Oh," she said. She wrapped an arm around her stomach and hoped she wasn't going to empty it onto the sand beside Morgan's feet.

Morgan's attention remained focused ahead of them. He took one breath, another – and when no further figures appeared he rose fluidly to his feet and continued to ease himself forward, as if he hadn't just killed two men in a matter of seconds. As if their corpses weren't lying there in the blazing sun, flies already buzzing to settle in the pools of blood around them.

"Keep an eye behind us," he said without looking at her.

She nodded jerkily. There was no one there and she didn't know what she would have done if there had been. She didn't think she could fire her gun – not now she'd seen what would happen if she actually hit her target.

She didn't realise Morgan had stopped until her shoulder jogged his and she felt his hand against her mouth, her breath humid beneath his palm. His breath tickled her ear as he whispered, "They'll be waiting." He nodded at the corner of the building, now only a pace away. "They know we're here. I'm gonna have to go for it, but I need you to keep them occupied."

She felt a rush of fear so intense it made her light-headed. The corpses of the two men he'd killed were only feet away and she could smell the blood and something fouler. One of them must have soiled himself as he died, no dignity in it.

Morgan studied her face. "Fire blind," he said. "Put your hand round the corner and pull the trigger. I don't need you to kill them, just distract them."

"OK. I can do that."

"Ready?"

She nodded and he held up three fingers. He clenched one back into a fist, then a second – and then he launched himself forward into a long low roll.

The first volley of gunfire shocked her into motion. Her hand shook so hard as she pushed it round the side of the building that she could barely squeeze the trigger. But she did and the gun recoiled brutally, almost snapping her wrist until she remembered to bring up her other hand to support it.

There were screams mixed in with the gunfire and shouts of rage. The building was immovable against her side, but the spirit world was still there, one with the timeless desert. She could slip into it and away and she wouldn't have to kill or be killed.

"Now!" Morgan shouted.

She froze, looking towards the horizon. PD's body might be here, it might not. The shofar might be found, or it might be far away. She was risking so much for a very small chance of success.

"Alex, move it!" Morgan roared.

She kept squeezing the trigger as she threw herself round the corner, barely registering that it was clicking on empty. Her legs kicked something soft and she leapt over it instinctively before she realised it was a body. Not even a corpse. The man's pleading eyes met hers as his hands clasped over a stomach that had been ripped open, his guts coiling into the sand around him.

"Got too close. I had to knife him," Morgan said.

She lost it, doubling over to heave her lunch onto the sand.

She felt Morgan's hand rubbing soothing circles against her back. She couldn't look at him. She looked around instead, at the bodies littering the ground. There were six of them, no seven. She wondered if any of the bullet holes she could see in chests and heads and legs had been put there by her.

"OK," Morgan said. "We gotta move."

She nodded, swallowing the burn of bile in her throat. The door a was third of the way along the wall. It hung half open, a body wedged into the gap between wood and frame. Morgan grabbed one of the limp arms then gestured at her to take the other. The flesh was still warm beneath her fingers and she had to look away as the head flopped on the loose neck and she had a brief glimpse of a dark-skinned, round-cheeked face.

As soon as they were inside, Morgan ran, zig-zagging through a seemingly endless network of corridors. She was glad to let him, happy to have him take charge, take responsibility.

Without warning, he wrenched open a door and pulled her inside, leaving it open a crack so he could peer at the corridor behind. She could hear nothing but the harsh rasp of her breathing and the more controlled *hush* of his. "Where are we?" she asked.

He shrugged and she felt the tension and fear of the last half hour transmute into a sudden, disproportionate rage. "Then why the fuck did we fight so hard to get here?"

"Had to get away from the entrance. Scene of the crime, know what I mean?"

The *crime*. Yeah, that's what it felt like. She swallowed and looked away, though she felt his eyes on her for a long moment. She turned her face away when he touched her cheek with a tentative finger.

"You did all right," he said. "But if it's any consolation, you're the worst fucking shot I've ever seen. I killed those men, not you."

"But you killed them *for* me."

He shrugged again and this time she let it pass. She didn't know what she expected him to say, anyway. This was his job.

"So what now?" she asked.

"You came because you can walk through walls, right? But you can't do that here and you sure as hell can't shoot a gun. You're not gonna be much help to me. Why not stay here and let me go after the shofar?"

"And let you destroy it without giving me a chance to use it?"

"Fine," he snapped. "Just keep your head down."

She sighed. "No. I'm sorry, you go ahead. Will you come back and find me when you're done?"

He nodded, turned to the door, then turned back again. "I think you're right – Lahav doesn't want you to use the shofar. But it's me who's getting it and I will."

She smiled at him and he smiled back. Then he slipped through the door and was gone.

There was a small single bed in the corner of the room. She sank down on it, the hard mattress giving only a little beneath her but the white cotton sheets releasing the comforting smell of fresh laundry. She wondered whose room it was. Had Maria spent her last night as herself in a room like this?

"As a matter of fact, yes," Raven said.

He leant against the door, legs crossed at the ankle.

"You knew," she said. "Why the hell didn't you just tell me?"

"I could have, I suppose. Then I imagine you would have felt obliged to come here yourself, all guns blazing. Except for the fact that you didn't have a gun. Or any back-up. And then they would have captured you – or just shot you. No, I think they would have taken you prisoner. And then they might have tortured–"

"Jesus – stop!"

He grinned at her, unrepentant.

Despite herself, she felt better for his presence. She could still hear the muffled sound of gunfire and she couldn't tell if it was approaching or receding. She rested her elbows on her knees and her chin on her fists. "Morgan's got no spirit self," she told Raven. "What does that mean?"

"That's a good question."

"Are you going to answer it?"

"Nope."

"Right." She lowered her head until it was resting between her palms. "Are you *my* spirit self?"

"Ha! Now that's a *very* good question. But you know the answer – you know who I am."

"Then who am I? You said you didn't choose me, but that could just mean I was already chosen."

He cocked his head. "Do you worry about where you'll go to when you die?"

Alex blinked, unprepared for the question and not sure how to answer it. The only church service she'd ever attended was midnight mass. She'd never worried about heaven and hell because she'd never believed in them. And now... she hadn't taken the time to think through what the things Morgan told her really meant.

Where was she going when she died? She hadn't been a terrible person but then she hadn't been a terribly good one either. She thought about Lahav, the man who contained a being inside him straight out of the Bible. *I have to trust him*, Morgan had said, and she thought she understood why: because his very existence proved the promise of heaven and the threat of hell real. But Raven existed too, and he wasn't a part of Lahav's book.

"When I die, I want to go where you are," she told him. "I think I belong there – in the spirit realm."

"You do," he said. "And *that's* why I came to you."

"OK. I guess I can live with that."

"That's the plan."

She studied him, the face which was so expressive and yet gave so little away. He was still here, and she knew that meant something. "There's something else I've got to do, isn't there?"

"The only thing you have to do is the thing that you do."

"I see the spirit world, but I can't see much here – just those walls."

"Then look at them and tell me what you see."

She blinked her eyes closed on the mundane world and opened them again on the other. The inner walls were like the outer with complex woodwork inside them, spirals and radiating lines that seemed breakable but held fast against her hand when she pushed against them.

"What do you see?" he asked. "What does it look like?"

She tried to see what he wanted her to, but there was nothing beyond the wood, the delicate swirls almost like a spider's web.

Suddenly, she understood what he meant. She sprinted through the door, careless of the noise it made as it slammed behind her.

CHAPTER SEVENTEEN

Coby handled the hire car awkwardly, his left hand reaching for a gear stick that wasn't there and his foot tapping at a nonexistent clutch pedal. He'd never been to the Mojave when he lived in America and he found that he liked its stark simplicity. It was a land that could kill the careless.

Was he being careless, though, following a stranger's instructions? Whoever left the recording *had* saved his life. And he was sure the Croatoans had the shofar. They had it, but he didn't think they understood how it could be used. He had something to offer them, and he suspected they knew it. If they didn't... He felt the lump of the Glock 9mm holstered under his arm.

As it always did, the thought of killing sped his heart and caused a warmth in his groin. He indulged himself in memories of the old man he'd strangled, then put the fantasy away. He wasn't an animal. The things that gave him pleasure didn't control him.

The road that led to the Croatoan centre was narrow, only one lane wide. It dead-ended outside the fenced perimeter of the compound. One way in, one way out and it would be easy to block it.

The fence was high and razor-wired, clearly intended for more than show. The gate was sturdier still with huts for security guards to either side of it. But as he cruised closer he saw that it had been forced open, the metal buckled by some strong force.

He stopped the car and drew his gun, debating simply reversing and leaving.

But the shofar might be here. He *had* to find out.

He kept his gun in his hand as he slipped out of the car into the parched desert air. As soon as he was clear of the air-conditioned interior he smelt blood. His gut clenched, half in pleasure and half in fear, but he'd made a decision now. He would go on.

The first body was only a few feet inside the fence. A high-calibre weapon had taken him out, the exit wound a bloody mess in his back, white ribs and torn muscle glistening in the midday sun. There were a dozen or more bodies in the fifty yards between the fence and the stuccoed building, but after Coby had watched in silence for a long minute he was sure they were all dead.

He knelt beside one and flipped him over. Blood oozed over his fingers and he tried to wipe them clean on the man's own khaki T-shirt, but the fluid was too tacky, sticking to his skin like glue. He looked at it a moment, red against white. Most of his recent kills had been bloodless. He'd forgotten how much he liked to see his hands this way.

He shifted his attention from his own hand to the dead man's face. It was broad and wildly bearded, the eyes a little too small so that it seemed piggish, not fully human. There was a swastika tattoo on his neck and SS lightning bolts on his arms beneath the ragged sleeve of his T-shirt.

The Croatoans weren't neo-Nazis, or at least that wasn't their public face. Coby guessed this man must have been part of a group attacking the cult. He examined a few more bodies, finding one more like the first – bearded, over-muscled and heavily-tattooed – and the rest young and clean-cut.

So. The neo-Nazis seemed to have got the best of the fight out here. The Croatoans had been foolish to step outside when they had a defended position within their own building. Coby wondered what had driven them to do it.

Gravel crunched beneath his sneakers as he walked towards the building. The door was ahead of him, open onto gloom, but he went to the left of it, towards the floor-to-ceiling windows which took up a large section of the wall. The glass was crazed in places but unbroken, almost certainly bullet-proof. Coby's heart sped as he walked, knowing how exposed he was to anyone inside. But bullet-proof glass worked both ways.

The windows reflected the desert back at him as he approached, and his own face, pale beneath his brown hair. The gun was a blur of darkness in his hand. When he was only inches away from the glass he cupped his hand over his eyes and peered in.

He guessed the place was a canteen of some sort. Tables were ranged at one end in front of a series of silver serving hatches, and cushions lay on the floor in rings. Plates were scattered about, as if the residents had been interrupted in the middle of their meal.

There were bodies scattered over the floor, too. The pools of blood looked black in the gloom. Coby saw that one of the bodies was twitching, some life still left in it. Not for long, though. The man's left hand dangled from the wrist by a thread – a knife wound, probably. And there was another cut beneath his ribs. It must have missed his heart, but it had caught something else essential, the liver or a kidney. It would be a painful death.

It took Coby a moment to register the one living figure in the room. The man stood by the door, more still than the dying man on the floor. He was looking straight at Coby and when their eyes met he smiled and beckoned before turning and leaving the room.

Coby stared at the slaughter for a moment longer then turned and headed for the door. The man had been expecting Coby and whatever he wanted to say, Coby wanted to hear.

He was waiting for Coby in the hallway just inside the front door. "Shaman," the man said. "It's a miracle."

Coby frowned as the stranger bowed to him. If there was a trick here, it escaped him. The man seemed to know him, though Coby was sure he'd never seen him before in his life.

Was it possible that, by some bizarre coincidence, he resembled the cult's leader?

"Stand," he said, injecting an authority he didn't feel into his voice.

The man squared his shoulders like a soldier before his commanding officer. He was young and startlingly handsome with thick black hair and crystalline blue eyes. But there was something... wrong about his face. The animal part of him sensed it and it prickled the skin on the back of his neck.

"The shofar," Coby said. "Do you know where it is?"

"Of course." The man looked puzzled, as if Coby wasn't behaving quite the way he expected.

"I need you to bring me to the shofar," Coby said, trying for a gentler tone. "It's very important."

The man nodded. "Yes, we organised it the way you asked. There's been a high... price." He looked to his left, through a doorway that led to the canteen and the corpses on its floor. "But they – well, they're replaceable We've funnelled the intruders through the building. They're trapped – but they're near the shofar. It seemed... but those were your orders."

"I had my reasons," Coby said, unable to imagine what they were.

Morgan stood in the doorway to a small bedroom. The room was windowless, ensuring no threat behind him. He had line of sight to the cross-corridor ahead, and he'd cleared the way back of all hostiles.

It was a perfect defensive position, but moving forward meant exposing himself to fire from an unknown number of enemies. He could feel his heart racing and his blood surging. He'd long ago learnt to find a kind of pleasure in the risk. Soldiers like him were gamblers and it was the possibility of losing which made the game worth playing.

Which didn't mean he *wanted* to die. He held himself still, gun braced and aimed at the corner where his last assailant had disappeared with a yell of pain after Morgan winged him.

Nothing. Morgan let the seconds stretch into minutes, aware of how waiting could wear on a person during combat. The fearful anticipation of action would eventually turn into a gnawing compulsion to do something *right now*. Inexperienced fighters could often be lured out of secure positions by that impulse.

After ten minutes of waiting, his own patience had been exhausted. He eased out of the door, footsteps silent on the tile floor. He slowed and pressed his back to the wall as he neared the corner. Then he listened, extending all his senses like an animal. But he still heard nothing, not even the betraying whisper of breath.

He counted one heartbeat, then two – then leapt and rolled, bringing his gun to bear as he rose.

There was nobody. He could see blood, tacky drops drying on the ochre tiles. If the Croatoans truly meant to stop him, they'd have set up their own defensive position here. He should have been unable to move on without exposing himself to their fire. But they weren't here. They *wanted* him to follow – to lead him onward, as they had been since the moment he first crossed the fence.

"Fuck!" he said, already running back. He leapt over the corpses of the men he'd killed, pawns someone had sacrificed in a larger game. There was a door at the end of the corridor and he rammed his shoulder against it, sucking in a breath at the pain.

It held fast. He grunted, angry but not surprised, then stepped back to put a bullet through the lock. It shot through clean, but when he pressed against the door again, it failed to shift. A kick jarred his knee but achieved nothing. The way back had been barred.

He had no choice. He had to go the only way they'd left open for him: forward, into the jaws of the trap.

Alex followed a trail of corpses. Her gun trembled in her hand and a distant shot caused her finger to tighten reflexively on the trigger and put a bullet in the floor only inches from her foot. She yelped and holstered her weapon.

The spiderweb runes in the walls were all around her. If she stared at them too long, she began to feel their power drawing her in. This whole building was a trap designed for a spirit traveller, and she wondered why it had been built that way, when Hammond claimed she was the only spirit traveller in the country. Had the place been designed specifically for *her*? But it wasn't new, or not entirely – it had to be a few years old. Could someone really have been planning to draw her here for that long?

A shot rang out, somewhere behind her this time, and she heard a shout of rage that might have come from the big, bearded leader of the militia. They were all being herded towards the centre of the compound and whatever waited for them there. There was more gunfire, even nearer this time. A shock of adrenaline liquefied her guts and tensed her muscles, urging her to run. She gritted her teeth and fought it, focusing on the walls and the runes inside them, trying to understand what they meant.

When she looked more closely, she could see the pattern in them, loops and swirls repeated from floor to ceiling, but no two quite the same. She thought about a concert she'd been taken to by her father – some political function where he thought his chances of re-election would be improved by the presence of his pretty young daughter. The music had been by Bach, a tune that circled round and round but never quite returned to the beginning, always a little changed. She remembered feeling frustrated as she listened to it, silently willing the melody to complete – to finally *end*.

She pressed her hand against the wall but it remained unyielding. Understanding it wasn't enough; she needed a way to get past. To end it, she supposed. How had the Bach ended? She seemed to recall that eventually it *had* returned to the beginning, bringing a sense of completeness that had been oddly satisfying. But where did this place begin? She studied the endlessly repeating pattern and sighed. She didn't know.

Another volley of shots sounded behind her, and this time she obeyed her animal instincts and ran. She'd been running for a very long time, she realised. And the compound was large, but it wasn't *that* huge, was it? The pattern in the walls was twisting the space inside them, turning the corridors into the same endlessly repeating loop, like one of those Escher prints her second-grade math teacher had liked so much, stairs you could climb forever and never reach the top.

She tried to wrench herself out of it, to return to the finite building in the mundane world. It was useless. Something held her here, either the building's power or her own undisciplined abilities.

Her footsteps slapped against the tile, a hypnotic rhythm. She lost herself in it and only slowly realised there was now a syncopated beat. Other footsteps were approaching – but these people were in the real world. They were all around her now. She could hear the desperate rasping breath of men who were exhausted and very afraid.

She grasped hold of the sound and pulled herself towards it. For a moment she felt herself suspended, neither here nor there. There was a tearing sensation as something inside her ripped itself free, and she found herself exactly where she'd started, but no longer alone.

Jimmy cursed and turned his gun on her as all around him his men yelled in shock. She raised her hands. There was a killing rage in Jimmy's eyes and she waited for the bullet and the pain, but after a second he lowered the gun.

"Where..?" he said.

She smiled, though she knew it looked sickly. "I told you I can walk through walls."

His men muttered and he stared at her. "That's... some power, lady. The good Lord don't give gifts like that often."

She thought about Raven, but that wasn't the lord Jimmy was talking about. "Yeah, I know I've been blessed."

She'd emerged into the real world in a meeting room. The carpet was scuffed beneath a glass-topped table and the lights in the ceiling were the harsh neon kind that made everyone look unwell. Jimmy's men were pale and blood-spattered and there were far fewer than she knew he'd brought to the compound. One man clutched his arm against his chest, its wrist mangled and red. Another was supported between two of his fellows, his head nodding down towards his chest as his eyelids drooped.

"We've walked right into their trap," Jimmy said.

She nodded. "Do you think the shofar's even here?"

"Lahav said it was."

"He could be wrong."

His men didn't like that, but Jimmy took time to consider it as he scratched a finger through his beard. "He coulda been mistaken," he said eventually. "What he is lives inside a man, and no man's perfect. But close up he can *sense* it, and he sensed it here. That's why he couldn't come hisself – it's lethal to him."

"Then they must be using it to lure us in."

"Why? What do they want from us?"

"Not hard to figure, is it?" one of the other men muttered, a redhead with an acne-scarred face. "They want to kill us."

Jimmy shook his head. "I don't buy it, brother. We lost half the men they did and we're in their base. If they wanted rid of us, there musta been an easier way.

"But they wanted us *here*," Alex said, looking at the runes swirling through the walls around them. They wanted *me* here, she thought.

"Then here's the last place we wanna be," Jimmy said. "Think you can walk us through these walls, lady?"

His small blue eyes bored into hers, more intelligent than she'd given him credit for, and she could only shake her head. "I'm working on it."

"Work faster," he said as a sudden explosive shock shook the door on its hinges. One of the men grabbed Alex and they rolled together to the side of the room as the door exploded inward in a shower of wood-chips and shotgun pellets.

Alex let the same man lead her by the arm as they fought onward, deeper into the trap. She knew she'd be safer in the spirit world, where bullets couldn't touch her. But she remembered the endless spiral and thought about walking it eternally and kept herself in the mundane world, where the worst that could happen to her was death.

There were fewer Croatoans to face them now. Alex looked down at their young faces as she walked over their corpses and wondered that they'd been happy to sacrifice themselves just to bait a trap. They hardly needed to die anymore; she and her allies could only go forward. But they kept on fighting, as if they didn't realise that they'd served their purpose.

A bullet tore past her ear, clipping the lower lobe. The blood dripped to the floor and the wound stung and then throbbed. Another room, another gunfight, and now Morgan was with them. He quivered with tension, his face hardened by the blood smeared across his cheek and brow. She saw other splatters of blood on his T-shirt and soaking one leg of his jeans, but from the easy way he moved she guessed that none of it was his.

And then the seemingly endless corridor ended and there were no more young men and women to throw their lives away against the militia's guns. There was just one person in the room: a curly-haired man. Though she'd never seen his face, she knew that he was the same figure who'd haunted her for seven years – the aura of danger he carried was unmistakable. His spirit self didn't surprise her, a grinning fox with blood around its muzzle, but his human face was more ordinary than she'd expected, the only unusual thing about him the pale hazel of his eyes.

He looked at them in shock, as if bringing them here hadn't been part of his plan. But in his hand he was holding a curling ram's horn with a gilded tip.

"Coby," Morgan said. "You work fast."

"I had friends."

"So do I – and they're here and armed. Give me the shofar."

"Or I could just use it," Coby said. "Drive all your spirits from all your bodies. Leave you empty."

"I already am," Morgan said. "The shofar doesn't work against me, so hand it over before someone gets trigger happy.

I don't need to kill you, but I really don't have a big problem with it."

Coby's eyes flickered around the room, but there was no help for any of them there. It was a white box: no furniture, no windows. One of Jimmy's men tried the door through which they'd entered. He pushed then kicked and it remained stubbornly closed.

"You're trapped too," Morgan said to Coby.

Alex thought he'd deny it, but he remained silent, and after a second he passed the shofar to Morgan. Morgan's hands shook as he took it, and she wondered what the artefact meant to him. It seemed to shiver the air around it, as if it burned with some unknown heat. But the Croatoans wouldn't simply have left it here for them to find, it made no sense.

At first she didn't notice it, a spreading yellow-green stain against the white. But when she felt the harsh taste against the back of her throat, she knew what she was seeing. A mist was settling over the room and the people in it. She coughed as she inhaled it.

"Gas," she gasped. "They're gassing us."

The men took a moment too long to react, gazes still locked on the shofar. By the time they turned, their hands were already clutched to their chests as they were shaken with racking coughs.

Jimmy's eyes locked on hers, small and bright and desperate. "Lady, it's now or never. Get us out of here."

She drew a breath and choked on it. Her head felt light and her eyesight was greying. The runes mocked her, a knot she couldn't untangle. But they were at the centre of the pattern now and finally she saw it – the end of the thread that bound this place together and trapped her inside it.

Her lungs burned with the poison gas and her eyes were blurry with tears. She forced herself to keep them open, on the spirit world and the mundane, as she reached out her hand towards the runes and the loose thread in the spirit trap. Her fingers passed through the physical wall and tried to close around something that wasn't quite real. She resisted the urge to tighten them and tightened her mind instead, squeezing it hard around the idea of a knot, and the way everything would just unravel once it was loosened.

Her head ached, her flesh felt bloated and her heart was beating hard and erratic, an unhealthy beat. She ignored it all and just pulled. The pattern of the runes tightened, and tightened – and then it all just fell apart. The runes frayed and fragmented and the building vanished from the spirit world, where it was never meant to be.

But it was still there in the real world, along with the poison gas that was killing everyone inside it. She tried to gasp in a breath and it burned down her throat and into her lungs, toxic and unnourishing. She needed to escape to the spirit world now. She could survive only a few more seconds here before her body starved of oxygen and died. She reached out with her mind as she turned to take a last look at Morgan and the men around him, ready to leave them behind.

A memory jabbed at her conscience: PD's face as she'd shut the door on him and left him for their enemies. There'd been no betrayal in his eyes. He hadn't known what she was doing. But she would see it in Morgan's face now if she left him.

She'd see it in all their eyes. There was no time, no finesse and barely any energy left in her. She summoned everything she could and cast the net of her mind over the room and everyone in it. And then she reached out to the spirit world and pulled herself towards it, dragging everyone behind her.

CHAPTER EIGHTEEN

Morgan felt a dislocation that tumbled him to his knees. One second his throat was burning and his heart straining against the poison he'd inhaled, and the next it was all gone. The building had just... disappeared. He was kneeling on rocks and sand. The sharp edges of flints pressed into him through his jeans, as real as anything he'd ever felt.

The men of the militia were still there. His eyes were half-blinded by the sudden noonday sun and their expressions were hidden from him. They'd all wanted Alex to save them, but he doubted any of them believed she really could. And they had the shofar. He looked down at it in his hand, the horn a slightly paler brown than his skin. Holding it was odd. The thing felt like it was vibrating, but he could see that it wasn't. He didn't doubt how powerful it was.

Jimmy stood with his back to Morgan. His tall body was hunched over, giving him the profile of a great bear, bestial and on the point of violence. "Where are we?" he growled.

Morgan shrugged. "Away from the poison gas. Back near the town, maybe?"

"We're exactly where we were before," Alex said. "But we're in the spirit world."

She turned towards him, bringing her face into sunlight. He scrambled to his feet so he could back away from her. Her eyes were pure black, round like a bird's. Her face, pretty before, had become a caricature of itself, the cheekbones too prominent, the nose sharp and beak-like.

She frowned at him. "What's the matter? I saved you, didn't I?"

"You look..." He shook his head. "What *are* you?"

Her frown deepened as she brought her hands up to her face, groping it. "What do I look like?"

"Your face is... sharper. And your eyes are black, like–"

"–a raven's." She looked resigned rather than shocked. "Of course. We're in the spirit world. What you're seeing is my spirit self."

Jimmy turned and it was only because he was prepared this time that Morgan managed not to take another step back. The militia leader's face was barely human at all. His jaw had elongated and his nose flattened and darkened. His fair hair was now light fur extending from his hairline to his back and down his massively muscled shoulders.

Around him, his men were staring at each other in horror. Some of them had pointed, fox-like ears, others had tails. None of them were unchanged.

"So what do I look like?" Morgan asked Alex.

Her bright black eyes blinked at him. "You look exactly the way you did before. What *are* you, Morgan?"

His gut clenched, but it only confirmed what he'd already known. "I'm a man without a spirit. I've got no soul."

Alex was still staring at him when Jimmy picked her up by the collar of her blouse, lifting her until she was nose-to-nose with him. "What have you done to us?" he shouted. His mouth was too full of teeth.

"It's not me," she gasped. "It's this place. Look at me. It's me too."

He snarled but lowered her until she was able to support herself on the tips of her toes. The nine other men who'd made it through the compound clustered around her, hostile and scared.

Morgan put a hand on Jimmy's unnaturally broad shoulder. "Let her go, man. She saved our lives. She's right. It's this place that's fucking you up, not her."

Jimmy's grip loosened a little. "How do I know you're not working with her?"

"Because Lahav told you I was all right. Come on – you know *I'm* not the bad guy.

They turned to look at Coby. He stood at the edge of the group, fox muzzle dripping blood onto the sand. Morgan suddenly became very aware of the shofar in his hand and the other man's covetous eyes on it. "Don't even think about it," he said. "This is going to Lahav and you're going to prison."

"If any of us ever get out of here," Coby said. He looked at Alex. "I know about spirit travelling – I've studied it. The effort it took to bring us here must have pretty much burned you out. There's no way you're taking us back right now."

Jimmy's massive, hairy body was quivering with rage as he turned to her. "Lady, is that true? Have you trapped us in this godforsaken place?"

Her strange black eyes were bright as she looked at Jimmy. When he'd first met Alex, Morgan felt he could trust her. She'd seemed a little out of her depth, not like the other players who jockeyed for position in the occluded world. Now her bird eyes and sharp nose gave her face an entirely different cast. Not evil exactly, but certainly not trustworthy.

"This is the spirit world," she said. "The place shamans and wise men visit in their dreams. But I can travel here in the waking world and I *can* take you back, just... not right now. I need time to recharge."

Jimmy growled and Morgan grabbed him, holding him back from her.

"You're saying this is... the afterlife? Heaven?" Morgan said.

Alex shook her head. "It's not heaven or hell. I don't know, it just *is*."

"There's nothing *but* heaven and hell," Jimmy snarled. "Anything else is an illusion sent by Satan to tempt us."

Alex raised an eyebrow. "Have it your way. Then let's just say we're in an antechamber to hell. I've been here before and I know the rules."

"I don't like you, Miss CIA," Jimmy said. "Seems to me you feel right at home in this hell-hole."

She shook her head, standing her ground. "I'm just a traveller. Try to remember, though. I brought you here – and I'm the only one who can bring you back."

"Is that a threat?" Jimmy bared his sharp teeth.

"Of course it was a threat," Morgan snapped. "And it's a good one, because she's right. We need her to get out of here. Unless you want to be stuck in whatever the fuck this place is forever, looking like – well, like that."

Jimmy frowned and Morgan realised the other man hadn't even considered what the place might have done to him. "Big teeth," Morgan told him, "and a hairy back – like a bear."

Jimmy looked to his men and paled when they nodded.

"I don't think we can take being in this place for long," Morgan said to Alex. "It's freaking out a bunch of big armed men with guns and I'm not too keen on it either. When are you gonna be strong enough to get us out?"

Her sharp-planed face suddenly looked a lot less sure of itself.

She opened her mouth to reply, then shut it again as he grasped her shoulder and shook his head.

When they stopped speaking, other sounds became much clearer. Morgan could hear the wind as it combed through the scrubby bushes of this nowhere land. The other men's breathing was harsher, punctuated by brief trills and chirps of birdsong.

And beneath all that was another noise, unpatterned and hard to identify. It sounded like speech, but there were no words in it, just a faint, high chittering.

The others had heard it too. They peered into the desert, but Morgan already knew there was nothing there. Then he saw one of the men look down at his own arm. It was bare, the muscles knotted beneath unevenly tanned skin. Something was moving on it, just a flicker of light, and the man screamed.

It was his tattoo which was moving. The black swastika on his arm was slowly revolving, tearing the skin as it moved. In five seconds it had turned a complete circuit and the man's forearm was a bloody mess, yellow fat glistening above the corded tendons.

There were more screams and Morgan didn't need to look around to guess the rest of the militia were suffering the same agony. They were all covered in tattoos. He spun to face Alex to find her staring at a tall, dark-haired man in horrified fascination. The tattoo of a snake on his arm was writhing – and rising. The head tore away from the skin, leaving a ragged hole in the flesh beneath. The snake's tongue flicked out to lick the blood from the smooth whiteness of his ulna.

"What the fuck is happening?" Morgan yelled to Alex above the man's terrified whimpers.

"It's this place," she said. "Symbols here *mean* something. And the symbols in those tattoos... They mean pain and hate and death."

She trailed off. The snake had torn itself free of the militiaman's arm. Its scales were slick with his blood as it crawled over the body of the man who'd birthed it. He'd passed out from the pain, or maybe the blood loss. A chunk had been torn out of his arm exactly the size of the snake slithering towards Alex.

The serpent reared up, black tongue flickering, and Morgan realised almost too late that it meant to strike. His knife flashed and the snake lunged right onto the blade. Its head bounced against Alex's leg before falling onto the rocks.

She gasped in a shuddering breath. "Jesus. Thank you."

Morgan looked down at the shofar in his hand, stroking its rough surface. It could banish spirits, but he couldn't be sure he'd drive away the right ones. Jimmy and his men had souls – would they want to risk them to escape death?

He was still looking at the horn when a body barrelled into him, pushing him to the ground as the gun was knocked from his hand. He stared up into Coby's wide hazel eyes as the other man's fingers scrabbled for the shofar. Morgan held on grimly and Coby gave up on that and put his hands around Morgan's neck instead, squeezing so hard he knew he only had seconds of consciousness left.

It was fading already when he heard Alex shout, "Let him go!" Her hands pulled at Coby's where they were clawing into Morgan's throat. He knew it was useless. She didn't have the strength.

"Fuck!" she said. And then she did something Morgan sensed but couldn't see, and Coby was just... gone.

Morgan blinked up at the blue sky above him, sucking in relieved breaths, until Alex reached out and pulled him to his feet.

"What the hell did you do to him?" he said.

She shrugged. "I don't know. I just threw him away."

"Back into the real world?"

"I don't think so. It was too easy – almost like the spirit world itself was pulling him somewhere else."

There was a flicker of movement behind her and for a moment Morgan thought it was another attack. Then he heard the scream and remembered why Coby had thought this was a good moment to attack. Jimmy's men were dying. One had his arms spread out from his sides, motionless, as he watched the tattoos on his body glow. As they brightened from a dull red to a bright orange, Morgan saw a horned circle, a spiderweb, a five-pointed star and many different variations on the swastika.

"I tried to get the fucking things taken off," the man said suddenly, looking into Morgan's eyes. "The laser treatment costs thousands. I didn't have any money." His expression tightened as the tattoos on his arms burned brighter still. There were more on his stomach and legs, glowing through the fabric that covered them.

"I'm dying, aren't I?" he whispered as his skin began to blacken around the tattoos. The scent of burning flesh filled the air and he whimpered.

"I'm sorry," Morgan said helplessly, but he didn't think the man heard. He'd started screaming as his tattoos burned white hot. They were sinking into his skin now, like living brands. A ring of wire around his bicep flared and ate away at him as the hand beneath twitched and then stilled when the nerves which governed it were severed. When the arm fell to the ground a few seconds later, Morgan had to look away.

He found himself facing Jimmy. The big man's eyes were frantic, scanning his fallen men, the wreckage of his militia. "Dead," he said. "I killed 'em all."

"You couldn't have known," Morgan said. "And we'd have died anyway if we stayed there."

Jimmy's pale skin was waxy, flecked with droplets of sweat. "We were doing God's work, weren't we?"

"Yes," Morgan said with all the certainty he could manage.

Jimmy nodded, his head dropping at the end of the motion to hang against his chest, as if he no longer had the strength to lift it. For a moment, Morgan thought he was flexing his shoulder muscles in preparation for some final burst of action. Then, as the T-shirt on the other man's back rippled and tore, he remembered the demon tattoo which lay beneath it.

Jimmy looked up again, throat stretched tight in a yell of agony. The T-shirt fell to the ground as two bat wings spread from his shoulders to flap behind him. The copper smell of his blood wafted from them and droplets of it scattered across the dun sand beneath him.

Jimmy's hand reached out, and after a moment's hesitation, Morgan took it. The fingers tightened painfully around his as Jimmy yelled his agony again and the figure that was ripping itself from his back twisted and pulled more of his essence out of him. "Why?" he whispered.

"I don't know," Morgan said. "People don't always get what they deserve."

"But I repented," Jimmy gasped, falling to his knees. His small blue eyes glared into Morgan's for one final moment of rage and pain. Then the life went out of them as his head dropped and another rose behind it, dripping with gore. Its ears twitched and a forked tongue snaked out of its mouth to wet its black lips.

"Hello, Morgan," it hissed.

He stumbled away from Jimmy's corpse and the thing that had gestated inside it.

The demon raised its neck. Threads of Jimmy's skin grew taught and then snapped as it shook first one clawed hand and then the other free.

There was a hard pressure against Morgan's bicep and for a moment of irrational panic he thought it was the demon's doing and jerked away.

"Morgan," Alex said. "Snap out of it!"

He stopped struggling and turned to look at her. "You've got to help them. This is *your* place. Do something!"

Her expression was wild. "For god's sake, it's too late for them. Look at them! We have to get away from here."

Morgan looked at the carnage; a few of the corpses still twitching, others barely recognisable as human. And he looked at Jimmy's crumpled form, kneeling in the dirt. The demon tattoo had freed itself almost entirely from his back. Only its feet still remained as two-dimensional imprints on the skin, and as Morgan watched, they began to bulge free, nails like rhino horn ripping out congealed lumps of flesh and blood as they freed themselves.

The demon laughed, a ringing, almost childlike sound. "I'm come-ing," it said.

Morgan tucked the shofar through his belt, grasped Alex's hand and ran.

Coby was flying. The desert whisked by beneath him and there was nothing he could do to stop himself. In this place, Alex had a strength he could only dream about. He thought for a moment that he'd returned to the real world and that he'd die when he hit the ground. But he just kept on flying and as the landscape changed beneath him he knew he was still in the spirit world with its impossible, twisted physics.

One moment he was flying over bare sand and rocks, the next there was thorny vegetation beneath him. He noticed no moment of transition and failed to notice it again when the scrubland became meadow. The grass waved in a wind he couldn't feel and he realised that it was no longer Alex's will which was moving him. Some other, even stronger force drew him on. He felt it tug at his chest and the heart beneath it and he understood that wherever he was going, it must have some powerful hold over him. He knew that was how this realm worked, the psychic significance of places more important than their temporal or physical location.

The grass, silver and delicate, became the robust golden stalks of wheat undulating over rolling hills. The sky grew more blue, high clouds scudding across it too fast, and he knew that he wasn't just travelling through space. Time was passing too – or retreating. With every inch and second that went by the shofar grew more distant and with it his hopes of immortality. There was nothing he could do. The spirit world wanted him to go wherever it was sending him and even Alex wouldn't have the strength to fight it.

The wheat grew and darkened as the landscape flattened and he was finally set down on his feet. He looked around him and saw that he was walking through the high fields of corn which had surrounded his childhood. When a road appeared beneath his feet and then houses to either side he found himself in his home town for the first time in seven years.

His old high school squatted ahead of him, grey and unwelcoming, and he realised where and when he was – and understood why the spirit world had drawn him here. It had brought him to the moment that was the central truth of his life, a black hole in his past. His entire existence lay within the event horizon of this day, and he could never escape its terrible gravitational pull.

Children fled past him, screaming but not seeing him. It surprised him how small they were. He'd remembered his victims being taller. It was a little disappointing to see what easy targets they'd been. The police had established a perimeter around the building, hunkered down behind their guns and cars, but not one of them saw him as he walked past. He was still cloaked in the spirit world and would remain there until he'd done what he came here to do. The years he'd spent studying the realm and its rules allowed him at least that much control, though he could never have entered it without Alex's help.

In the entrance hall, he found his first kill. He remembered the shock of it. Like a jolt of 100 per cent proof alcohol in his stomach, it had taken a little while to transmute into pleasure. Mrs O'Grady lay where he'd left her, the wreckage of her skull facing the ceiling, her face pressed to the floor.

He smiled and walked on, understanding a lot of things now: why he'd been sent to the Croatoan centre, who his saviour in San Francisco had been.

The nameless jock he'd killed on the stairs was next. He hadn't stayed to enjoy that murder the first time. Now he paused to examine the boy's smooth face. He was so incredibly young, a life ended before it had even discovered its purpose.

Sirens began outside the school, but they didn't worry him. He wasn't truly here and they wouldn't catch him – either of him, even though back then he'd meant to die. Something had and would intervene.

The door to Mr Skeete's classroom was shut. He remembered that he'd kicked it closed behind him, trapping his classmates inside with him and his guns. He eased it open, careful not to make a sound. He remembered that he hadn't heard himself coming.

His younger self stood in the centre of the carnage, the barrel of a gun pressed against his temple beneath the George Bush mask.

"If you knew where you were going," Coby told him, "you wouldn't be in such a hurry to get there."

The gun hesitated, shook a moment, and then lowered. "I don't believe in hell," the 17-year-old said.

He smiled at his own naivety. "That's OK, they believe in you. And now they know about you and so do a lot of other people. The cops are here. You need to get out."

A hand reached up to remove the mask and beneath it he recognised the look of faux toughness on his own face. "I only bought a one-way ticket today."

"Don't worry – I'll cover the round trip." He stooped to pick up the shell casings from the floor and passed them to his younger self. He took the George Bush mask and slipped it on Joshua Heligman, then wiped the grips of the guns and put them in his hands. He pulled the boy's finger on the trigger to fire one round before he released him, ensuring there'd be gunshot residue when the police checked.

When he'd finished, he held out his hand, and his younger self shrugged and took it. He remembered the strange compulsion he'd felt to trust the man who'd approached him in the school, and the almost dreamlike journey which had followed. At the time, he'd attributed it to shock and the adrenaline high.

Together, they retraced his path through the school, past the body of the jock and around O'Grady's slowly stiffening corpse. When they reached the gate he saw that a SWAT team had arrived and were preparing to enter the building.

His younger self tensed as he tried to draw away and retreat, but he held himself fast. After a moment, he felt a different sort of tension in the fingers clasped in his as they walked straight through the police line. No eyes or guns lifted to follow them and no one asked who they were.

"They can't see us," the younger him said.

He nodded and kept on walking, past the outer ring of police cars, flashing lights reflecting red and blue from the puddles of rainwater on the tarmac. When they were out of sight of the school, only a block from his childhood home, he released his own hand.

"You're safe now," he said. "Just keep your mouth shut and they'll never catch you. They'll blame it on Josh instead and you get the added bonus of watching his family fall apart from the shame."

His younger self nodded. His eyes were a little wild, his hair mussed where the mask had pressed against it, but he seemed to understand. Coby knew that he did – he had. He wouldn't be caught.

They stared at each other in silence for a long moment. "Who are you?" his younger self asked finally.

He shrugged, knowing he wouldn't answer, and turned to walk away. He had a lot to do and learn in the next seven years, a lot of things to get ready. He needed to track down Alex, the spirit-travelling CIA agent, and make sure she'd be there on that crucial day – along with Morgan and everyone else.

"Wait!" the younger him shouted. "Where are you going? Where can I find you?"

He smiled but didn't turn. "Wait a while," he said. "We'll meet again."

Morgan could hear the wet flap of the demon's wings behind them. Alex's hand was slick with sweat in his and fear coiled tight in his stomach, ready to unravel into unreasoning panic if he let it. The demon was faster than them. There was a giggling laugh then a whistle of wind as claws slashed through the air and he felt five lines of pain open across his shoulders.

He spun and fired and the demon laughed louder as the bullet travelled an inch from the barrel, then dropped to the ground.

"No good," Alex gasped. "This place. Driven by will. Bullet... has none."

Morgan dropped his gun and drew his knife, but when he slashed with it the creature flapped higher. It screeched in mixed defiance and pain and he saw a strip of leathery skin hanging loose on its left wing. But he'd been hurt worse than it was and in a war of attrition he knew it would win.

Fighting was futile. Running was suicidal. "What the hell do we do?" Morgan said.

Alex hid behind his shoulder. "We've got to escape."

"No shit!" he yelled, slashing again at the demon. Its return stroke opened a raw line of blood along his forearm. "How about you get us out of here?"

"Sill too weak after Coby," she gasped. "And I might pull that thing with us."

When he snatched a look at her, her black bird eyes were blank, her attention focused inward. The demon seemed to sense her inattention and swivelled in midair as its talons lunged towards her face. Morgan cursed, dropped the knife and jumped at the creature, grabbing its claws in his hands.

The nails pierced his palms. He stifled a yell of pain and held on grimly. The demon struggled against him for a moment, the upward pressure of its wings almost lifting him from his feet. Then it laughed again and stopped struggling. When he caught its eye he could see it had realised what he already knew: with their hands locked, his face was unprotected from the pointed teeth which filled its mouth to overflowing.

It struck, lips stretched inhumanly wide. He ducked his head and the teeth only scraped his cheek as they passed. A droplet of drool fell from them and burned his skin like acid as the demon drew back its head to strike again.

"Let him go!" Alex shouted.

There was a note of command in her voice Morgan had never heard before and he obeyed without thinking. The demon flew back and up, wings pumping to counter a force which was no longer there.

"Think of a maze," Alex said, grabbing his arm and spinning him to face her.

"What?" he tried to pull away and turn back to the demon but she was stronger than she looked.

"A maze. Any maze. Trust me!" she yelled.

Morgan didn't, but now she'd said it he couldn't stop the thought. He remembered one rainy school trip to Hampton Court Maze, the hedges drooping and dripping and some of the boys getting in trouble for trying to cut their way through.

And then Alex had hold of his hand and was pulling hard – and he felt himself moving, but not quite physically. There was a blur of yellow below him and blue above and then a jolt he felt all the way down his spine as they stopped.

He'd expected to be somewhere else entirely, but they were still in the desert. The wastelands stretched into the distance as featureless and unwelcoming as before. And when he heard the flap of wings he saw that the demon was with them as well.

"You don't shake me that easily," it said.

Its wings rose and its claws extended as it prepared for another dive. Morgan had lost his knife in their sudden move, but he prepared to face it, fingers clawed in a weak imitation of the demon's. He resisted Alex's tug on his arm. He couldn't let himself be distracted from the demon's attack.

"Come *on!*" she said, pulling harder.

The demon giggled and dived and Morgan hesitated only a moment before letting Alex drag him out of its path. Its red eyes glared into his as its wings pulled it up and round for a second pass, but now Alex was running across the sand and Morgan was pulled after. They topped a rise, the demon inches behind them, and suddenly the sands were spread out in a vista beneath them. For a moment he thought it was an illusion, then he realised the complex network of swirls and lines really were there, writ large over acres of the desert in piles of rock.

"The Topock Maze," Alex said. "We can lose him here."

The lines of rock were barely a foot high. Even if it hadn't been able to fly, they would have been no barrier to the demon. But Alex was yanking Morgan's arm and gravity carried him down the slope towards the maze in a run that teetered on the brink of a fall.

The demon hissed and struck. Its talons caught Morgan's head, tearing out a chunk of his hair and scalp. He yelled and would have spun to face it, but the momentum of his run was unstoppable and he felt it strike again and miss, a rank breeze brushing the back of his neck as its claw passed by. Then they were at the bottom of the slope, the entrance to the maze in front of them, a gap between two low lines of stone.

On the level ground Morgan finally got control of their headlong flight. Dust and rocks skidded beneath his feet as he crunched to a halt inside the maze. Alex pulled at his arm but he ignored her, turning to face the demon hovering at the bottom of the slope.

"I think it can still see us," he said dryly.

She smiled. "You'd be surprised."

The creature could certainly hear them. Its pointed ears twitched and then its wings pushed the air down in one powerful stroke as it launched itself towards them. It giggled, flapped harder – and struck something Morgan couldn't see.

The demon's laughter morphed into a scream of shock and rage. Its claws struck and struck again at the invisible barrier, scrabbling futilely against air.

"I need to start listening to you," Morgan said.

Alex shrugged. "I wasn't sure it would work. But the Mojave Indians built this place to trap evil spirits. I thought in the spirit world it might actually work."

Morgan nodded and let her lead him through the twists and turns of the maze. In a moment of curiosity he reached out his hand to hover above the line of stones on the ground. There was no resistance.

"Why don't we just walk straight across?" Morgan asked as they turned left and then right and were suddenly only a few feet from the start of the maze. The hovering demon grinned as it heard them and Morgan teetered for a moment on his toes before Alex grabbed his collar and pulled him back as the creature dove and rebounded from the invisible barrier.

"Best not," Alex said. "We need to respect the metaphor."

"OK," he said. "But this place is fucking huge. Do you know the way through?"

"We should just find it automatically. *We're* not evil."

Morgan wasn't so sure. It seemed to him he might be exactly the sort of thing this place was designed to trap.

Alex's eyes cut to him, black and unreadable. "Worried?"

The sounds of the demon grew faint, but Morgan couldn't tell if they were making progress. They twisted and turned and the maze went on and on and it all looked the bloody same. Then, just when he'd stopped expecting it, the end came.

They halted between the low walls of stone, gazing at the desert beyond.

"If we step out, is that where we'll end up?" Morgan asked, nodding at the scrubland stretching to the horizon.

"Maybe. I think it has a lot of exits."

"Could one of them lead out of the spirit world?"

"Let's see," Alex said, taking his hand and stepping forward.

CHAPTER NINETEEN

Alex felt a dizzy sensation of falling as she stepped from one place and into somewhere else entirely. There was the hard snap of something out of alignment slotting back into place, and she knew they'd left the spirit realm – at least for now. She looked at Morgan, unchanged beside her, and was relieved to see the shofar still tucked in his belt.

"We're back," she said. They were in a desert far bleaker and more barren than the one they'd left. There was no greenery, just rolling sand dunes and, in the distance, mountains. "I think this is Death Valley."

"But why did it bring us here?" Morgan said. "There's... nothing."

"Not quite nothing." She pointed to her left, where the sand was churned, spoiling the silken smoothness of the dunes. It was too fine to hold prints, but she guessed the trail had been left by a vehicle, maybe more than one. Though the sun was nearer to the horizon than its zenith, it was still hot enough to steal her breath. She knew how dangerous that kind of heat could be and they had no water with them. Her fair skin would burn agonisingly if they didn't find cover soon.

"Whoever that is, they've got to be going somewhere," Morgan said. "We need to follow them."

Alex looked at the tracks which led towards the horizon in either direction. There was no way to tell which way they'd come from and which they were going. "Or we could wander around for hours and then die of heat exhaustion. Why don't I take us back into the spirit world?"

Morgan shivered. "No thanks." He walked away before she could protest, following the broad trail to the top of the nearest sand dune and down.

Alex trotted to catch up with him, cursing as the sand slipped away in sheets beneath her feet and she lost almost as much ground as she gained.

"How the hell are you walking so easily?" she asked Morgan.

"I've spent a lot of time in deserts."

"I thought you were British."

He rolled his eyes as she drew alongside, gasping for breath. "We have got passports, you know. Anyway, I was in the army."

"In Iraq?"

"Afghanistan. And other places."

She heard something in his tone that told her he didn't want to elaborate and she didn't press him. They walked in silence, not even the sound of the wind to disturb the perfect stillness.

Alex knew she was sweating, but the parched air snatched up the moisture before she could feel it. The painful band of a headache tightened around her temples and although she knew they were moving they didn't seem to be getting anywhere.

When she heard the faint sound she thought at first that the wind had picked up. Then the pitch rose and she knew what she was hearing. "PD's here."

Morgan frowned at her.

"My partner. The coyotes."

As if her voice had summoned them, the creatures loped into view around them. Alex knew they weren't hostile but she didn't like the wildness in their eyes. The people trapped inside the animal bodies were burning with rage and she didn't want to be its target. "Easy," she said. "We have what we need to help you. We just need to find your real bodies."

The lead coyote lifted its head and howled.

"Do you think he understands?" Morgan asked.

"I hope so. But he's losing himself in the beast."

The air filled with the musky odour of fur as the creatures kept pace beside them. The sand dunes gave no chance at a long view, and Alex had no sense of how long they'd travelled or how much further they needed to go.

The sun had sunk lower in the sky, acquiring the first hint of red, when Morgan stopped. He held out his hand to halt Alex beside him. The coyotes seemed to understand some need for caution. The leader sunk to its belly and the others clustered behind it, eyes swinging between Alex and whatever lay ahead.

"Do you hear that?" Morgan whispered.

She cocked her head, then nodded. "Voices." They could be anyone, but knowing the way the spirit world worked, they were almost certainly someone connected to all this. The maze would have spat them out into this particular part of the real world for a reason.

She didn't like the idea of walking into whatever was waiting with only Morgan beside her. He'd lost both his gun and his knife in the spirit world. But her mouth was so dry she found it hard to swallow and she was beginning to feel light-headed, a combination of heat and thirst. If they didn't chance it, the desert would finish them off anyway.

The dune in front of them obscured what lay beyond, but the voices grew louder as they drew nearer. Alex thought she recognised at least one of them. "That's Coby, isn't it?"

Morgan nodded.

She hesitated a moment then walked forward, to the top of the rise and over. The coyotes howled when they saw what lay beyond, a high desperate note that went on and on. Alex tried to see what had spooked them, but it was just a ring of young people, probably Croatoans. They were dressed in Native American costumes, beads and buckskin.

She couldn't see Coby's face, but there was a shock of curly hair on a man with his back to her and she knew it was him.

"Coby!" Morgan shouted. "I've got the shofar. You know what it can do, so don't fuck me around." He held the horn above his head and the gold around the mouthpiece glinted in the sunlight.

The people in the circle shifted and turned to stare at him. Alex saw the skulls beneath their beautiful faces and knew these were the true leaders of the cult, the body-hopping spirits of the old in fresh young bodies. She thought some might try to rush Morgan before he could use the horn. They didn't, though. And they didn't seem entirely surprised to see them. A shiver of unease passed down her back, and then the curly-haired man turned.

It both was and wasn't Coby. He had the same features and the same wide hazel eyes, but there were crow's feet around them and his skin had lost the glow of youth. He was holding another man, a knife against his throat.

"PD," Alex gasped.

"Yes," his captor said, "I know what you're thinking and I am Coby. And yes, I will kill your partner's body if you don't do exactly what I say."

"I'm not giving you the shofar," Morgan said. "I'm sorry, Alex."

Coby smiled. "I don't want it. I want *you*, Alex. Or are you going to sacrifice this man again to save your own skin?"

"Wait," Morgan said. "Tell us what the hell happened to you."

Alex guessed he was stalling for time and was happy to let him. *Could* she sacrifice PD again? But if she saved him at the cost of the shofar, the whole world would suffer. She'd have sacrificed the greater good to salve her own guilty conscience. Wouldn't that be worse than the original crime?

"Alex happened to me," Coby said. "She pulled me into the spirit world, where events aren't ordered by time, but by their psychic significance, their weight. There was one event – one day in my life – that outweighed all the others. Once she pushed me away with all the force of her considerable power, it was inevitable I'd return to it."

"The day you murdered the other kids in your class," Morgan said. And then, "*You're* Laughing Wolf. Jesus, you've lived these last I don't know how many years twice. And the second time you knew everything you found out the first time. You set the trap in the Croatoan centre to draw Alex there so she could send you back in time to set the trap. You probably set up the whole fucking cult just to draw us there. You wanted to go back to the beginning."

"You're a clever guy," Coby said. "When I was younger, I underestimated you. Now I know I need you."

"Need *me*? I've already spoken to Dee for you. I thought it was Alex you wanted now."

She looked between them, agonised. The knife pressed against PD's throat and the coyotes paced as if they were caged. The leader's lips were pulled back in a fierce snarl and Alex could see PD's face behind the beast's, equally feral. She thought he understood everything and was judging her for her hesitation.

"I need you both," Coby said, "but Alex first." His face hardened and his hand tightened on the knife. Droplets of blood gathered beneath the blade and fell on PD's white T-shirt. The man possessing his body whimpered but didn't try to pull away. With the blade pressed against his jugular, any movement would have killed him.

Morgan turned to Alex, the shofar clasped against his chest. "Don't listen to him. His promises aren't worth anything. PD's already dead. You tried. Let it go."

"He's right," she said thickly to Coby. "I've got absolutely no reason to trust you. I'm not putting my life in your hands along with PD's."

"I'm not asking you to. I just want what I've always wanted – a chance to escape what I know is waiting for me at the end of my life."

"You don't deserve to escape it," Morgan said. "And it's not like it's gonna end there. If you're immortal, you can do anything you want."

"I don't want much. I enjoy killing, why deny it? But I like it personal, one victim at a time. Even if I live forever, the people I kill will be nothing, a blip on the radar. Malaria kills a thousand times as many every day. If you're really so concerned about innocent life, Morgan, why don't you devote your time to finding a cure for that?"

"Listen to him," Morgan said to Alex. "Listen to the shit he's spouting. You *can't* let him live forever."

"Summon the spirit world, Alex," Coby said. "Just draw it in. The circle is here, we're ready to perform the ghost dance to evoke paradise." He caressed PD's face with his free hand, smiling. "We've even got a direct descendant of Jack Wilson here to make the metaphor complete. All we need is for you to take the metaphor and turn it into reality."

He gestured to the circle around him, a sharp jerk of his head. The Croatoans linked hands and began to turn as the low hum of a chant throbbed through the desert air.

"Don't do it," Morgan said. "If he gets to Eden he gets the apple – it's game over."

The coyotes snarled and howled and the circle below moved faster. Their feet churned the sand into a fine yellow fog.

"But Eden's got a guardian, hasn't it?" Alex said. "And you've got the shofar. I've got to save PD. I owe him."

Morgan turned to her and for a moment she saw violence in his eyes. Then it faded and his hands dropped. She didn't think he could kill her in cold blood.

Coby smiled. His hazel eyes were hidden in the shadows beneath his brows as the setting sun dyed his skin red. "Use the dance," he said to Alex. "Jack Wilson knew what he was doing when he taught his people to perform it. He just wasn't as powerful a spirit traveller as you. He could never pull Eden all the way through, though he spent all his life trying. Visualise paradise, Alex, and the dance will bring it to you."

"Eden," she said. "The *biblical* Eden?"

Coby's mouth quirked. "If that's the easiest thing for you to picture."

She could see him vibrating with energy. Coby thought he'd won and maybe he had. "OK," she said, then shut her eyes and spread her hands wide in a welcoming gesture.

She did exactly as Coby had asked – she pictured the perfect little glade she'd imagined as a little girl when she'd first heard the story of Eden. She visualised the apple trees, side by side, old and gnarled, leaves bright against their cracked bark. And then she smiled and pictured the serpent. Coby thought he could escape the judgement he was owed, but if she could contrive it he'd find himself facing it anyway.

She felt the power build and build inside her until it was too much to bear. Her arms dropped and her eyes opened. Her neck hairs stood on end, springing back up when she ran a hand down to smooth them, as if the air was filled with static electricity.

The coyotes must have sensed it too. The one which contained PD's spirit cocked its head, ears pricked, then lifted its head and howled. The others joined him. She realised, with a lurch of alarm, that they were howling a perfect counterpoint to the chanting of the Croatoans below.

She took an unconscious step towards them, tried to pull up short and instead stepped forward again, drawn by the power of the dance. Whatever she'd set in motion here was out of her control – or Morgan's. He walked forward beside her, the tense set of his jaw revealing both his struggle against the movement and its futility.

Alex stopped beside Coby near the edge of the circle and Morgan flanked the cult leader on the other side. Her eyes met Coby's for a moment, but the pale hazel was unreadable. Then the other man looked back into the centre of the dance and the expression on his face made Alex's stomach churn.

The Croatoans were running now. Sweat beaded on the beautiful young faces and gathered in the armpits of their buckskin tops. The coyotes had moved to circle them, a snarling, feral outer ring. The Croatoans sensed them and the skulls beneath their perfect skin grinned at the beasts.

At first she thought it was a shadow in the centre of the circle and looked up to see what had cast it. There was nothing, and when she looked back down the stain had grown and she saw that it was grass.

It was a vibrant, emerald green, a colour she'd never seen in the desert, not even after a rare rainfall. The grass grew and spread. She felt it sprouting beneath her feet and nearly overbalanced, taking a step back onto sand only to have it too erupt into growth. The air was filled with the bright, fresh smell of it.

The cultists must have seen it too, but they kept running, faster than should have been possible. The power which had raised the hairs on her neck intensified. She couldn't tell if it was a consequence or the cause of the Croatoans' inexhaustible energy.

Coby was laughing. He sounded disbelieving and Alex wondered if he'd planned this all these years but never quite thought it could happen. Morgan gazed around him with a soft smile on his lips. He looked entirely relaxed, and she didn't understand how he could be until she realised she was smiling too, as flowers bloomed among the blades of grass, pinpricks of blue and the occasional daisy, like a child's drawing of the sun.

Something larger disrupted the grass as the grass had disrupted the sand. It grew like a piece of time-lapse photography, first a slender sprouting stem, then a sapling and finally a tree. Green fruit inflated on the tips of its branches and she tensed until the fruit darkened to purple and she realised it was a plum. To her left, another sapling grew, and the sweet smell of lemons wafted from it.

The circle of Croatoans finally broke, pushed apart buy the wildly growing plants around them. There was an explosion of sound, musical but discordant. A second later a flock of birds swooped towards the trees. The flock moved as one but was composed of a hundred different sorts of bird. She saw the common brown of starlings, a red-breasted robin and a bluetit. Before it was lost in the foliage, she glimpsed the pink feathers and long, insectile legs of a flamingo.

She looked at Morgan. "Did I do this?"

"Well, it sure as hell wasn't me."

She laughed. She knew she should be worried, but something about this place seemed to stifle dark emotions. She felt joy and gritted her teeth to fight it. She'd let Coby get very close to his goal and she had to make sure he didn't reach it. She looked for him among the branches – and heard the first scream.

They were in an orchard now, the other people lost in the dappled shadows of the trees. It took a moment for her eyes to make out the shapes of the nearest Croatoans and the black holes of their open mouths. She ran towards them, propelled by an instinct to help someone in pain that overrode who these people were and what they'd done. But when she reached the nearest woman she stopped and stared. It was Maria – her body, at least.

Maria shrieked as her hands clawed at her face. It had changed. She was still the same person, with the same gap between her front teeth and the same soulful dark eyes, but now small furrows radiated from them and her skin was no longer perfect. It looked a little dry and weathered. Older. Coby's transformation had happened to her too, but Alex didn't think it had the same cause.

"What's happening to me?" Maria said.

"The spirit world hates lies," Alex said. "You being young and pretty was a lie. This place is correcting that."

A small coyote slunk forward and whined when it saw Maria. Alex's righteous satisfaction faded into nothing. "Oh god, I didn't think."

"It's their bodies, isn't it?" Morgan said. "Think this'll reverse when we get out of here?"

Alex shook her head helplessly as Maria continued to age in front of them. Her body twisted, stooping as her bones lost density and grew brittle and her tendons tightened. Her face was a mass of wrinkles, her hands liver-spotted and gnarled with arthritis. And she still kept aging.

"In her real body she had cancer," Alex said. "She would have been dead by now if she hadn't stolen Maria's."

The woman in Maria's body understood what Alex was saying. Her screams trailed into whimpers and she held out her wizened hands imploringly towards them.

Alex shook her head and backed away. "Everyone ages and everybody dies."

The old woman's eyes narrowed and her almost lipless mouth twisted. "See if you feel that way when your own time comes." She looked as if she intended to say more, but only a dry rattle emerged, terrible and terminal.

As the body slumped to the ground it kept aging. Skin stretched tight over bones as the flesh beneath melted away. By the time the corpse lay on the perfect green grass it looked weeks dead.

"We have to find PD," Alex said. Her chest felt so tight she could barely breathe.

Morgan looked at her and she knew he thought it was already too late. She turned her back on him and walked between the trees. More bodies lay beneath them. The musk of decay wafted on the breeze but the ripe smell of the fruit quickly overrode it. Alex didn't think this place liked death or unpleasantness. It wanted you to forget them. She had to concentrate very hard not to let her mind drift into a formless daydream of happiness.

Some of the Croatoans were still alive, though barely. They passed an old man on his knees beside a cherry tree, dry retching into the grass. When he raised his head at the sound of their passage Alex saw that he was blind, his eyes eaten away by disease.

"I'm sorry," Morgan said to her.

"Don't be sorry!" Alex snapped. "PD's body could still be alive."

"But in what kind of state?"

They reached the centre of the orchard, a small clearing where the sun shone down brightly. Alex realised that, impossibly, it had returned to the height of its daily arc. In this perfect place it must always be noon. The clearing was on a slight rise, allowing a view over the trees to the landscape beyond. They were still in the Mojave. She could see where the greenery gave way to the brown of desert. Bare mountains ringed them.

Coby stood at the other side of the clearing. His head turned from side to side. For the first time since the ceremony started, he looked less than completely composed. Among all the fruit hanging from the branches around them, Alex couldn't see a single apple.

"Where is it?" he said to Alex. "You didn't finish it. Finish the fucking summoning."

"Where's PD?" she asked.

He shrugged and looked down at his feet. A body lay there, spine arched in the final agony of death. The skin was thin and mottled and the hair gone, but Alex recognised the shape of cheeks and nose. She felt a pain in her chest that might have been either grief or guilt.

"Once I got here, they were surplus to requirements," Coby said.

Alex glared at him. "You don't even care, do you?"

"I just don't like to share, especially something as important as immortality."

"But you *should* care," Alex said. "What can you threaten me with now?"

She enjoyed his look of consternation. It was transmuting into anger when the ground beneath her shifted. She staggered back and watched the earth gape open. There were two holes and her heart stuttered when she saw the thick bole of a tree push through each of them. Coby smiled triumphantly.

The ground rolled beneath her as if the roots of the trees ran very long and deep. The trunks were already full thickness when they emerged from the ground and the branches tore out of the soil with them, buds sprouting into leaves as they rose. The apples which grew beside them were green with red cheeks. They looked like they'd be crunchy and sweet.

A figure sat beneath the trees, cross-legged.

"Raven," Alex said bitterly. "Trust you only to show up once it's too late."

"I don't know why you're acting all surprised," he said. "You invited me here."

"I didn't," she said and then remembered. When she'd thought of the Garden of Eden she'd imagined the serpent. She'd thought she understood what Raven was, but she'd made the mistake of taking the spirit world's metaphors for literal truth. She knew of the trickster god called Raven and that was how he'd appeared to her, but he was a far more universal principle.

"You're real," Coby said to him. "I always wondered if the dreams were just dreams."

"Real*ish*," Raven said.

"You know him," Alex said to Coby, and then to Raven, "You're *helping* him. I thought you were on our side."

Raven arched his brows. "Now whyever would you think that?"

CHAPTER TWENTY

Morgan didn't know who the man beneath the tree was. It didn't matter. The apples were within Coby's reach and Morgan had to stop him. Coby must have realised the same thing at the same time. He lunged towards the tree as Morgan lunged towards him – and both of them found themselves inches from a wall of burning flame.

Morgan felt the blaze blister his skin even in the brief second he was near it. He reared back, a hand curled around Alex's arm to pull her with him, when he realised the flame wasn't moving.

He turned to see Lahav approaching through the trees. The angel was still inside Meir's body, only the red of his eyes burning through the other man's hawk-nosed face. As Morgan watched, the light from his eyes spread its glow to the rest of his face. Behind him, the outline of wings took shape. They were flaming too, and so was the dagger in his hand which quickly grew to the length of a sword.

Morgan stared at Coby, expecting the other man to be afraid. He was, a little – but he also looked calculating. When he caught Morgan's eye, he smiled.

Lahav strode on to the edge of the clearing. His bones blazed white beneath his skin and Morgan thought he saw a flicker of pain in the human host's eyes before they burned into steam and only the glowing eyes of the angel were left beneath. His skin sizzled and there was a smell of scorched flesh before it was also gone and there was only the smooth marble of what lay beneath. It was a deep brown shot through with veins of gold. The angel was very beautiful, but inhuman. His hair was flame and his wings stretched high behind him, brushing the tops of the trees and setting the nearest leaves smouldering. There was a sound around him like a musical note from a scale humans weren't meant to hear.

"Uriel," Coby said. "Though I gather you prefer a different name now."

"Did you really think you could escape me?" Lahav said. His voice was melodic too, but the tune was an ominous one.

"I *can* escape," Coby said.

Lahav shook his head and raised his sword. He took a step forward, then another. On the third, he halted. His smooth forehead wrinkled as he looked down at his own feet. The grass was curled around them and there was a writhing as vines rose and twined themselves around the angel's legs. Lahav's flames singed the greenery and its hold weakened as he pulled himself forward. But more grew to take their place and he was stopped again. His gaze rose and blazed into the man Alex had called Raven.

"I am the guardian of paradise," he said. "You can't stop me, deserter. You have no right to be here."

Raven smiled. "But I can slow you down. And since I made this place, I rather think you're the one who's trespassing."

"*You* made this place?" Morgan said. "I thought..."

"That God made it? Yaweh? El Shadai? El Elyon? Adoni? Why create something so tempting and then forbid you to take it? I know he's bit of a bastard, but that's beyond the pale even for him."

"Blasphemer!" Lahav said. "Hashem created the trees as a test." His rage seemed to give him strength and he tore his leg from the vines which clutched it and took another step forward.

"You have to stop him," Coby said to Morgan. "That's why I let you have the shofar, don't you see? It needs the most powerful note to drive a being like him away, and only you can sound it. Anyone else... It would drive their own soul out of their body before they could complete it. You can do it, though, Morgan. That's what Uriel didn't understand – he was putting the means of his own destruction in your hands when he sent you after the shofar. And if you get rid of him we can all eat the apples and it won't matter that you don't have a soul. You won't need a second life. Your first will go on forever."

"I made a bargain with you, Morgan Nicholson," Lahav said. "Your help in exchange for a soul. The bargain stands." He dragged himself another step forward, leaving embers and a charred trail of dead vegetation behind him.

"And what about my life?" Morgan asked.

"If you aid me you'll have proved your worth and I will spare it."

"How do I know I can trust you?"

"I never deal in untruth."

"He's right, you know," Raven said. "His kind can't lie, especially not here, where lies have consequences. Well, you've seen that for yourself. Oh – here's a thought. Since he can't lie, you can ask him anything. Why don't you ask what he'll do to Alex here if you don't stop him?"

"Her life is forfeit," Lahav said. There was no regret in his voice, or any other human emotion.

"But she didn't do anything!" Morgan said.

"She summoned Eden."

"I had no choice!"

Lahav turned his burning eyes on her. "There was a choice."

"Only if I let PD die."

"And where is he now?" the angel asked.

"She couldn't know that was going to happen!" Morgan wasn't sure why he was defending her. He hadn't agreed with her decision. But he didn't think she deserved to die for it.

"This is what they are," Raven said. "No compromise. No half measures. No sympathy with weakness. No room for human foibles. Just a terrible and absolute justice."

"You must not listen to the serpent," Lahav said. "He tempted mankind once before, and you suffered for it."

Raven's tongue flicked out to wet his lips. It was forked and he winked when he saw Morgan notice it. "I made the apples to free you," he said. "When you were ignorant, they used you as cannon fodder – conscripts in the pointless war they love to fight. But once you'd gained the knowledge of good and evil for yourselves, they couldn't fool you into fighting their battles any more."

"Lies," Lahav said. "The woman must die and Eden will fade with her." He took another step towards them. His face was beautiful but terribly cold.

Morgan stared at Raven, who was also the serpent. Did that mean he was the devil? But Morgan didn't sense the same evil about him that had drifted from Belle like a rank smell. And his eyes didn't burn with the dull glow of hers or the fierce fire of Lahav's – they were bright and black, just like Alex's had been in the spirit world. "What are you?" Morgan asked him.

"They'll tell you I'm a deserter from their war."

"And is that true?"

Raven shrugged. "I remember it differently, but isn't that the way with memory? We all remember the version of events that suits us best."

"There *is* a real version, though," Morgan said.

"Is there?" Raven looked at Lahav. The angel held his sword upright in front of him and the barest glow of its heat warmed their fronts as the ring of fire surrounding the trees scorched their backs. "Well, this is the story I choose to tell myself. When mankind ate the fruit of knowledge the armies of heaven needed a new way to force them to obey. If they couldn't rule humanity in this life they could control them with threats of what would happen in the next. They took some of this realm and made heaven and hell from it. And so I made another tree – the tree of life."

Morgan nodded. "Because if people live forever, they don't have to worry about what happens when they die." He looked at

Coby and thought that some people *should* have to worry about that.

"Heaven is a reward for the righteous," Lahav said. "Hell a punishment for the wicked. He twists the truth to suit himself."

"Well..." Raven said to Morgan, as Lahav took another stride forward, more confident now. "Eden is meant to stay in the spirit realm, the realm of dreams. If you eat the apple there, it's your spirit which lives forever. Or rather, it remains bound to the spirit realm and returns there when you die. But once bitten, as they say, and the forces of heaven got the jump on me. They put Uriel here to guard the apple before I could get anyone to eat it."

"My god," Alex said. "That's what this was all about. You were using me to open the way to this place. But what happens if we eat the apples here, while the spirit world is in the real one?"

"Real immortality," he said. "Not an ideal solution, but needs must when the devil – well, you know what I mean."

Lahav took another step closer. Two more and he'd be within reach of them. Morgan and Alex backed away, until they were standing beside Coby. He didn't like that image: siding with the killer against the angel.

"You can't be expected to judge right and wrong," Lahav said to him. "You were made by the Adversary, not Hashem, but you can be made whole. Don't listen to the tempter. Mankind wasn't made for freedom. You need our guidance – or you might all be like Coby."

"Are you like Coby?" Raven asked Morgan. "Do you want what he wants? Or is everyone different? Should you all have the freedom to choose, either good or evil?"

Morgan remembered the choice he'd made, when he'd rejected his father and the path the old bastard had chosen for him. He'd thought that by rejecting them he was accepting Lahav and what he stood for. Now he wondered. Alex had called herself a conscientious objector in their war. That seemed to be Raven's way, but that didn't seem quite right either – an abdication of responsibility. Coby had abused his freedom and there were a million other people in the world who would too, if Raven had his way.

Lahav was moving faster now. Raven's smile had dropped and the hands he'd rested against his crossed legs were twitching. His power was fading and if Morgan didn't act to stop Lahav soon he'd have made his decision by default.

"Tell me," he said to the angel. "What happened to Meir when you came here?"

"He burned. I was too great for him to contain in his place."

"But he helped you, didn't he? He let you possess him. Don't you care that he's dead?"

A single frown line wrinkled the marble forehead beneath its crown of flames. "He did his duty and he will have his reward. You can have it too. All you need do is stand aside. Their deaths will be my doing."

Alex shook with fear as she turned to Morgan, but she raised her chin defiantly. "Just remember, you'll be buying your soul with my life."

Lahav stood in front of her, dead vegetation beneath him and nothing to restrain him. She could have run, but Morgan could see she knew it was hopeless. Lahav was too fast and too strong and Raven's power was spent. Nothing could stop him. Nothing except Morgan.

The angel raised the sword above his head in a quicksilver motion – and Morgan grabbed Alex's arm and pulled her out of range as the down stroke cut into the earth, burying the point a foot beneath the soil.

"Tell me how to stop him," Morgan said to Coby.

Lahav put back his head and roared as he pulled the sword out of the ground. The heat of his breath shrivelled Morgan's hair into cinders.

Coby looked dazed. "Blow," he said. "Tekiah Gedolah."

"What–" Morgan said as Lahav's sword swung. He stumbled back, not quite fast enough. A line of fire open along his chest, the cut cauterised as it formed.

"Just do it!" Coby shouted.

Morgan put the shofar to his lips as the sword rose again. He didn't have enough time – only a second till it fell, but the instrument seemed to understand his urgency. It sucked the air out of him to emerge as sound and something else far more powerful.

The note was deep and mournful and it froze everyone where they stood. Coby's face paled and Alex fell to her knees, clutching her chest as if her hands could keep her soul inside. But Morgan wasn't aiming the shofar at them – not with his mind and not physically. The sound blasted directly into Lahav.

The beautiful features shifted slightly, the eyebrows rising in shock or maybe reproach. And then the note blasted through them and they were torn from his face. Flames swirled and sparks rose and the note went on. The outline of the angel shimmered like a mirage and his proud nose and perfect ears melted as if they'd burned in his own fire. His wings fragmented into fiery feathers. They floated away on the wind as cinders.

And then there was nothing left of him. Only the scorched earth testified that he'd ever been there.

Morgan felt his lips burn and the shofar itself melted into slag and dripped to the earth through his hands. "Is he dead?" he gasped. "Did I kill him?"

Coby laughed. "Who cares?" He reached out and plucked an apple from the tree that was no longer guarded by a ring of fire.

Morgan reached for him just as his teeth closed on the flesh of the fruit. Coby swallowed and Morgan dropped his hand, knowing it was too late. He turned to Raven.

Raven shrugged. "That's a bit of a nuisance, isn't it? Good luck dealing with it." He smiled and was gone.

Morgan watched Coby finish the apple and realised he'd have to do the same. Though he was afraid of what faced him when he died, he wasn't sure he wanted to be immortal. But Coby would need to be stopped, or at least contained, and only someone else like him would stand a chance. Morgan sighed and reached for the nearest fruit.

"Leave it!" a new voice said. It was low and course and for a crazy second Morgan thought it might be God himself. Then Alex said "PD" and he saw who was standing behind Coby.

The creature stood on two legs, but it wasn't human. Its limbs had joints in the wrong places and it was covered in grey-brown fur. The eyes above the black nose held intelligence and a feral rage that made Morgan take a step back as it grabbed Coby and held him tight.

"Get out, Alex," the creature growled. Its voice was unclear, its teeth too sharp and tongue too long to make human speech comfortable. "He's holding the nut flush. You can't outdraw him – only the board can beat him. Send this place back where it belongs and him with it."

Coby struggled in his arms, no stronger than a normal man but dangerous because he didn't need to fear injury or death. The other coyotes stood in a ring around them, growling. Morgan wondered why they didn't also assume more human forms, but maybe it took an extraordinary strength of will. Or maybe they'd been too long in their animal bodies and had forgotten how it felt to be a person.

Alex looked agonised. "But what about..."

"I can't go back," PD snarled. "You saw to that."

"I came to help you!" she said, suddenly sounding angry. Morgan didn't think she was a woman who could sustain guilt for long.

"Too late, kid," PD said. "I'm out of chips. Go!"

Coby was struggling like a wild thing. His nails lashed out at the half-human creature holding him and left deep red scratches behind. One missed PD's eye by an inch as he whipped his head aside. PD was tiring and Coby never would.

"He's right," Morgan said to Alex. "We have to go. We can't let Coby out into the world. Imagine what he'd do."

Alex hesitated and Coby twisted and turned to free his hand. It latched onto PD's thigh, gouging a lump a flesh from it and tearing an inhuman howl out of his throat.

"Oh god," Alex said. She began to back away. "PD, I didn't mean to hurt you – you've got to believe me."

He didn't answer, all his attention focused on the struggling man in his arms. Alex looked at him one second longer, then turned with Morgan and fled across the clearing towards the orchard beyond.

"You're wasting your time!" Coby shouted after them. "I've got eternity to find a way to get out."

His voice faded as they ran between the trees. "Can you do what he said?" Morgan asked Alex. "Can you send Eden away?"

"I'm trying." She was crying and he looked away.

He stumbled as his footing shifted beneath him. It felt like quicksand, but when he looked down he saw that it was the grass. It was moving – retreating.

"It's working!" he said.

"It's hard." A single drop of blood rolled from her nose to her lip. "I don't know if I can–"

"You have to!" Morgan snapped.

They ran on, over sand now rather than grass, but the trees were still there and Morgan heard another howl behind them. It sounded anguished. He was afraid Coby had hurt PD badly enough to gain his freedom. He could be only minutes behind.

"Get rid of the trees!" he yelled. "For fuck's sake, get rid of it all!"

She groaned in agony. Ahead of him, a bough of plums twisted as if it was alive as the fruit turned from purple to green then shrank and disappeared.

"That's it!" he said. "Keep doing that."

She nodded, droplets of blood flying left and right. Her nose was still bleeding and her tears were red too. He thought this might kill her and wondered what the point of what he'd done had been if she was going to die anyway. But he didn't tell her to stop.

She let out a yell that sounded like it ripped her throat coming out. The tree in front of them pulled itself back into the earth as boughs turned to twigs and the trunk shrivelled into a sapling. It happened to another tree, and another, and they kept running.

Morgan felt the air rasping in his lungs. One moment it was cool and filled with the scent of fruit, the next hot and dry. He saw one last tree ahead of them, a narrow strip of wood plunging into the ground like a nail. They ran past it, and for one moment more the sun blazed above them, and then it went out.

He stumbled to a halt. Alex slowed too, then started to collapse. When he caught her he could feel that she was exhausted and hoisted her into his arms. He turned them both so they could look behind them.

The false sun had gone and it was night in the desert. The moon shone instead, and in its pale light they could see nothing but bare sand for miles in every direction. There was no Eden – and no Coby.

Morgan wiped sweat from his face and smiled a little. "We did it."

Alex was limp in his arms. "Yes," she said. "We did."

EPILOGUE

They made their way back to San Francisco, the last place Alex thought the CIA would be looking for her. She thought about going to see Caesar and Sofia to tell them their daughter was dead, or as good as. She couldn't face it, though – and wouldn't it be better to let them live with at least a little hope? Her body was battered and her mind was aching as if it had taken a beating too. It had used all her reserves to escape from Eden and she wasn't sure she'd ever fully recover the energy she'd spent. Even if she still had all her powers, she didn't dare use them. If she returned to the spirit world, she risked letting Coby out of it.

And she risked facing PD. His fate hurt and she was trying very hard not to think of it as a death. Something of him did live on, but despite what she'd done, he hadn't forgiven her. There was a lesson in that. She was still trying to decide what it was.

Meanwhile, here she was, stuck in the mundane world. She'd chosen a diner in the sleepy Noe Valley, a place where nothing too remarkable ever happened. She knew she couldn't stay in town long, though. Or in the country. Hammond would want to know what had happened to PD, and she didn't want to tell him that either. She wasn't going back to the Agency.

"Did I do the right thing?" Morgan asked.

She laughed and he frowned. He looked tired too. She'd seen the long burn on his chest from Lahav's blade, though he'd covered it with a fresh T-shirt, and she knew he must be in a lot of pain.

"Well, I'm still alive" she said. "Personally, I count that as a win." His frown deepened and she laughed. "That not enough for you? We also disbanded the Croatoans – stopped them stealing anyone else's bodies. We didn't save the people they'd already taken but they're in the spirit world now. Maybe they'll find a way back to themselves."

"You think?"

She shrugged. "I don't know. I'm just glad it's over and we made it."

"That's not all that matters, though, is it?"

"Isn't it? I thought that was the point of what happened in there. Do what's best for you, let other people deal with their own shit and don't let any higher power tell you how to run your life. You destroyed the guardian of Eden – now anyone can be free of heaven or hell if they want to."

"But you sent Eden away," he said.

"Back into the spirit world. If you visit it there in your dreams, you can eat the fruit the way Raven meant you to."

"Was he the devil? Did I pick a side in there – the wrong one?"

"Raven isn't on either of their sides," she said. She'd come to accept what the god had done. He'd acted according to his own principles, which was all she could have expected of him. And he wasn't a hypocrite. He'd used his own freedom from moral constraints to give humanity their own.

Morgan still seemed troubled. "I don't know. I just... I don't want to live in a world that's run by people like Lahav. But I don't want people like Belle in charge either. And Coby... we stopped him getting back here but he got off scot free. What happens to him now?"

She took a mouthful of eggs Benedict before she answered. It tasted great and she took the time to appreciate it. She hadn't been sure she'd have the chance to do something this ordinary again. "Coby's trapped in the spirit world," she said finally. "Forever, I guess."

"And what will happen to him there? Will he pay for what he's done?"

"I doubt it. I think... Actually, I think he's sort of a god now."

He looked horrified. "A *god*?"

"Yeah. He can't do anything terrible, not really, but he can appear in the dreams of people sensitive to the spirit realm – the way Raven did to him. He can influence people, inspire them, at least those who are open to his way of thinking."

"Inspire them to be like him?"

She nodded. "If that's the way they're already inclined."

"Jesus. The god of serial killers."

She studied him, his over-serious face and soft eyes. "What does it matter, anyway? We did the best we could and we both escaped, even if we're not going to win any popularity contests with our respective employers. We can go far away and get on with our lives."

"Not me," he said. "I'm going back to the Hermetic Division."

"You're kidding, right? You totally screwed them. You'll be lucky if they just lock you up."

He shrugged and looked away. "I don't think anyone should be able to get away with just anything. Because of what I did, all kinds of people like Coby might not have to pay in the next life. I can't change that now. But at least I can make sure I pay for what I've done in this one."

"Count me out," she said. "I'm heading for the hills."

He smiled finally. "That's OK. I'm still not sorry I saved you."

Acknowledgements

Enormous thanks to Jared Shurin and Anne Perry for helping with this book, going massively above and beyond for the last book, and being almost as bonkers about my kitten as I am. Thanks too to Jon Oliver and Jenni Hill, without whom the whole thing wouldn't exist. Carrie O'Grady, Matt Jones and many other friends deserve my gratitude for putting up with me endlessly talking through story ideas with them. And thanks to Jason Arnopp and David Derbyshire for being so understanding about me failing to acknowledge them in the first one. Finally, I need to thank Fiona Singh, who's never been mentioned in one of my books and really should have been. She's my oldest friend – and the one who remembers my childhood for me.

Rebecca Levene

Rebecca Levene has been a writer and editor for eighteen years. In that time she has storylined *Emmerdale*, written a children's book about Captain Cook, several science fiction and horror novels and a *Beginner's Guide to Poker*. She has also edited a range of media tie-in books. She was associate producer on the ITV1 drama *Wild at Heart*, story consultant on the Chinese soap opera *Joy Luck Street,* script writer on *Family Affairs* and *Is Harry on the Boat?* and part of the writing team for Channel 5's sketch show *Swinging*. Recently, she was head writer on the video game *Rogue Warrior*, whose lead character was voiced by Mickey Rourke. She's now launching the Infernal Game, her own series of supernatural thrillers.

The Infernal Game

COLD WARRIORS

REBECCA LEVENE

Visit www.abaddonbooks.com for information on our titles,
interviews, news and exclusive content.

 UK ISBN: 978-1-906735-36-4 • £7.99 Abaddon
US ISBN: 978-1-906735-83-8 • $9.99 Books

Follow us on twitter: www.twitter.com/abaddonbooks

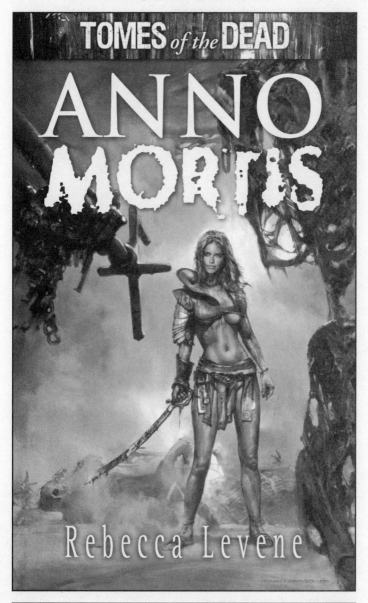

TOMES of the DEAD

ANNO MORTIS

Rebecca Levene

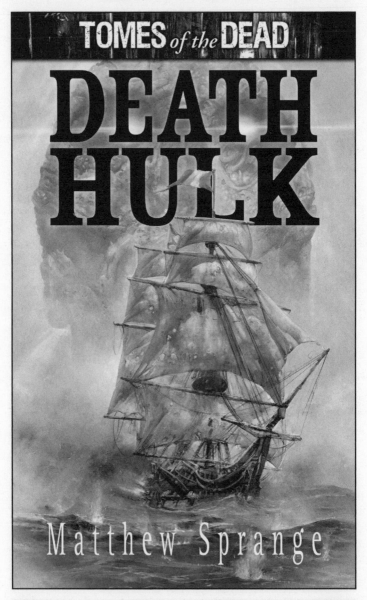

TOMES *of the* DEAD

DEATH HULK

Matthew Sprange

ISBN: 978-1-905437-03-0
UK £.6.99   US $7.99

Abaddon
Books

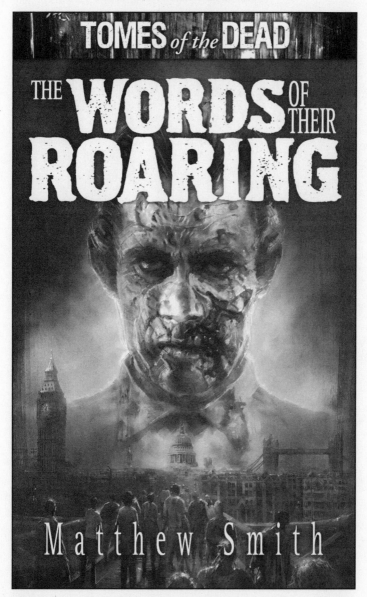

TOMES *of the* DEAD

THE WORDS OF THEIR ROARING

Matthew Smith

ISBN: 978-1-905437-13-9
UK £.6.99   US $7.99

Abaddon
Books

TOMES *of the* DEAD

THE DEVIL'S PLAGUE

Mark Beynon

ISBN: 978-1-905437-41-2
UK £.6.99   US $7.99

Abaddon
Books

ISBN: 978-1-905437-72-6
UK £6.99   US $7.99

Abaddon
Books

TOMES *of the* DEAD

TIDE OF SOULS

SIMON BESTWICK

Visit www.abaddonbooks.com for information on our titles,
interviews, news and exclusive content.

ISBN: 978-1-906735-14-2
UK £.6.99   US $7.99

Abaddon
Books

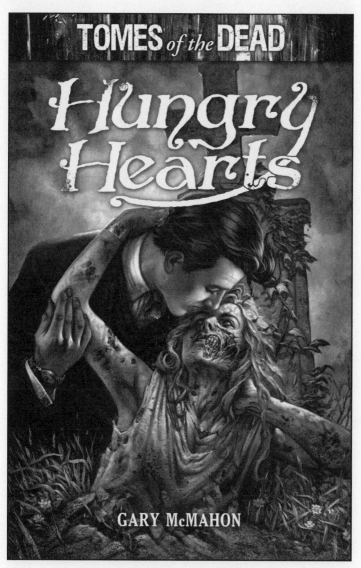

TOMES *of the* DEAD

Hungry Hearts

GARY McMAHON

Visit www.abaddonbooks.com for information on our titles,
interviews, news and exclusive content.

ISBN: 978-1-906735-26-5
UK £.6.99   US $7.99

Abaddon
Books

Follow us on twitter: www.twitter.com/abaddonbooks

TOMES *of the* DEAD

EMPIRE OF
SALT

WESTON OCHSE

Visit www.abaddonbooks.com for information on our titles,
interviews, news and exclusive content.

ISBN: 978-1-906735-32-6
UK £.6.99   US $7.99

Abaddon
Books

Follow us on twitter: www.twitter.com/abaddonbooks